Minding Mama

Winner of Mayhaven's Award for Fiction

A Novel

Minding Mama

Winner of Mayhaven's Award for Fiction

A Novel

Marilyn Arnold

Mayhaven Publishing

All Rights Reserved and Assigned to:
Mayhaven Publishing
PO Box 557
Mahomet, IL 61853

Hardcover Edition
Cover Art & Design: Aaron Porter & Doris Wenzel
Copyright © 2004 Marilyn Arnold
ISBN: 1878044-77-X
LOC Number: 2004112469

Softcover Edition
Cover Art & Design: Aaron Porter & Doris Wenzel
Copyright @ 2006 Marilyn Arnold
ISBN 13: 978-193227822-4
ISBN 10: 193227822-2
LOC Number: 2004112469
Printed in Canada

Dedicated to the fine folks in Kanab, Utah, and to all the daring souls (you know who you are) who have pulled such a stunt as Dorie June Grimes pulls in this novel.

One

This was going to be no picnic. Dorie June Grimes knew that before her husband said it, but he had to say it anyway, didn't he? Backing onto the street in a lower middle class Atlanta neighborhood, she jerked the wheel hard and pointed the nose of her faded red Toyota pickup west. Dorie's mother, Ruetta Ansell Flatray, sat hunched beside her in flowerdy seersucker pajamas, all wrapped in a yellow hand-tied quilt that exposed only the sagging oval of her face and the top of her white head. Ruetta Flatray was going home at last. She was two hours dead, and ripening. There was no time to lose. Forty-eight hours was the most Dorie could hope for. She thanked her lucky stars that if her mother had to die, she had chosen early March and unusually cool weather for it.

By Dorie's calculations, the drive from Atlanta, Georgia, to Jericho, Utah, would take a good forty hours. Dorie Grimes could not afford to ship her mother in the regular manner of dead persons, so she was driving her. A promise is a promise she had told her husband Cleve when he questioned her sanity. Cleve had said why not bury the old woman ("broad" was the word he used) here in Atlanta? Ruetta was dead, he said, and wouldn't know the difference. Well, I'd know, Dorie had snapped back, and then she had begun bathing her mother for the last time. She didn't want her mother arriving in Jericho unwashed.

Dorie had dressed her mother in the elderly woman's almost new pajamas because they were the nicest article of clothing Ruetta owned. Ruetta was eighty-five, and her wardrobe had gone downhill with her health. The quilt was added as an afterthought, in deference to a woman who in life believed wearing pajamas after 7 a.m. to be indecent. Now that she thought about it, Dorie realized that she should probably have packed her mother in ice for the trip. But how on earth could an ordinary person of limited means lay hold of an insulated, waterproof body bag? Or even an ice chest with the necessary capacity?

Maybe Dorie would have invited Cleve along if he hadn't been so insulting, and if she thought she could stand him and his tongue in a small space for forty hours straight. Then again, he could have driven the lot of them in that rattletrap station wagon of his, and Ruetta could have ridden in the back seat where she wouldn't show so much. After all, Cleve wasn't working these days. He wrenched his back on the job two years ago October, and he found idleness so agreeable that he took it up full time rather than return to janitorial service at the airport. When his workers' compensation ran out, he was contented to let Dorie support him and the boy.

"The boy," as Cleve called him, was their only child, Clarence Ross. Clarence was thirty-five. Dorie had given birth to Clarence when she was twenty and mainly ignorant of the facts of life. When his wife threw him out three years ago, he moved in with her and Cleve. Until he could get on his feet, he said. Apparently he has misplaced his feet, permanently, Dorie had complained to Cleve last week. Or maybe he's saving shoe leather, she added with a smirk. Cleve had not appreciated her humor. He sided with Clarence Ross. Indolence loves company.

In fact, Dorie had taken off work from the beauty salon to make this trip. An errand of mercy, it was. A labor of love and a budget breaker. By working six days a week, she was just barely able to keep food on the table to feed the four of them. But it wasn't her idea of a good time, standing on her feet doing perms and shampoo-sets the livelong day. She wasn't getting any younger either. Fifty-five. That's how old she actually was. She could hardly believe it. Of course, she was a lot younger than Ruetta because after Ruetta had Marva Grace, Dorie's older sister, she entered a dry spell. It was seven years before Dorie came along, the only one who gave a tinker's toenail about her mother.

Given that Marva Grace and Dorie were her only options, it was Dorie that Ruetta had turned to when Demont Ralph, the girls' father, passed on to his reward eight years ago and was buried in Jericho, Utah. Jericho, a kind of last outpost that squats in the red rock desert just above the Arizona border and the Grand Canyon, is where Dorie had attended the last two years of high school and cheered for the Jericho Cowboys. She never developed an attachment for the place, and Marva Grace had left the nest before Demont and Ruetta moved there from Wyoming to get out of the wind. Dorie really hadn't a choice in the matter, but Jericho isn't what she'd have chosen if she had. Her mother could never understand why neither of her children elected to make their homes in Jericho, which she always referred to as a little piece of paradise. Dorie herself was fond of saying that Jericho wasn't the end of the earth, but you could see it from there. As it happened, Cleve rescued her. When he was young and footloose, and still believed in gainful employment, Cleve spent a year in Jericho, with the BLM; when he went back to Atlanta, Dorie went with him.

Well, Dorie had said to her mother after Demont Ralph died, you can come to Atlanta and live with Cleve and me if you want. I couldn't cut Cleve loose from Atlanta with a hacksaw. You can have Clarence Ross's room. Of course, that was before Clarence and his wife Mona Fay parted ways. "Irresponsible differences" was the only reason Mona Fay ever gave, and Dorie never corrected her. She was righter than she knew. When Clarence turned up wife-less and jobless during the fifth year of Ruetta's tenure, he was relegated to the green plaid sofa sleeper in the living room. Dorie figured he didn't expect Ruetta to last very

Minding Mama

long, and he'd just wait her out. Well, she fooled him. She fooled them all. And now here Dorie was, on the long road to Jericho with Ruetta perched next to her. Promises mean something in my family, Dorie had said to Cleve, implying that they meant little in his family. Which was correct because they didn't. Cleve didn't even attend his mother's funeral. She wouldn't know the difference, he said, and she had inconsiderately died in the middle of the NBA championship series.

Actually, there were two promises that put Dorie and Ruetta on the road together, the one Ruetta made to Demont Ralph, and then the one Dorie made to Ruetta. In a weak moment, she admitted to Cleve. But that didn't make it any less binding. First off, Ruetta had promised Demont on his deathbed that she would one day lie in sweet repose next to him under the trees there in the little Jericho cemetery, not too far from the New Hope Bible Church, amid the Pratts and Hamblins and Woolleys. (Dorie's eleventh grade biology teacher, on whom she had a secret crush until Cleve arrived, knew the names of the big trees they buried him under, but hardly anybody else did.)

The very day they buried her father Dorie vowed that if Ruetta would come to Atlanta and not expect her and Cleve to move back to Jericho, she'd see to it that Ruetta kept her promise to Demont. Of course, Ruetta always intended to return to Jericho before she died, fully expecting to wear down Dorie's resistance. That's why she never sold the old house, which had now been sitting vacant for eight years collecting spiders, mouse droppings, and unfriendly neighborhood comments. Ruetta seemed to forget that Dorie had a husband and a son. But here the two women were, traveling to Jericho together after all, though not quite in the manner Ruetta had envisioned.

Dorie wasn't five miles from home when two joggers swerved out around a parked car. Instinctively, she yanked the wheel hard to miss them. The rocking motion threw Ruetta against Dorie's shoulder and pitched the truck toward somebody's front yard. En route to the flower beds, the vehicle clipped a trash can and jumped onto the curb.

"Mama, stay put!" Dorie hollered, hitting the brake. "Why isn't your seat belt fastened?" Had Ruetta been alive and breathing, Dorie would have known why. Ruetta was not a tall woman, and she saw death by seat belt as less desirable than death by sailing through a windshield.

Feeling a little shaky, Dorie took three deep breaths and opened her door. Unlike her mother, she was large-boned, tallish, and broad, which was fortunate because Ruetta had required a good deal of hefting and hoisting lately. Most beauty operators of Dorie's acquaintance, at least those like herself who catered to the older perm and dye set, more or less looked the part, with their colored hair in a trendy style, their makeup thick and showy, and their clothing a size too small. Not Dorie. She couldn't be bothered with flashy makeup, and she wasn't about to squeeze her sturdy frame into some cutesy outfit. Her one concession to the vocation was bleached blonde hair piled high on her square

Minding Mama

head. Her hazel eyes, however, could take on a dreamy quality that seemed at odds with the stack of hair above them and the sometimes feisty temperament behind them.

Sometimes when Dorie studied her face in the mirror, it struck her that the eyes gazing back were better suited to somebody else—an unsuccessful poet, maybe. The purplish circles beneath the eyes, more pronounced of late, were definitely hers, however. She credited them to sleepless nights at her mother's bedside when Ruetta was fitful and suffering. So what if Dorie wasn't a four-star caregiver, she had done her duty. She didn't want any regrets down the road, she told Cleve.

As Dorie stepped to the pavement, two more joggers loped easily by, deep in conversation and heedless of anyone but themselves. They reminded Dorie of Clarence Ross. Clueless Clarence, she called him at the beauty shop, and the label could be applied just as handily to Cleve. Clueless Cleve. Satisfied with her invention, Dorie marched around the truck to the passenger's side where she tugged her mother to a sitting position, straightened the quilt around her, and fastened the shoulder strap across the inert body.

"There, Mama!" she exclaimed. "I should've checked that b'fore we left home. Might've known Clarence Ross wouldn't trouble himself."

Ruetta's head dropped forward, nodding her assent. Dorie made some minor adjustments and returned to her own seat, where she religiously fastened the belt. As she swung back onto the road, she was surprised to find herself singing—no, crooning, in her best imitation of Willie Nelson. "On the road again, just can't wait to get on the road again. . . ." For some reason, at this moment she felt more lighthearted than she had in years. How could she feel carefree when reason told her she should be grieving and fretting? Was she in what people called denial? Indeed, she had wept uncontrollably when her mother gasped her last breath a few hours back. But now, it was as though the both of them were freed from some terrible bondage and were off together on a lovely adventure. Besides, her companion was likely to be wholly agreeable, devoid of opinions, and easy to please on this trip. It would be a first. In any event, today Dorie was in charge, and there would be no running commentary on her driving.

Dorie had known for some time now, ever since she checked the rates for shipping a coffin with somebody in it, that one day she'd be making this journey. She and Ruetta had discussed the matter and plotted the course enough times that Dorie had it memorized. Resting on the dashboard was the USA road map she and her mother had marked carefully with a yellow felt tip pen. Follow I 20 to Tuscaloosa, then take US 82 across the rest of Alabama and on into Mississippi, Arkansas, and Texas. At Henrietta, just before Wichita Falls, join up with US 287. Stay on 287 until it merges with US 66 and I 40 east of Amarillo, and when the routes split at Amarillo go with I 40 to Flagstaff, Arizona. From there, take US 89 to Turner and then cross

Minding Mama

the border to Jericho. The Promised Land.

Ruetta had stressed repeatedly that there could be no diverting to the Grand Canyon or other points of interest on the westbound journey, since she would not be alive to enjoy the diversion and time was of the essence. Dorie could lallygag on the way back if she so desired. Ruetta didn't want any slip-ups, she said. Demont Ralph was out there waiting, and he wouldn't tolerate any slip-ups. He was a very particular man when it came to what Ruetta was supposed to do. Dorie had noticed that her father was less particular when it came to what *he* was supposed to do, but she wasn't about to criticize the dead. She had enough to do criticizing the living. When you shared quarters with the likes of Clarence Ross and Cleve, it got to be a full-time job.

* * * * * * *

Even anticipated departures seem to surprise everyone in the actual moment of transition, and needless to say, Dorie was ill prepared for Ruetta's death when it arrived. On the instant, time became the enemy, and she was hard pressed to get her mother ready and a few things packed for herself. There was no time to grieve after the first shocked outburst, no time even to think. Dorie remembered her last conversation with her mother regarding the trip, just yesterday. Twenty hours later, as though to prove her point, Ruetta stopped breathing. No dialing 911 either, Ruetta had insisted. When the call comes, let me go. And go she did.

"Now, Dorie June," Ruetta had said, "if drive we must, at least you've got the route down pat. What you need to do is get yourself a bag packed and ready. You're not goin' to have any time to spare. I only pray that sorry excuse of a truck we're takin' won't fall apart b'fore we get there. I'd rather go by fast freight, m'self, but neither of us has the cash. Every cent Demont Ralph left me went for buryin' him and buyin' me the space next t' him."

We could sell the Jericho house, Dorie had said to herself, knowing full well her mother would never assent to it. "I don't see why the rush," Dorie had said out loud. "You've thought you were on the verge of death ever since I was born. No reason to think you won't last another twenty or thirty years. You'll make the McGinnis Book of Records. Katie Couric will interview you on the morning show." She paused. "I don't want to bother about such things any sooner'n I have to."

"You don't want to bother about such things at all," Ruetta said. "Trouble with you, Dorie June, is you're lackin' in the milk of human kindness. The word 'charity' is missin' from your vocabulary."

Dorie resented the comment. "I took you in, didn't I? When Marva Grace wouldn't trouble herself to lift a finger? What's charity if that's not?"

"It don't count if you give the gift grudgingly," Ruetta said. Ruetta knew her Bible and she cited it whenever in her view the occasion called for it. She knew her Book of Mormon, too, but since she had weakened and joined up

Minding Mama

with the Mormons after Dorie left Jericho, she apparently figured it was pointless to draw her instructional examples from that book. Demont Ralph had held out and gone to his grave an infidel, though apparently he didn't object to Ruetta's religious activity.

"When you actually are dyin' will be soon enough for additional acts of charity," Dorie muttered.

"I tell you, child, this time it's for real," Ruetta had insisted, her voice raspier than usual. "The angels are waitin' in the wings. I can hear 'em singin'. Pack that bag and fill that gas tank. And don't forget my Bible and Book of Mormon. I want to be buried with those holy works right inside the coffin. For insurance. You and Cleve and Demont Ralph may be gamblers, but I intend to go with all m' bases covered."

It turned out that Ruetta was right this time, and the only task Dorie had accomplished ahead of time was the memorizing—that because Ruetta had drilled the route into her until she was rehearsing it in her sleep. After readying her mother for the trip, Dorie stuffed a dress, a pair of polyester pants, and a couple of indestructible knit blouses into an old canvas traveling bag for herself, along with pajamas, underwear, jacket, toothbrush, hair spray, lotion, and comb. She tossed the bag in the back of the pickup, where the leftover manure mostly wasn't, and with Clarence's help, loaded her mother into the front seat. Naturally, Cleve was nowhere to be found, and the pickup was no better prepared for the pilgrimage than Dorie was.

Marilyn Arnold

Cleve's cousin had borrowed the truck last week, and it came back short on gas and long on the smell of cow manure. It happened every year when he started thinking about a garden. Most years the thinking and the manure were as far as he got. Even without the manure, Dorie couldn't have put Ruetta in the back and let her arrive all windblown and weatherbeaten. And the alternatives, such as stuffing her mother into a cardboard refrigerator box, were just as bad. Downright disrespectful, in fact. At least Dorie didn't have to bring much in the way of accessories for Ruetta, who wouldn't be needing a change of clothes any time soon. Nor would she be requiring extra restroom stops, either, a decided advantage for people on a tight schedule. Dorie had learned over the last eight years that an elderly person's bladder has about as much elasticity as a dime store balloon at the north pole. I'll buy gas first chance I get, Dorie told Clarence Ross when he shut the door on Ruetta.

In the rush Dorie neglected to pack a lunch, though she had called Marva Grace with the news. Marva Grace hadn't batted an eye. Dorie knew that without seeing it. From Marva's reaction, or lack thereof, you'd think she lost a mother every day of the year, and that daughters drove their dead mothers across the country at the drop of a hat. She could have offered to pay the freight, but she didn't. Keeping her eyes on the road and her left hand on the wheel, Dorie rooted around in the lumpy straw handbag stowed on the floor beneath her legs. In point of fact, it was

Minding Mama

Ruetta's extra handbag, appropriated two or three years ago when the strap tore loose on Dorie's own stained white vinyl one. A high school graduation gift, as she recalled. Her hand found the tan nylon wallet with the velcro closure that had served Cleve for two decades before he discarded it and she rescued it from the trash. She dumped the wallet's contents in the lap of her serviceable blue denim skirt, a favorite for travel because it didn't bind the way pants did. It had an elastic waist, too. On her feet were the off-white sandals Clarence's wife had left by mistake the last time they visited before calling it quits. Clarence Ross said keep 'em, so she did. Naturally, they were a little short because Mona Fay was not a large woman; but with sandals what did it matter? Your toes could hang over the edge without hurting anything, unless you happened to stub them, which she did once on a grocery cart.

As she drove, Dorie counted the wrinkled bills and the change. In all, it amounted to about fifty-six dollars, give or take a little—mainly this week's tips. The wallet also held a VISA credit card that, if she was lucky, wouldn't max out before she got to Jericho. She'd sell the spare tire and take up prayer if push came to shove. Dorie hoped to borrow from her sister for the return trip, assuming that Marva Grace would trouble herself to show up for the burial and that guilt over her inexcusable neglect of her one and only mother was substantial enough to translate into a small loan. Marva Grace had the good sense to marry a man who was destined to be rich. Dorie couldn't remember

why she herself had married Cleve, other than to escape
Jericho, but she knew she didn't marry for money because
he didn't have any. Who knows, maybe she did it to show
her older sister that money wasn't everything. That was
before she knew it was.

So Dorie had fifty-six dollars cash. Well, she told herself, since Ruetta won't be eating much this trip, or stopping for souvenirs at every tourist trap, that amount should
cover food. Economy-wise, there was something to be said
for traveling with a dead person. And besides, Ruetta
Flatray dead was better company than either Cleve or
Clarence Ross alive.

* * * * * *

At the next junction, Dorie pulled off the interstate to
get gasoline and to check the oil. The pickup had been
burning oil lately, and though she didn't know what that
meant, she knew it wasn't good. She longed for the old
days when women, and men too for that matter, didn't have
to pump their own gas and add their own oil, or pay extra
for somebody else to do it. The only convenience Dorie
could see in convenience stores was for the owners and
their hired help. They never had to dirty their hands or
brave the elements. Cleve had showed her how to check the
oil with the dipstick, so she did that while the gas was
pumping. The oil was okay. So far, so good. Dorie hung the
gas nozzle on the pump and went inside to pay and use the

Minding Mama

facilities. When she returned to where her pickup had been, the vehicle and Ruetta had disappeared, presumably together.

If Ruetta had been able to operate a car, which she never had, Dorie might have assumed that her mother had returned to life and driven off. Although in her present state Ruetta wouldn't favor such detours, when alive she had always fancied side trips. She and Dorie never went straight to any place. One time they traveled eighty-three miles out of the way to see a two-headed cow Ruetta had read about in the newspaper. Another time it was a barn somebody had painted in green and white stripes that people said made the cows dizzy. On this occasion, however, Dorie knew she could safely assume that someone had stolen the Toyota and acquired Ruetta in the bargain. Worst of it was, the tank was full. They wouldn't run out of gas any time soon.

Dorie dashed to the street and looked both ways. Then she ran back into the convenience store.

"Somebody's stolen my truck!" she cried. "While I was in here, paying!"

The fat-faced man behind the counter, who looked to be forty or so, blinked at her from behind round, black-rimmed glasses. "You don't say, stole your truck, eh? Well, well. You'd better call the *Po*-lice. That happened here oncet before, as I recollect." He pointed to the door. "Pay phone's outside."

The last thing Dorie wanted was to have the police

involved. They'd grill her about transporting a dead woman in her vehicle and likely cause her all kinds of delays. They might even accuse her of killing her mother, or stealing a body! She wasn't absolutely sure, either, about the legality of rolling across several states with a dead person sitting as pretty as you please in the passenger seat. What Dorie did know was that she had no time to spare, so once again she ran to the street and began flagging down cars. Most of them zoomed around her as if she didn't exist, but a couple of people stopped. No, they said, they hadn't seen a red Toyota pickup making tracks out of here.

Then at last a Dodge Caravan transporting clientele from the Sleepy Manor rest home came under the freeway instead of off it. The driver, a balding man in a blue windbreaker and a bow tie who seemed to welcome any diversion, however small, stopped and asked what the trouble was. As a matter of fact, he had seen such a vehicle, he said, up the road a couple of miles, off in the grass. The door was wide open, and a teenage boy in overgrown shorts and a backwards baseball cap was sprinting away from it like he'd seen a ghost.

"He had," Dorie replied, but declined to elaborate. "That sounds like it," she amended. "I hope he left the keys."

"Want me to take you?" the fellow offered. "There's room back there by Wallace." He turned and shouted. "Move over, Wallace, a pretty lady is coming to sit by you."

"By me?" squeaked an elderly gentleman in an overcoat and a cap with the ear flaps down. "Well, tell her not to get fresh. I'm a married man, you know."

"When did you get married, Wallace? I thought you were a bachelor."

"Got married last week," Wallace replied. "To Elizabeth Taylor. Needed somebody to mend m' socks."

Dorie slid open the van door and squeezed in beside Wallace. He wasn't about to make space for her, but she could stand anything for two miles. At last the van slowed to a stop. When the driver came around to let Dorie out, she could see that the Toyota's door was open and the engine was running. Ruetta sat there unperturbed, enjoying the scenery.

"That there your mama?" the driver asked as Dorie walked toward her vehicle.

"Yes, it is. Thanks kindly for the lift," Dorie answered, climbing into the little pickup.

"Glory be, he stole the truck and your mama sat there and let him?!" the man called out.

"She's real old," Dorie called back.

"Why d'you s'pose he left in such an all-fired hurry?"

"Nature's call, most likely," Dorie shouted and drove off, bumping up through the lumpy grass. In her rear view mirror, she could see the Sleepy Manor van driver, still standing there, scratching his head.

Two

Glancing over at her mother, Dorie Grimes could see that the quilt had been pulled back from Ruetta Flatray's ashen face. Clearly, the youthful carjacker had made Ruetta's acquaintance and concluded that this was not the vehicle for him after all. On reflection, Dorie could see that a lot of people might object to traveling with a corpse, even a small, inoffensive one like Ruetta. This particular thief had lasted a scant two miles before he bailed out, scarcely a fair trial in Dorie's view. For just plain calm and quiet, and a sense of companionship, too, you really couldn't beat this arrangement. And, as Dorie noted before, the expense was minimal. Of course, as Clarence Ross observed, having a longstanding familial attachment to the corpse probably helped.

As the miles sped by, Dorie took the opportunity to discuss a number of things with her mother, subjects she hadn't cared to broach when Ruetta was alive. Some things

Minding Mama

you don't discuss with your mother until after the fact, when her opinion comes too late to change anything, as with Dorie's youthful marriage to Cleve. Other things you don't bring up until, as in the present case, your mother is unable to express an opinion. At least not an opinion you can hear. Dorie was currently wrestling with a knotty personal question which she now presented to her mother. Should she pull out and leave Clarence Ross and Cleve to fend for themselves permanently? What would they think if she never came back? Would they try to track her down? After all, she was their meal ticket. She could see why some people would jump at the chance to enter a witness protection program. You could get rid of a lot of baggage that way, though it had its downside, too.

"I'm just plain tired of feeding those two and cleanin' up after them," Dorie told Ruetta as she swung out to pass a brown UPS van. "If I had any gumption, I'd clear out or throw them out. You've lived there, you know how they are. Maybe I should move to New Mexico and become a tourist guide at Carlsbad Caverns. What do you think, Mama, would I make a good tourist guide?"

Normally, Ruetta would have dismissed such a notion, but today she didn't object. She even seemed to concur, Dorie thought. Suppose her immortal soul was hovering up there by the ceiling light, listening in. It could nudge me, couldn't it, or knock on the dashboard? Once for "yes," twice for "no." But then Dorie remembered that at times Ruetta didn't think Cleve was so bad. "I've seen worse," she would say. "He used to come in and bring me a cherry popsicle when you were at the salon."

* * * * * * *

On the outskirts of Birmingham, Dorie pulled off the highway and into a fast food place where she could drive through and not have to leave Ruetta alone in the truck to be scrutinized by every teenager and four-year-old who passed by. And maybe kidnaped again. Not that Ruetta would ever mind being kidnaped. Dorie had the distinct impression that her mother would love to be whisked away by somebody more exciting than her middle-aged daughter. Ruetta regularly accused Dorie of leaving her get-up-and-go, along with her congeniality, at the salon. In fact, Ruetta probably hated to see the juvenile delinquent who stole her, along with the truck, depart before they really got acquainted and she had a chance to give him a Bible lesson or two and a lecture on the evils of smoking and premarital sex. At the drive-up window (this establishment allowed a customer to address a warm body instead of a menu board that crackled with static), Dorie ordered a hamburger, small fries, and a chocolate milkshake.

"You want two a' those?" the gum-chewing girl at the window asked.

"No, just one set," Dorie replied.

"That your mama over there?" the girl asked, peering across Dorie at the inert form opposite her.

Minding Mama

"No, I'm just making a delivery to the rest home."

"Like, she sure don't look very good, does she?"

"They all look this way, trust me." Dorie didn't turn her head an inch.

"Mebbe, she'd, like, want somethin' t' drink?"

"No thanks, she's fine. Just bring the burger." Dorie clamped her lips together in a thin line.

"I could, y' know, call a doctor or somethin'?"

"Forget it!" Dorie cried, her eyes boring a hole in the windshield. She shoved the pickup into low gear and roared off the premises. "It appears that from now on, if I want anything to eat, I'll have to park in some remote alley and leave you on your own, Mama," she said. "Wish I'd brought one of your hats to doll you up, make you look more presentable to prying eyes."

* * * * * * *

Evening had arrived when Dorie approached Tuscaloosa where she was to change from the interstate to US 82. She was hungry and tired, and found it a relief to get off the busy thoroughfare. Before long she spotted a small grocery store with a white frame Baptist church across the street. The church parking lot was empty, so Dorie stopped there and maneuvered the pickup to put Ruetta on the side next to the grass and bushes. "I won't be a minute," she told her passenger, and then walked over to the market with her straw handbag dangling from her wrist.

29

Marilyn Arnold

Dorie was learning all kinds of tricks to keep her mother from the public gaze. At the last gas station, she paid at the pump and parked Ruetta behind the station, out of sight, while she made a quick visit to the restroom. On a bench in front of the grocery store sat two old black fellows and a white, the three of them in overalls, smoking pipes and cackling to each other. One of them smiled and tipped his hat to her as she went past. Something about the gesture made her smile, too, and she remembered the strangely carefree mood that had offset her grief this morning. It will be okay, she told herself. Everything will be okay.

On her return to the Baptist parking lot, Dorie plunked down on the grass with her bag of food—apples, oranges, crackers, bottled water, Country Time lemonade, cheese, potato chips, and licorice. Ruetta Flatray hated licorice. Said it stained the teeth and the breath for three days, and so it was forbidden in the Flatray household and any other household Ruetta happened to occupy. Now, however, with her mother's sense of smell no longer influencing the menu, Dorie could indulge to her heart's content. Biting into a licorice twist, however, she realized that she had lost her taste for it. Ruetta's edicts had intimidated Dorie's palate. Maybe after Ruetta had been deposited in Jericho, Dorie could get reacquainted with licorice.

Her hunger satisfied, Dorie flopped back, stretching and yawning. She must have dozed off because when she opened her eyes, a girl she had never before laid eyes on was sitting cross-legged by the open grocery bag munching

Minding Mama

a piece of licorice. Dorie sat up.

"Hey, girl, what you doin'?!" she demanded. Dorie judged the girl to be fourteen or so.

"Jus' eatin' licorice, is all, ma'am. I ain't doin' no harm." The girl uncrossed her brown legs, got to her knees, and began a careful examination of the contents of Dorie's paper bag. "You ain't got no doughnuts, do you? I crave a doughnut. My stepmama's the same way. Eats 'em three times a day and twice on Sunday. She fasts ever' Sunday morning else she'd eat 'em then, too. Says she aims to get pardon for her sins by way of fastin' on Sundays. She belongs to the First Church of the Lamb and Him Crucified. My daddy says he wouldn't be caught dead inside no church with that long of a name."

Dorie noticed that the girl's legs, like the shorts above them and the short T-shirt above the shorts, were none too clean. She didn't know why they were dirty and why the girl was here eating licorice barefooted, but all indications were that the girl was not likely to hold back much information. Dorie could see a pair of scruffy sandals in the grass by the bag, and figured she knew whose feet they belonged to.

"Well," said Dorie, groaning as she struggled to her feet, "I've got to be on my way." The girl didn't move. "You can have the licorice," Dorie said.

"That your mama in that there truck?" The girl continued her exploration of the grocery bag.

"Yes, it is."

"She don't look none too good, do she? She been sick?"

"You might say so, yes." Dorie bent and picked up the bag by one corner. The girl's eyes followed it, almost wistfully, Dorie thought.

The girl's frizzy brown hair, pulled into something resembling a ragged ponytail, and her thin frame and soulful eyes tugged at Dorie's heart. Dorie had to be on her way, but here was this girl. Why didn't she go home and bathe herself and eat? Dorie found an apple in the bag and handed it to her.

"You go along, now, y' hear? It's gettin' dark. Time for you to go home."

The girl sat back down with her legs bent under her. "Cain't go home. I run off," she said. "I got tired a' them folks back there. It was Lily Dawn this and Lily Dawn that all the livelong day. My stepmama, she rode me somep'n awful, and my daddy was off drivin' truck mos' of the time. Those boys a' hers scairt me spitless, them and their evil eyes and nasty mouths. Who knows what they mighta tried next?"

Dorie frowned. "You heading west or east?" She did not want this girl latching onto her. She had enough worries of her own without acquiring a batch of new ones.

"East's where I've been, an' west's where I'm goin'. I'd sure favor a ride in that direction."

"Well, I'm headin' west myself, but I've got Mama. No room for anybody else. Besides, I'd be in trouble with the

Minding Mama

law if I took you with me. I hear it's illegal to transport a minor such as the party here present across state lines. I've got no time to get busted on this trip."

The girl looked pleadingly at Dorie. "I wouldn't be no trouble, ma'am. I'd scrunch up real small. Your mama wouldn't even know I was there."

Dorie laughed darkly and moved toward the pickup. "She sure wouldn't, she's dead!"

"Dead!" The girl stopped following Dorie and took the licorice twist from her mouth, which now had black juice showing in both corners. "No wonder she looks so peak-ed." The girl paused. "How is it, ridin' next to a dead person?"

Dorie opened the pickup door. "Fine and dandy, thank you. She's better company than most. We've been travelin' for hours and haven't had so much as a harsh word between us. It's a record for me and Mama."

The girl dropped her eyes and began pulling up grass with the toes on her right foot. "I wouldn't mind if'n I could set by the window," she said.

Finally Dorie gave in. What was one felony more or less? she asked herself. In any case, she couldn't dilly dally here any longer. She'd drive until her eyes wouldn't stay open and then grab a catnap. The girl could talk and keep her awake. So the two of them shifted Ruetta to the middle of the seat, a location seemingly designed for the specific torture of the living, but one not likely to trouble the dead all that much. They managed to get the center seat belt fastened around Ruetta's waist; without a shoulder strap, however, she slumped over a little. The girl commented on how nice the quilt and pajamas were, and Dorie said she always thought it paid to take pains.

Between Tuscaloosa, Alabama, and Columbus, Mississippi, Lily Dawn—that was the girl's real name—entertained Dorie with her life story, in all its colorful details. She told how she was born in Milledgeville, Georgia, but they moved, and how her real mama ran off with a drummer in a band when she herself was nine and her daddy married this other woman who already had twelve and thirteen-year-old boys who gave her the evil eye because she was now fourteen and turning into a young lady and they were seventeen and eighteen and turning into you know what. As it happened, Lily Dawn had a grandmother in Turner, Arizona, and she had decided to try for that place. All she knew is that it was by a great big dam with lots of water, so she figured she could spot it easy.

"Won't the police be looking for you?" Dorie asked.

"Naw. My daddy he's on a run, and my stepmama is thinkin' good riddance t' bad rubbish, meanin' me. Nobody start lookin' 'til my daddy gets home nex' week. I'll call my daddy then, tell him I'm at Grandmama's."

"Assuming you get there," Dorie muttered.

Lily Dawn had forgotten when she left home three days ago that she would need money and clean clothes and food, not to mention transportation and a place to sleep. This nice old couple who had been to Disney World gave her a ride to somewhere in Georgia, and fed her, she said, and then these girls who had stolen their daddy's Chevrolet picked

Minding Mama

her up and brought her as far as Tuscaloosa where the police caught up with them, and she slipped out and ran into the brush.

One night she slept in the back of a car somebody left unlocked on the street, and the other night she partied all night with the girls who had stolen the Chevrolet and some beer and Doritos from a convenience store while she herself distracted the clerk. Lily Dawn said that she hated to be a party to theft, and anyway she would never dare steal Doritos because the bag was too puffy and too rackety. Anybody could see it or hear it when you snuck out of the store. She was assigned the clerk because the girls said she had to be good for something and she had no shoplifting experience.

* * * * * * *

At Columbus, Mississippi, Lily Dawn ran down in the middle of a sentence, and Dorie heard her head clunk against the window. Dorie fought sleep as far as Winona and then stopped for gasoline at an all night station that looked as tired as she was. She had to add oil this time, and Lily Dawn slept right through the banging down of the hood.

"She's a sounder sleeper than Mama in her current state," Dorie commented aloud.

Dorie held on as far as Greenville, on the banks of the Mighty Mississippi, at which place her eyes rebelled and refused to stay open. She swung around to a lakeside park and drove up to an empty picnic table. Only half-conscious, Dorie lifted her bag from the truck bed and set it on the table, punching it a little to make a sort of pillow. Then she stretched out on the table. Twenty minutes is all I need, she told herself. Twenty blessed minutes.

Fortunately, the table was hard enough that twenty minutes was all Dorie could stand. Unfortunately, every joint protested when she sat up and swung her legs over the side to find the bench. With effort, she stood, stretching both arms to the sky and then reaching for her toes. It was a mistake. When she tried to stand straight again, her back refused to cooperate. In something of a bent hobble, she limped to the pickup and on the third try managed to heave her bag over the side and into the truck bed. The moon was in its first quarter.

"Hoo, huh, whuzzat?" a raspy male voice hollered, and Dorie saw the dark shape of something human, or nearly so, rise up out of the truck bed like a frightened spook.

Dorie screamed, threw both arms in the air, and fell back on the roadway. In the process, her body unbent itself without her help. She decided that was how the expression "scared stiff" originated. Somebody actually was. Somewhere in the semi-darkness she found her voice and her feet.

"Who are you? What d' you want? Get outta there!" she yelled. "That truck bed is covered with manure. You want manure all over you?" For the life of her, she didn't know why she thought of the manure.

Minding Mama

The dark shape in the bed began shaking and brushing itself off. Then it talked. "Why, lady, I don't mind the manure. Truth be known, it's kinda warm and softlike. Too bad most of it's blowed out. This here your truck?"

"Yes, it is, and I want you out of it. The smell alone is enough to . . ."

"Truth be known, I lost m' sense of smell in Korea or somewheres. Jungle fever or some such. Corporal Loyal Bunce, at your service, ma'am." The shape in the truck bed saluted. "Looks like you got two passengers already. One more wouldn't hurt, would it? I've got me a trombone here, I could entertain." The shape patted something that must have been a trombone case. "I play ol' Matilda on street corners an' people drop money in her case. It ain't much, but it's a livin'."

"One more passenger would be two too many," Dorie said, "now git!"

Dorie meant to elaborate, but she was interrupted by a low, gurgly snarl coming from the back of the truck bed. The snarl issued from the mouth of a very large dog that now labored slowly to its feet and made a feeble stab at baring its fangs in the moonlight. The way it stood there, swaying, Dorie could tell that it was ancient. The same vintage in dog years as its owner, or older.

"Appears to be not one but *two* of you, not countin' the trombone," Dorie observed wryly. "You must be in a terrible fix if I'm the best you can do." Something about the pair got to Dorie. She attributed her vulnerability to repressed grief, lack of sleep, and the deferred influence of Ruetta's love affair with 1 Corinthians 13 and other equally trying passages. Oh, what would it hurt? she argued silently. What have I got to lose? Certainly not my dignity. That evaporated years ago. No one living by her own consent with Cleve and Clarence Ross Grimes could make any claim to dignity. "When did you come aboard, anyway?" she inquired gruffly. She really did want to know so as to take precautions in the future.

"Oh, back there t' the service station, when you was inside. Looked to me like them two up front was sawin' logs, so I hopped in. I hunkered down real low. Luckily, you was pointed the direction I wanted t' go."

"Yeah, luckily," Dorie muttered. "I'm havin' nothing but luck today." When she opened the door, Lily Dawn stirred and sighed, but didn't waken. Dorie turned back to Loyal. "Make yourself comfortable, but if you make any trouble, you're gone, y' hear? History!"

"Oh, yes, ma'am. I won't be no trouble, and neither will Petunia. She's a good watchdog."

"Yeah, I'll bet. I can tell she's a regular spectator, that dog. When she's awake." Dorie got behind the wheel and closed the door. "If any more strays show up, I'll have to get me a trailer," she said, turning the ignition key. "Talk to me, Mama," Dorie pleaded as she rammed the Toyota into gear. "You're the only sane person in the bunch, and that includes me!"

Minding Mama

* * * * * * *

The encounter with Loyal Bunce and Petunia the mongrel dog had produced enough adrenaline to get Dorie nearly to Texarkana before she started nodding again. A stop for gasoline in Crosset had helped, too. But if Lily Dawn didn't wake up soon and start talking, Dorie would have to wake her. Just past Lewisville, Dorie shook herself out of a doze and glanced in the rear view mirror. Even in the semi-darkness of pre-dawn, she could hardly mistake the patrol car beneath the flashing light. The unwelcome vehicle was obviously on her tail and nobody else's. There was nothing to do but pull over, so she did.

Panic set in as the officer approached, scowling behind his patrolman's gold-rimmed glasses with those intimidating twin blue mirrors. Oddly enough, Dorie's first thought was of Loyal. Was it illegal to transport a human being in the back of a pickup in the state of Arkansas? She'd plead ignorance and throw herself on the mercy of the court. On the other hand, why not plead ignorance of Loyal's very presence? After all, she had driven with him and the dog for some miles totally oblivious, hadn't she?

Dorie's next thought, logically, was of her mother, for whom such deceptions were no better than out-and-out lies. Maybe worse because deceptions were premeditated, while some lies were born in the heat of the moment. At times, traveling with Ruetta Flatray was like being escorted by your own nuisance of a conscience. There it was, in plain sight, where Dorie couldn't ignore it, much less shove it out the door. A quick glance indicated that Ruetta's face was not wholly covered. Since it was too late to make adjustments now, Dorie did the only thing she could do under the circumstances. She coughed and leaned forward, hoping to block the patrolman's view of her mother. Her last thought was of Lily Dawn, who was bound to wake up any minute and start dispensing more information than the officer would think to ask for. There was no time to coach her. Luckily, the girl had no knowledge of the latest adjuncts to the Grimes touring company, the sorry-looking pair in the back. Ruetta was another matter entirely.

Dorie rolled the window down—it was stuck and would go only part way—as the officer approached. "I wasn't speeding, was I officer? This wagon won't go all that fast," she added with a lame smile.

The officer's face was concrete. "No, ma'am, you weren't speeding, you were weaving back and forth. Exit the vehicle, please, and bring your car registration and your driver's license."

Dorie began rummaging through her handbag for her driver's license, which she usually kept in her wallet, formerly Cleve's. This was no TV version of a tobacco-spitting southern lawman outside her window. The precision of the fellow's speech and the set of his jaw gave her such a case of nerves that she dropped the wallet between the seat and the door and had to open the door to find it. The truck registration, if by some miracle it still existed, was probably in

Minding Mama

the glove box in front of Lily Dawn. Along with who knows what else. The last time Dorie opened the woefully small box it took her ten minutes to re-stuff the thing and get it closed up again. That event very nearly triggered an unfriendly letter to the Toyota people. And now, here she was, facing yet another adventure with the box, this time before an unsympathetic audience. To make matters worse, she would have to get at it via Lily Dawn's door, waking the girl in the process. The officer eyed her in what she regarded as a hostile manner when she explained about the registration. She circled the front of the pickup, thinking to draw his eyes away from both the cab and the truck bed. He chose to follow her, however, and she noticed that he unsnapped his gun holster. Do I look like a dangerous criminal? she wanted to ask him.

If Cleve had been here, Dorie told herself, none of this would have happened. I wouldn't have been driving tired, Mama would have been resting comfortably in the back seat of the station wagon, Lily Dawn would be asleep in some parked car in some city completely unknown to me, and Loyal would be crossing the country in somebody else's pickup with an arthritic dog named Petunia and a trombone named Matilda. I wouldn't even know they existed. They'd be somebody else's worry. Dorie longed to turn the clock back forty-eight hours and start over. If she did that, Ruetta wouldn't have died yet. Maybe she'd have held off a day or two and given Dorie a chance to think things through and fully consider the hazards of traveling with a

41

corpse, even if it was a relatively friendly one.

When Dorie opened the door on the passenger side, Lily Dawn, who was sleeping heavily against that same door without her seat belt fastened, tumbled out and landed in a noisy heap on the ground. Dorie screamed and lunged toward the girl, wrenching her back once again. Roused by the commotion, Loyal and Petunia woke up and joined in the chorus. All that was lacking, Dorie mused, was a contribution from Ruetta and Matilda. Bent nearly double, and her ire raised, Dorie turned to the patrolman.

"See what you've gone an' done?" she cried. "You've woke up everybody but Mama. Lucky for you she's not wearin' her hearing aid! And my back's gone out to boot! What have you got to say for yourself?" Dorie was surprised at her boldness and the clarity of her mind.

The patrolman stumbled back a step, sputtering something resembling an apology. Clearly, he was unprepared for the onslaught.

Dorie leaned over Lily Dawn and stroked her head, winking furiously at the girl. "Are you all right, Mindy Lee?" she asked, fussing and comforting with exaggerated concern. "If you're hurt, your daddy and me can sue the state of Arkansas for false arrest and harassment and bodily harm. You hush up, now, daughter. Don't say another word. We'll get some bandaids and iodine for those scrapes."

Then Dorie turned to Loyal who was threatening to crawl from the truck bed and defend the ramparts with the trusty Petunia at his side. "No, Papa," Dorie said firmly, measuring every word, "you and Petunia stay there. I'll handle this, and we'll still get to the reunion on time. I promise. When did I ever break a promise to you, my own daddy?"

"Whatta ya mean, 'daddy?'" Loyal yelled, then caught Dorie's frantic facial signals. "Well, if'n you say so," he grumbled. With obvious reluctance, he saluted Dorie and dropped to the truck bed, sprawling across a still protesting Petunia and thumping the trombone case over and over with his left hand.

Dorie turned to the patrolman, energized by indignant wrath. "Well, I hope you're happy," she said accusingly. "Mindy Lee's all dirty and hurt, my back's gone out, you've upset Papa"—with her right forefinger Dorie made circles in the air around her right temple, indicating that "Papa" wasn't quite right in the head— "and we're all in danger of being late to the family reunion."

"But, but, I was only . . ."

"Since when does an officer of the law, a servant of the people, have nothing better to do with his time than make trouble for a family of strangers in a strange land?" Dorie was pleased to find a use for one of her mother's Bible phrases. It seemed to make an impression on the baffled patrolman.

Dorie pressed her advantage. "If anybody's broken any laws around these parts, officer, I'd have to say it was you. Any weavin' you think you saw me do musta been a heat warp on the pavement, or a figment of your imagination." Dorie could hardly believe her own eloquence. She should have gone on stage. She could have brought the house down. In fact, she found herself actually enjoying the little drama and almost reluctant for it to end.

"If you want t' bend down here and sniff my breath," she cried, "you're welcome to it! The worst you'll find there is the smell of licorice." She put her hand over her heart. "Alcohol has not crossed my lips in thirty years," she said with all the pious flourish she could muster.

The patrolman backed up another step, both hands up to shield himself. "Look, lady," he stammered, his composure crumbling, "I'm going to pretend this never happened. I never saw you weave, I never pulled you over." The man couldn't escape fast enough. "You just get on your way and go to that reunion, ma'am. I only hope it's across the border. The state of Texas may be big enough to survive the likes of you, but the state of Arkansas sure isn't."

Dorie waited until the patrol car was just a speck in the distance before she allowed herself to breathe.

Three

Slumping weakly against the side of her much abused Toyota pickup, Dorie June Grimes exhaled profoundly and shook her head. Where she had scraped up the nerve to bullyrag an officer of the law like that was a mystery to her. It's a wonder he didn't bust her on the spot (or on the nose!). Dorie wasn't alone in her perplexity. In front of her sat Lily Dawn slowly awakening to the fact that she had toppled from the truck onto hard ground. The girl craned her neck right and left, uttered a dazed little sigh, and rose stiffly to her feet. Seemingly oblivious to her surroundings and to recent events, she staggered forward a step, then rubbed her shoulder and began examining her damaged knee and elbow. In the truck bed, Loyal Bunce released Petunia's jaws from the vise of fingers that had been holding those jaws clamped shut for several slobbery minutes. Loyal found his voice before Petunia found hers.

"Well, little lady, you sure outfoxed Johnny Law that

45

time! That was mighty quick thinkin', mighty quick. Couldna' done better m'self." He paused. "An that ain't all," he said, extracting a crumpled ball of red bandanna from his pocket and noisily blowing his nose into it. "You tol' him we was a fambly! Me 'n you an' the others. It's a long time since I had any fambly but Petunia, leastways any that'd own up to it."

Dorie and Lily Dawn looked at Loyal but didn't speak. He dropped his eyes and changed the subject. "I cain't believe your mama slept through the whole thing. She mus' be deefer than a fence post!"

It was the first time Dorie had really seen Loyal in the daylight. He looked much worse than even her unflattering image of him, worse than Lily Dawn, if that was possible. No doubt he smelled worse, too, though that would be going some. His gray, stringy beard had fared no better in the wind than his matching hair, and his deep-set eyes were all but hidden beneath his wild gray eyebrows. Loyal's cheeks, which sank sharply below the bone, combined with bad teeth and an unhealthy pallor to make him look at least as dead as Ruetta Flatray in the front seat. Dorie could see now that he was no taller than she was, and his bones were so meagerly covered that he looked like a skeleton that had been dressed at a yard sale and left in a cow pasture for a year or two. His faded denim jacket was only a few degrees cleaner than his jeans. No wonder the patrolman had turned all of them loose! It would take an iron constitution to conduct a body search of this raggle-taggle bunch. Loyal was armed for germ warfare, as overpowering in its way as her theatrics.

"Oh, she's deaf, all right," Dorie answered Loyal wearily. "I believe most dead people are."

"Daid! You say she's *daid!* You mean I been travelin' with a daid woman?" Loyal bent down and squinted through the streaky cab window. Then he tried to stretch around and look in the open door. "Well, I swan," he sighed, dropping to the truck bed. "This's a first, an' that's the truth."

Lily Dawn tried to lick her scraped right elbow, and failing that, she licked her left forefinger and applied the murky spittle to the offended area. Dorie privately questioned the application of a mud poultice to an open wound, but she withheld comment. A rare thing for her, she admitted. Then it occurred to her that the makeshift first-aid kit might still be in the glove box. It was a gift from Cleve on their twenty-fifth anniversary. She remembered the event because Cleve had made the kit from an old tin Schilling spice can—rosemary, she thought—he had emptied for the purpose. He had then stuffed the can with twenty-five bandaids and a tiny tube of first-aid cream. One bandaid for each year, he grinned. The can was missing. Cleve had apparently repossessed it.

What Cleve didn't know was that the rosemary hadn't gone bad. That was how rosemary smelled. That's why rabbits won't eat it in your yard unless they're starving to death. Her mother had discovered that fact in Jericho with the wild rabbits that raided her garden on a regular basis. They seemed to think she was sent to earth for their personal pleasure and convenience. In Dorie's view, then and now, a spice can full of bandaids that smell for all the world like rosemary was a sorry excuse for a silver anniversary present; but since Cleve had forgotten the previous twenty-four anniversaries, she supposed that anything was better than nothing. He had then returned to form and forgotten the next eleven, which gave added value to the one in thirty-six he remembered.

Lily Dawn looked up from her elbow, noticing to her surprise that the world was inhabited by people in addition to herself, people who did not have scraped elbows but were a sorry sight just the same.

"Who on earth's *that*?" she exclaimed, pointing at Loyal as he shuffled about rearranging what remained of the manure in the truck bed with his feet. "Hey Dorie, where'd that dirty old man come from, and what's he doin' dancin' around in *our* truck?" Petunia's head appeared. "An' what's that critter with him? Does he bite?"

"You mean the man, or the dog?" Dorie asked, pretending to look them over. "So far, neither of 'em bites, though I suspect both could if pushed to extremes. And as for dirt, missy, I'd say you're runnin' a close second, and I'm not such a distant third. The only respectable person associated with this entire enterprise is Mama. Ordinarily, she wouldn't be caught dead in such company." Dorie hesitated while her brain registered that remark and then she looked in at her

Minding Mama

mother. "But that's just how you've *been* caught, isn't it, Mama?"

The girl was not interested in metaphysical questions. "Why'd you call me the wrong name and wink all crazy-like at me when that lawman was here? You forget my name already? My mama use t' call me wrong half the time because it was my daddy named me. He named me after his mama 'stead of hers, and after the time of day I was born in. When she was mad at me, though, she never missed my name."

Dorie checked her own image in the smudged glass of the door and circled the cab to the driver's side. "Get in, child. First gas station past the state of Arkansas, we're goin' in and cleaning up as best we can. Y' hear me? I don't like bein' taken for trash one bit, even if it does save me a ticket or worse!" She turned to Loyal, who had settled himself and Petunia against the cab. "You all right back there?" Dorie called. She didn't wait for his reply, but wondered how his bones stood the ride, even cushioned by manure and the rubber mat Cleve had installed after only ten years of good intentions.

Fixing the quilt around Ruetta so that her face didn't show, Dorie spoke to Lily Dawn without looking at her. "Why'd I call you Mindy Lee? Suffice it to say I don't like tellin' fibs any better'n you do, but if anybody asks, you're my baby girl, and him back there, he's your granddaddy. You got that? And we're headed for the Flatray family reunion. Flatray. That's Mama's last name."

The girl didn't respond, but Dorie could feel her disapproval.

"Sometimes a righteous fib at a dangerous moment can save good people a whole lot of grief," Dorie explained, but she knew the girl wasn't buying it. Dorie could hear her thinking, *How can I be your girl when I don't look nuthin' like you or him? And besides, a fib is a fib, no matter how you dress it up.* "Your mama ever read you the Bible?" Dorie asked.

Finally, Lily Dawn spoke. "My mama didn't read me much, but my daddy, he took me to Bible school sometimes."

"Mine read me the Bible all the time. Made me sit there and listen if I wanted any supper. And that was even before she joined the Mormons."

Lily Dawn was horrified. "She's one a' *them*?" The girl shrank from Ruetta as though from a carrier of the plague or worse.

"Yes, she is. Don't change the subject. And don't worry, it's not contagious." Dorie found herself dipping again into the well of her mother's faith. "You ever hear the story of Rebekah, how she fooled her husband Isaac into givin' the birthright to Jacob 'stead of Esau?"

"She done Esau wrong, an' Isaac, too. I alluz felt bad for Esau."

"I did, too, but Jacob had to have the birthright or the Lord's plans would've gone to smash."

"Why didn't the Lord just make Jacob be born first? Save a lotta trouble and all that lyin'."

Minding Mama

Dorie glanced across her mother at Lily Dawn in surprise. The girl had a head on her. Clean her up, and Ruetta Flatray might have liked her for a real granddaughter. Ruetta already had a couple of those, but they didn't pay her any more attention than their mama, Marva Grace, did. Never having discovered that there was life after cheerleading, they were still trading on their former glory.

"I don't know why the Lord didn't make Jacob be born first," Dorie replied finally. "Maybe he wanted to see if Rebekah and Jacob would do what he said, no matter what. I think he must get tired of us arguing with him all the time, tryin' to talk him out of what *he* wants and into what *we* want."

"Like I used t' do with my daddy."

"Yeah, and like I used t' do with my mama."

Lily Dawn fell silent. A moment later, as if to affirm that good mamas should be listened to, she patted Ruetta's knee, bony and spare even under its thick quilt. Then, in something of a recoil, Lily Dawn drew her hand away and dumbly contemplated it. Her face revealed that she had reflexively touched a dead Mormon and that the gesture had shocked her. Ruetta Flatray, however, didn't seem to mind at all.

* * * * * * *

Crossing the border into Texas was a great relief to Dorie Grimes. Surely, here was a state large enough to absorb her pickup and its assorted contents without undue notice. But serious fatigue was setting in. Her eyelids weighed a pound each, and her back hurt. Lily Dawn, off in dreamland again, was no more help than Ruetta. Maybe less. After all, Dorie could invent dialogues with her mother because by now she pretty well knew how her mother would respond to just about anything. Well, at least the truck cab smelled better since the last stop. Along with gas and oil and other essentials like corn dogs, nachos, and cokes, Dorie had purchased a small bar of soap. She and Lily Dawn used the facilities to clean up a little while Loyal and Petunia stood guard duty. It would be Loyal's turn with the soap when Dorie stopped for a break at the first public park they came across. Petunia was a lost cause.

"Mama," Dorie said quietly, "why couldn't you of died early in the morning so's I could've been fresher when we started?"

Signs advertising various commercial enterprises in the next town began to appear, and Dorie allowed as how a place big enough to advertise would have a public park somewhere in the middle of it. She was right. There it was, with tables, swings, slides, and enough grass for a person to stretch out on for a few precious minutes. Half asleep already, Dorie left the pickup in search of a likely spot in the trampled grass. She warned Lily Dawn not to leave Ruetta and to fend off the curious while she herself grabbed a quick nap. The girl was also instructed to entertain Petunia while Loyal was indisposed. They'd eat a bite, Dorie promised, when she woke up. Apples and oranges that she bought yesterday, mostly.

They all needed the vitamins, she said, wondering as she spoke why she was concerning herself with the nutritional needs of such as this sorry pair of vagrants. What were these people to her anyway? Here today, gone tomorrow. She did need to keep her own strength up, however, and a diet of coke and chips could hardly be considered health-promoting. So far as she could tell, coke's principal contents after sugar were bubbles and caffeine, both of which have their place in civilized society, she supposed, but don't appear anywhere on the government's official food pyramid.

Dorie didn't know what awakened her, but she sat up with a start and looked around. Loyal was nearby, dawdling in a swing, peeling an orange and depositing the peelings in his jacket pocket. Clearly, he had made some effort to tidy up before abandoning the project as a lost cause. Dorie labored to her feet and turned toward the pickup. There, before the open passenger door in single file, stood six or seven children, obviously waiting for something. Moving slowly down the line was Lily Dawn.

"What's she doing?" Dorie screamed at Loyal.

"Looks like she's chargin' admission, don't it?"

Dorie grabbed the lunch bag and ran for the pickup. She arrived in time to hear Lily Dawn's pitch.

"One touch for a nickel, three touches for a dime!" the girl announced. "Come touch the dead lady. One touch for a nickel, three for a dime!"

Dorie grabbed Lily Dawn by the arm, shaking a few nickels and pennies loose, and pushed her toward the cab. The children scrambled to recover their investment from the grass. "Don't you have any respect for the dead?" Dorie screeched. "That's my mama. We're not runnin' a side show here. Nobody sells admission to my mama!" She slammed the door and turned to Loyal, who had followed her to the pickup. "Get in!" she cried. "We're outta here. Where's the dog?"

Loyal pointed. Petunia was perched in the driver's seat, her muzzle hanging on the half-open window, her tongue dripping saliva down the door. "That dog has alluz wanted t' drive, so I let her in," he said. "I shoulda put her in the circus."

* * * * * * *

It was after 3 p.m. Wednesday when Dorie and her flock passed through the town of Claude not twenty miles from Amarillo. She had been fighting sleep ferociously, slapping her cheeks, singing, drinking cokes, shaking her head. The only thing holding sleep at bay was worry about the pickup. Was that intermittent whir new or old? And that occasional clicking, had it always been there? Every unfamiliar sound sent adrenaline coursing through her system.

"Car trouble beats caffeine hands down for keepin' a body awake," she informed the sleeping Lily Dawn. "Hey girl, here's hoping we miss rush hour traffic at Amarillo. At least we'll soon hit the interstate. Once we get past Amarillo,

Minding Mama

it'll be clear sailin' to Flagstaff. The population'll be more sparse, too."

Getting no response from Lily Dawn, Dorie addressed Ruetta. "You'll be safer now, Mama, 'cause the towns are fewer and farther between. Not so many gawkers."

As if on cue, the pickup coughed and lurched. Dorie managed to pull onto a dirt side road before the engine died. She pumped the gas pedal to no avail and coasted to a bumpy stop in the grass and weeds along the roadside.

"We've stopped," Lily Dawn said through a gaping yawn.

"Brilliant deduction!" Dorie replied.

"We outta gas or what?" The girl scratched her ribs.

Dorie checked the gas gauge. The needle pointed below the E. She turned the ignition key off and slumped over the steering wheel. "I thought sure we'd make it to Amarillo. Must've been that cotton-pickin' head wind."

"Whatta we do now?"

Dorie raised her head. "Well, actually, this would be a good time for you to turn yourself around and get on back home. You're supposed to be in school, anyway. I musta lost my senses, bringin' you along."

"Next week my school's got spring vacation. Anyways, I cain't go back. Them boys an' their evil ways'll do me in, an' my stepmama she'll beat on me." The girl reached across Ruetta and grabbed Dorie's arm, pleading, "You saved me. You're a savior on Mount Zion! I learnt about them kind in Bible school an' you're one."

Dorie shook her head. "I'm no savior, girl, on Mount Zion or anywhere else. Any good in me comes from this woman here between us. Who knows, maybe she's been directin' things from the other side, assuming there is an 'other side.' She thought most things happen for a purpose."

"Even runnin' outta gas?"

"Maybe, maybe not. Who knows? Anyway, I got to think for a minute. I need time to think." Dorie opened the door and climbed out.

There to greet her was Loyal, on his knees leaning over the side panel of the truck bed firing a barrage of questions. "Why'd we stop here? Where are we? What's goin' on?"

Dorie wanted to smack him. "It seems this vehicle won't go without gas," she snapped. "We ran out. You've got two options. You and Petunia can take Matilda and go your merry way, or . . ."

"Or what?"

"Or you can stay here with Mama while I take Lily Dawn and flag a ride into Amarillo for help. What'll it be?"

Loyal stood and saluted with solemn precision. "My name ain't Loyal fer nuthin'. Me an' Petunia'll stay with the ship."

Dorie softened. "Okay, good. Now, about Mama. I think we better move her out of the cab and put her in the back, outta sight, in case somebody comes snoopin' around. Let's get her out and set her there in the grass whiles I see what's behind the seat to cover her with. At

Minding Mama

least we made it off the highway." Dorie turned to Lily Dawn. "Out with you, girl. Undo Mama's seat belt."

Dorie had forgotten about rigor mortis, but of course it had set in. Ruetta Flatray was permanently molded to the shape of a small truck seat. After much twisting and wriggling and a little well-aimed cursing, the three of them managed to pry her loose from the cab and set her carefully on the ground. They propped her against a rock, and Loyal tied Petunia to a splintery old power pole so she wouldn't, as he put it, be "worryin' the body none." Ruetta was, as Loyal also observed, "dead weight," and unable to assist with the transfer. Brushing away an errant tear, Dorie found an old canvas tarp behind the seat, which they fashioned into a little shelter behind the cab. Tugging and lifting, they finally got Ruetta into the truck bed and under the tarp. Dorie hated to see her proper little mother treated so. On the other hand, any break in the routine was always a party for Ruetta.

"She's in fetal position, ready for being born again inta the heavenly kingdom!" Loyal exclaimed.

Dorie didn't appreciate the observation, though she knew Loyal meant no disrespect. "That'll keep her out of sight and out of the sun 'til we get back," she said. "C'mon, Lily Dawn, we've gotta get on that highway and get us a ride into Amarillo, fast." Dorie grabbed her handbag, straightened her hair and blouse, and started off.

"When we goin' t' eat? I'm gettin' hungry," Lily Dawn complained, trailing behind Dorie.

"You shoulda thought of the fact that you'd require food on a regular basis b'fore you run off," Dorie replied.

* * * * * * *

A good many cars roared by as Dorie and the girl stood there, waving at the traffic. Then finally one slowed and stopped, a faded black Ford Taurus, anything but new. It held two people, a man and a woman who looked to be in their late twenties. They both smiled all friendly-like and said hop in. She was in a bare midriff tank top and shorts, and he wore jeans and a Hard Rock Café T-shirt. The man, a blond with short hair, was driving and the woman, a long-haired brunette, was opening beer cans, of which several empty ones had accumulated on the floor behind the front seat. The full ones were apparently up front. Dorie calculated the risk and climbed in anyway, pulling Lily Dawn after her. "Beggars can't be choosers," Dorie sighed under her breath. It was one of her mother's favorite mantras after she took up residence with Dorie and Cleve.

Once inside the car, Dorie realized that Ruetta was wrong. Even beggars could be choosers, and she should have chosen to wait for another vehicle. The smell of beer was enough to make a sober person drunk, and the pair in the front seat were happier than she liked to see anybody who was in charge of a moving automobile.

The man turned around. "Where you headed? You got car trouble, or just out on the road?"

Minding Mama

Dorie tried to hide her anxiety. "Our truck ran outta gas back there, so we have t' go to Amarillo to get some," she said.

"Outta gas. What a pity," the woman chimed in, but she didn't sound all that sincere to Dorie. "That your girl there?"

"Yes, it is," Dorie lied. "Name's Mindy Lee. I'm Mrs. Lewis." She shot a warning glance at Lily Dawn.

"Well, well, outta gas. What a pity!" the woman repeated, and then she laughed.

Dorie squirmed as she moved a couple of empty cans to the side with her left foot. Lily Dawn eyed her apprehensively, and Dorie crossed fingers on both hands. "You goin' into town by chance?" she asked.

"By chance we are," the man grinned. "We got a little banking to do."

The woman giggled when he said that, and Dorie wondered what was so funny. Then the woman turned around and looked Lily Dawn over. "Glory be, girl, you look a little worse for the wear. When's the last time you saw a bathtub?" The woman waited. "S'matter? Cat got your tongue?"

"No'm, just ain't got nothin' t'say." Lily Dawn's eyes were riveted on her clenched hands in her lap.

US Highway 287 had joined Interstate 40, and the Ford Taurus exited on a street that the man said led to a shopping center. "We plan to use the branch bank comin' up," the man said, and the woman giggled again and took another swallow of Budweiser.

"We'd be much obliged if you'd let us off at the first gas station you see," Dorie said, forcing a smile. "We're on kind of a tight time schedule."

"Yeah, we got a dead woman!" Lily Dawn broke in.

"What's that?" the man asked.

Dorie poked Lily Dawn, hard. "She means we got to get to the funeral of her grandmama before they put her in the ground," Dorie said.

"Oh," the woman said. "Is it your mama?"

"Yes, it is," Dorie answered, sniffing and looking mournful to demonstrate her bereavement.

"Well," the man said, "we're in a smidgen of a hurry ourselves. Lucky the branch banks stay open later'n them downtown."

The woman giggled again and dropped her empty beer can on the floor.

"This ain't a trash bin up here, Sugar," the man said. "Stow that can in the back."

"Picky, picky," the woman complained, but she retrieved the can and dropped it to the floor between Dorie and Lily Dawn. It rolled to Dorie's side, and she left it.

"There it is, Amarillo's finest!" the man exclaimed, pulling into the parking lot behind a boxy looking bank and slamming the brakes in time to miss the hedge in front of him. He wiped his hand across his mouth and then across the front of his shirt. "You folks sit tight whilst we conduct our business. I got to get my li'l briefcases out of the back. C'mon, Sugarpie!"

Minding Mama

After the pair left, Dorie fidgeted a minute or two, then came to a decision. "Listen, Lily Dawn, I'm goin' to go look for a public telephone and call the AAA to pick us up and take us and some gas back to the truck. When you drive vehicles as old as ours, you keep your membership in the AAA paid up."

"What's the AAA? Ain't that for alcoholics?"

"No, it's for automobiles. It's got three A's instead of two. You stay here so's they don't leave us in case I can't get through to the AAA."

"I don' wanna stay in this here rattletrap. It smells bad."

"So do you, honey, so do you," Dorie said and started toward a convenience store she had noticed down the street.

Dorie hadn't gone 100 yards when she heard what sounded like shooting behind her. Turning, she saw two people in ski masks, one of them wearing a bare midriff tank top, the other jeans and a T-shirt, running across the bank parking lot. Seconds later, the black Ford Taurus went tearing by. As it flew past, Dorie caught a glimpse of Lily Dawn's panic-stricken face at the partly open back window.

"Lily Dawn!" she screamed. "Lily Dawn!"

Dorie was beside herself. Within minutes, police cars were at the scene, but rush-hour traffic was jamming their pursuit of the bank robbers. "I thought Bonnie and Clyde died a long time ago," Dorie said aloud. She was helpless to do anything but trust Lily Dawn to the prowess and wisdom of the Amarillo police. Most likely they'd send the girl home, and then she'd have to run off all over again. Of course, Dorie knew that if the police caught up with the robbers and rescued Lily Dawn, the girl would tell the first person she saw, and all subsequent persons, about Ruetta. Well, Dorie only hoped that Lily Dawn would be alive and *able* to talk. She'd rather have Lily Dawn alive and saying anything at all, than dead and saying nothing. Dorie was surprised to discover how much she cared about the girl. You'd think I was her mother or something, she told herself. Heaven forbid. There wasn't a thing she could do now except find some gasoline and get back to the pickup and Mama. She said a silent prayer for the girl and vowed to see about her on the return trip.

* * * * * * *

Nearly an hour had passed by the time Dorie Grimes found a phone, enlisted the AAA, and was roaring toward the pickup in the company of a large bearded man named Mike. It was an hour that she might better have wasted sleeping, if waste it she must. Mike wore greasy striped coveralls and operated a tow truck, which Dorie desperately hoped would not be necessary. Apparently, Mike had heard nothing of the robbery. At least he didn't mention it, and neither did Dorie. His only comments, unrepeatable in polite company, were directed at any driver who dared venture into space he himself intended to occupy. He and his rig were big enough to drive his point home.

Dorie herself had never argued with a tow truck, nor did

Minding Mama

she ever intend to. As they rolled along, Dorie noticed something that resembled greenbacks blowing up with the traffic. She wasn't the only one to notice. Cars going both directions were screeching to a stop and spilling out their occupants before the wheels stopped rolling. Whistling to himself, Mike was oblivious to the entire drama of blowing money and greedy scramblers. Dorie, however, could hardly be disinterested. She was pretty sure she knew where the stuff came from. The robbers had doubled back and had lost some of their booty along the way. Dorie wished she could reach out and snag a bill or two. Her money was getting low with three extra mouths to feed, if you counted Petunia.

When Dorie and Mike and the tow truck reached the dirt road where she had left the Toyota and Ruetta in the care of Loyal Bunce and Petunia, the pickup was gone. There in its place sat a black Ford Taurus. Dorie was dumfounded.

"My . . . my truck's gone," she stammered.

"Gone! Where could it of went to? Didn' you say it was outta gas?" Mike was not sympathetic.

"Well, yes. I thought so."

"You sure you wasn't in the Ford t'day, lady, and your old man was drivin' the pickup?"

Dorie glared at Mike as he pulled to a stop next to the Taurus. Then it hit her. *Mama!* Mama was in the bed of the pickup! And Loyal! Where was Loyal? And Petunia? And Lily Dawn? Did Loyal find some gas and steal the pickup? Would he do that? Did he take Lily Dawn, or is she dead? Where are the bank robbers?

Mike picked up his order sheet. "Look, lady, I got other calls t' make. You want the gas or not? You already paid fer it an' the deposit on the can. You better take 'em."

"All right, all right, leave 'em here." In something of a daze, Dorie descended from the tow truck and watched Mike unload the gas can, climb into his vehicle, and drive off.

Too stunned to cry, Dorie hurried over to the Taurus and looked inside. The beer cans were there, and a couple of empty canvas bags. The keys were in the ignition. "Oh, Mama," Dorie wailed, "how'm I ever gonna get you to Jericho? I don't even know where you are or who's got you." She dropped to the ground and buried her face in her hands. "At least you're covered, what with night comin' on an' all," she sobbed. "Mama, I've failed you. You're in the Lord's hands now. Maybe he can get you to Jericho. I can't seem to."

At that moment, Dorie became aware of footsteps approaching. Her first thought was that the cheap imitation of Bonnie and Clyde had returned, but she didn't care if they blew her to smithereens. I'd welcome it, she told herself. Anybody who fails her mama as bad as I did deserves to die a terrible death. But it wasn't the drunken robbers. It was Loyal and Petunia.

"Loyal!" Dorie cried, "what's happened here? Where's Mama? Where's Lily Dawn?"

"Well now, I don't know about Lily Dawn, but I 'spect your mama's gone off with the folks who left this here black car. They don't know they got her, but they do. I slunk into the brush back there when I seen 'em comin'. I

Minding Mama

made Petunia hush up, too."

"They took the pickup?"

"That they did, little lady."

"But it was out of gas."

"That didn't stop them folks none. The man, he siphoned gas outta the Ford there and put 'er in the truck. Got a mouthful, too," Loyal snickered.

"Did you see Lily Dawn?"

"Lily Dawn! I thought she 'uz with you. I didn' see nuthin' else. I crouched down on top a' Petunia an' hid m' head. Them folks started lookin' around all suspicious like, runnin' from bush t' bush an' cussin' a blue streak." Loyal looked up. "Whatya know, there's Lily Dawn now, comin' acrost the road on t'other side."

Dorie got to her feet and retrieved her handbag from a clump of weeds where she had dropped it. "Lily Dawn!" she cried, running toward the youngster. "Are you all right? What're we goin' to do, child? What's to become of us? What's happened to Mama?" Dorie embraced the girl and wept.

Lily Dawn squirmed free. "Them robbers got her, but I fixed 'em an' they're madder'n hops. I let loose all their money outta the window. Y'know, like Hansel and Gretel and them bread crumbs. My daddy he read me that story. I didn't have no bread, but I had them people's money. They threw the bags of it in the back seat with me. They didn't see me do it 'til I was about finished."

"How did you escape?"

65

"While they was takin' the gas outta this here car and puttin' it in the truck, I snuck out the back door an' skittered acrost the road real quick. I got in a ol' dry ditch and run 'til I found me some thick bushes to hide in. They run around and yelled some, but then they give up and lef' me. I didn' know Loyal was still here. I thought maybe he run off."

Loyal was offended. "Not me, I'm Loyal. I ain't never run off in m' life."

Lily Dawn looked at him. "Huh! Whatya call what you done when you took to the road?"

"That's differnt!" he insisted. "It ain't the same as betrayin' a trust. I ain't never betrayed a trust!"

"All right, you two. We've got other things to do than argue whether Loyal run off or not. We got to find Mama, pronto! It'll be dark soon. We gotta find her b'fore dark."

Lily Dawn spoke. "I bet them two drunk robbers will be chasin' that money, once they think the police are lookin' for them somewheres else."

"Tha's right," Loyal said. "They'll figger the police won't be lookin' fer anyone in a red pickup. I bet they'll be scourin' the roadsides. If'n we can spot 'em, we can trade 'em vehicles when they ain't lookin'. They're bound to be even drunker now 'cause they're so mad. I c'n hotwire this vehicle easy as pie."

Dorie opened the car door and leaned across the wheel. "You won't need to," she said. "They left the keys. Get the gas can and let's get this jitney started." Dorie turned to Loyal. "You're a genius. If you weren't so dirty, I'd give

Minding Mama

you a hug." She looked around. "Get Petunia. The two of you can ride in the back seat."

"I'll collect on that hug if I ever get me a real bath," Loyal grinned. "I'm fambly, ain't I? You said so y'self."

"Yes," Dorie agreed, "I s'pose you're family, and I owe you a hug. An' Lily Dawn, too. Now let's get movin'!"

Four

Lily Dawn and Loyal Bunce had guessed right. Two or three miles up the highway, there was Dorie Grimes's little red pickup off the shoulder and tilting rather precariously, she thought. The robbers hadn't bothered to park it properly or to check under the tarp in back for dead bodies. They had other things on their minds. Dorie hoped Ruetta hadn't shifted around too much, calling attention to herself and getting her pajamas all dirty. As it was, the undertaker would be hard pressed to extract or disguise the manure smell. Under the circumstances, cremation should have been an option, but Ruetta had made her opposition to that process crystal clear. Burial in one solid lump facilitated resurrection, she said. She didn't want to be sent to the end of the line when the graves were opened.

Of course, when Ruetta said these things, a close encounter with fresh manure was not in the equation. Manure had a way of making its presence felt into the next

Minding Mama

county, if not the next life. It was the skunk of the recycled vegetable kingdom. Loyal and Petunia were a case in point, an obvious case now that they were occupying the back seat of the robbers' Taurus. Even so, when Dorie considered how the pair would have smelled without the barnyard additive, she was inclined to be grateful for small blessings, as her mother would have advised. The manure was the lesser of two evils.

As they approached the pickup, Dorie could see what looked like the robbers dashing about in a field some sixty or seventy yards from her truck. They resembled tipsy participants in some primitive rite of spring. They weren't alone, either. The occupants of several other vehicles, parked every which way in front of Dorie's pickup, were out there competing with Bonnie and Clyde and the wind for the dancing greenbacks. A south breeze had blown the money across the highway, which saved Dorie the trouble of crossing the median in a low-slung car, a hazardous proposition and an illegal one which Lily Dawn was sure to question. Dorie was still finding travel with two consciences besides her own a little restrictive, even if one of them was somewhat incapacitated. Where Ruetta left off, Lily Dawn took up. They were a team, those two, and they had never been properly introduced.

"Here's hoping they've left the keys in the pickup," Dorie said, "although I might have a spare in my handbag somewhere. Unless Cleve borrowed it—Cleve, that's my husband, in case you're wondering."

"I could always hotwire her," Loyal offered from the back seat.

"I'd just feel better knowing that people such as them don't have a key to my vehicle, even if our paths were never to cross again."

"Are we gonna collect us some money, too?" Lily Dawn wanted to know.

"No, girl, we've got no time for that. Besides, that money's not for the taking. It belongs to the bank."

"Finders keepers, losers weepers," my mama used to say." Lily Dawn paused, then added, "Less'n it was somethin' of *hers* turned up missin'."

Dorie pulled to a stop behind her pickup. "Loyal," she said, "I'll get out and sneak up to the truck. If the keys are there an' Mama's there, I'll signal, and you and Petunia quick slither into the back with Mama and lay low." Dorie then looked at Lily Dawn. "You crawl out this side of the car, duckin' down. Sneak in the truck on the driver's side and skoosh over. Keep your head down so's they can't see you. Then I'll jump in and start her up. We'll shift Mama into the front soon's we feel safe."

"Gimme about two shakes extree," Loyal said, and pulled a Swiss Army knife out of his pocket.

"What you doin' with that thing?" Lily Dawn demanded.

"Never you mind, missy, jus' never you mind."

"Here's hopin' the robbers don't look this way," Dorie said, opening the door just wide enough to get out. "Times like this I wish I was about four feet tall and skinny."

Minding Mama

Dorie bent as far as she dared with her bad back and made for the pickup. After a quick check under the tarp, she carefully opened the door on the driver's side. Spotting the key in the ignition, she signaled c'mon to the others. Lily Dawn stubbed her toe on a rock and had to stifle a yell. It wasn't easy, either, to traverse the two gear sticks with her head down. By the time the girl reached the passenger's seat and Dorie arrived behind the steering wheel, Loyal and Petunia were in the back, sprawled flat against the tarp that covered Ruetta and the trombone. Loyal tapped on the cab to say they were aboard. A glance in the rearview mirror showed that Loyal had remembered the gas can, too. Dorie had to return the can and fill the gas tank.

Taking a deep breath, Dorie turned the ignition key and rammed the stick into first gear. Then she gunned the engine and spit gravel off the shoulder as she barged into the right lane of traffic between a Chevy Suburban and a semi. She hoped the semi would cover her escape and wondered if the bank robbers had seen her leave. Well, they could hardly give chase even if thcy had; and the more Dorie thought about it, the more she hoped maybe they had witnessed her little moment of triumph. It was a satisfying thought, though as a rule Dorie did not regard herself as a vindictive person.

With a few miles between her and the wild pair, Dorie relaxed and told Lily Dawn she could sit up straight now. She thought they were safe, and with the coming night they'd be even safer. The sun had dropped behind a dusty horizon, and in response to the ever-deepening sky, Dorie's eyelids begged to close. Her eyes felt like knots of raw ore. She wanted sleep more than she had ever wanted anything, except maybe that little spotted pony when she was eleven, but she could feel the adrenaline still pumping. Until her insides slowed down, she wouldn't be able to sleep anyway, not even if she had a feather bed and a clear conscience.

Just outside Amarillo, Lily Dawn had a thought. "What if they follow us?" she cried.

"They won't," Dorie said, jingling a set of keys in Lily Dawn's direction. "Seems I ran off and forgot to leave these keys in the Ford. Now, how could I have been so careless?"

"You stole their keys! What you gonna do with 'em?" Lily Dawn's ethical system hit a snag here. The Bible says thou shalt not steal. It does not say if stealing from robbers counts as a regular sin. Bible School hadn't prepared her to make such fine moral distinctions.

"Deposit 'em in the first trash can I see," Dorie answered, then added, grinning, "or keep 'em for a souvenir."

"What if they got another set?"

"Well, even if they've got more keys, I doubt they've got *two* spare tires." Dorie glanced over her shoulder. "Seems Loyal had a leather punch on that fancy knife of his."

Lily Dawn was shocked. "Y' mean he poked holes in them people's tires? That's against the law, ain't it?"

Dorie laughed. "I think the law is lenient toward somebody pokes holes in a bank robber's tires!"

* * * * * * *

Minding Mama

At the next exit, Dorie drove onto a side road and stopped in the cracked asphalt yard behind an abandoned warehouse. "I got to get Mama outta the back," she said. "I bet she's drivin' Petunia crazy. Poor Loyal's got his hands full."

"Well, three in the back an' two in the front suits me jus' fine. My daddy wouldn't cotton t' me travelin' with no dead person anyhow."

Dorie frowned. "Well now, your daddy's not in charge of this particular trip, is he?"

"No he ain't, but that don't mean . . ."

Dorie cut the girl off by opening her door. "Now, you get yourself out, Lily Dawn. We need your help, pronto. I don't want t' hear any more of your moralizin' today."

Just then, Petunia leaped from the truck bed and bounded toward the sagging rear door of the claptrap building, dodging assorted pieces of greasy machinery as she went. Dorie was surprised to see the dog display that much interest in anything.

"What's got into the mutt?" she asked Loyal.

"Squirrel," he said. "Squirrel run acrost there an' Petunia seen 'im. Lookee, she squeezed in there after 'im. An' listen to 'er. Don't she carry on, though?"

The smell of rancid oil and grease turned Dorie's stomach. This was no place to linger. "You've got to shut her up, or she'll roust out the whole town, and we've got to get Mama into the front seat where she belongs. Did Petunia bother Mama any?"

"Not so long as I wuz settin' on her tail, she didn't. It's when I stood up she spotted that there squirrel. Leastways I think it wuz a squirrel. Too dark t' tell fer sure." Loyal stretched both hands above his head and moaned. "How much futher we got to go t'night? M' bones is tired."

Dorie's patience was worn thin. "*You* don't have to go any farther. *I*, on the other hand, have to go 'til I drop dead or get to Jericho, whichever comes first. Now, help us with Mama, and then go get that mongrel. She'll raise the dead with her racket."

Loyal was offended. "She ain't no mongrel. She might be a conglomeration, but she ain't no mongrel!"

Dorie rolled her eyes and pointed at the tarp. "Undo that tie and scoot Mama out. It's not befitting the dignity of the dead to keep company with leftover manure and a leftover dog."

Getting Ruetta Flatray into the middle of the pickup's front seat was harder than getting her out of it. The three of them tried feet first and head last; but she had no give to her, and the gear sticks kept catching on her feet, threatening to tear her slippers. So they eased her out and tried head first, with Dorie working from the driver's side and Loyal and Lily Dawn working from the passenger's side. In the meantime, the clamor in the warehouse continued, rattling Dorie's nerves like a nest of exposed wires in a lightning storm. But at last they managed to get Ruetta settled and belted in her accustomed seat. Loyal wondered out loud when the dead woman might start to smell, and that was the

Minding Mama

last straw for Dorie Grimes.

"Soon enough!" she cried. "Now go get that dog and we're leavin' this place. All this grease and trash makes me want to puke! My nose has endured about all it can stand, what with the three of you. Bad as you all smell, I doubt you'd even notice if Mama did ripen a bit." She climbed in beside Ruetta, who had brought the scent of manure into the cab to compete with the unbathed essence of Lily Dawn. "There's a flashlight in the glove box if Clarence Ross didn't swipe the batteries from it for something or other. Find it and git!"

Lily Dawn, who usually had plenty to say, didn't enter this particular conversation. Silently she climbed into the passenger seat and straightened the quilt around Ruetta. The girl had seen enough of her stepmother's ire to know the warning signs. It had been a big day, and even if she was hungry, she didn't ask if they were going to eat any time soon. One thing was certain. Dorie was her best hope for getting to her grandmama's by the dam. She had to stick it out.

Dorie watched glumly as Loyal approached the ramshackle building and pulled a plank out of the door to get in. Petunia had other things on her mind and was paying him no heed whatsoever.

Within minutes, however, Loyal came bursting back through the door, flashlight waving wildly. "C'mere quick!" he cried. "You ain't gonna believe what I found in there! You ain't gonna believe it!"

Loyal's enthusiasm notwithstanding, Dorie knew that the

last thing she could possibly care about at this moment was what Loyal had seen in the old warehouse. All she wanted was to get gasoline and get out of the state of Texas. She still had to cross all of New Mexico and half of Arizona before Ruetta spoiled. Besides, they were all famished, and she had no time to spare on warehouse diversions. Lily Dawn, of course, had all the time in the world to spare on them, and she was out of the truck before Dorie could stop her. In the dim light, Dorie saw Loyal duck back into the building just before Petunia and the squirrel came tearing out again, screaming toward the wire fence surrounding the yard. The squirrel slipped under it, and Petunia screeched to a stop, yipping and whining as her lithe prey disappeared into the dusk.

When Loyal emerged from the building, he was carrying something, Dorie couldn't tell what. It appeared, however, that aiding and abetting burglary, not to mention breaking and entering, could be added to her rap sheet. Why not see how many more crimes she could tally in a mere forty-eight hours? Maybe she should go for a record.

"Lookee what I got here!" Loyal cried as he half-ran, half-stumbled toward where Dorie sat in the pickup with her mother.

Dorie informed Loyal that she had no interest whatsoever in whatever it was he had there, and that if he and Lily Dawn and Petunia weren't in this pickup in about two seconds she was leaving the lot of them. Didn't they know she had to deliver Mama to the mortician in Jericho by tomorrow afternoon? Did they think she could dawdle around here all night? Get in, she commanded, and they did, with Petunia still torn between the escaped squirrel and the departing Toyota. At the last minute, the dog opted for the pickup, jumping onto the tailgate as Dorie made for the street. Loyal looked ready to bail out if his dog fell short.

Herself, Dorie was in no mood for conciliation or conversation. Lily Dawn was obviously agitated and bursting to talk, but she held her peace while Dorie returned the gas can and got gas and snacks in Amarillo. Dorie didn't speak to either Loyal or Lily Dawn, but tossed each a packaged sandwich and a plastic bottle of apple juice. Lily Dawn ate in silence, occasionally sending a furtive glance in Dorie's direction. Then it was the I 40 on-ramp and full speed ahead to New Mexico. By the time Dorie stopped again, in Tucumcari, Lily Dawn was asleep and Dorie was feeling calmer. If she could wake Lily Dawn, stay awake herself, and abide the girl's conversation—and if her bladder cooperated—she could go nonstop to Albuquerque. She bought the girl a coke and herself a large coffee, but didn't disturb Loyal and Petunia who appeared to be dead to the world. Already she had forgotten about Loyal's "find" in the warehouse. She wished all her passengers were as little trouble as her mother.

* * * * * * *

Dorie realized that in some ways, she was gaining a new appreciation for her mother on this trip. In life, Ruetta was opinionated, yes, but she was never dull or self-absorbed.

Marilyn Arnold

She was fascinated by the world and its amazing variety. All it took was for someone to die and, by and large, the negatives of traveling with her vanished. What stayed, of course, were the guilt and the worry. Over the last eight years of living with her mother Dorie had become almost accustomed to the backseat driving, the complaints about the temperature, and the running commentary on the evils of fast food. As for the sermons on the state of Dorie's eternal soul, however, there had been times when Dorie wished her mother had never discovered the Mormons, or they her, whichever it was. Ruetta had always professed faith in God, but when she took up with the Mormons rather late in life, she acquired a whole new batch of views to express and a new enthusiasm for expressing them. It was odd, now, to have the older woman so accommodating and tranquil, even pleasant, when Dorie could feel her presence filling the cab of the truck like yeast in rising bread.

What with Ruetta and the others, this particular journey was taking on the character of a pilgrimage. The Jericho Tales. One thing was certain. It was more than an automobile trip, even though that's how Cleve and Clarence Ross referred to it in the abstract, before it happened. As if Dorie and her mother were merely planning a vacation together. Dorie admitted that in the beginning, the journey had assumed something of that character, but subsequent events had burst that fragile little bubble. If Dorie had been a religious person, she would have said the journey had become a kind of holy quest. She had heard about mythic

Minding Mama

searches for the Holy Grail, and only now did she understand something of what drove the heroic seekers toward their goal against all odds.

But Dorie knew she was no hero. And now, with all those miles still to travel, she found herself wishing yet again that she had never promised to bury Ruetta beside her mate in Jericho, Utah. At the time, the vow had seemed to Dorie only vaguely binding and something her mother would soon forget. That was before Ruetta moved to Atlanta and hammered it home daily, and before Dorie considered the logistics and checked a road map. She had made the promise partly to appease her mother and mainly to change the subject. Ruetta had a way of riding a subject to death, especially the subject of her burial. There were few topics she enjoyed more, unless it was religion, and few Dorie enjoyed less.

* * * * * * *

Once she was rattling along the interstate again, Dorie tried to coax Lily Dawn out of her shell. She had perhaps been a little too harsh, she realized, and wanted to make it up to the girl. It wasn't the girl's fault that they nearly lost the truck and Ruetta too. In fact, if the girl hadn't thrown all that money out the window, the truck and Ruetta might not have been found 'til a week from some Tuesday.

"Pretty smart of you to dump that money, Lily Dawn," Dorie ventured. "That's what got us Mama an' the truck back."

Lily Dawn eyed Dorie a little distrustfully, then turned to the window. Clouds had moved in and covered the stars. Dorie wondered what the girl was looking at out there in the dark.

"Want to find something on the radio?" Dorie suggested, desperate for distractions to keep her awake. She should have thought to bring some tapes. One of her patrons at the beauty shop had lent her some motivational tapes that the woman swore had changed her life. They told her how that she was a child of the universe and all she had to do was get in contact with these friendly aliens who swooped around in spaceships and spread love. If she just stretched out from the top of something high like a roof or a cliff and repeated these special words that normal people couldn't understand, why then, these aliens would hear them and answer her on the internet. They would solve all her problems for her and make her rich besides.

Dorie tried to explain to the woman that she and Cleve didn't have a computer, much less the internet, but the woman said it didn't matter, the tapes would help her anyway. Dorie thought maybe the tapes would have helped keep her awake if nothing else, and regretted not having brought them. She was not into all this outer space stuff and neither was Cleve. As for Ruetta? Not on your life. She believed that God and angels, not aliens, occupied the heavens.

Lily Dawn looked at Dorie and then punched the power button on the dashboard radio. Static. She left it there. Dorie knew the girl was making a statement. She tried again.

Minding Mama

"What kind of music do you like? Rock and roll? Rap? Country?"

The girl stared at the road pouring out before the headlights. "I likes gospel music the best," she said, and punched the button again. The truck cab became a silent vacuum.

Dorie was surprised at the response. "What kind of gospel music?"

"All of it," Lily Dawn declared. "I likes all of it. It 'minds me of when my daddy took me to Sunday School an' I felt happy."

Dorie hesitated, her eyes fixed on the converging cones of light that ran ahead of the pickup and were never caught. "Do you believe in Jesus?"

The girl thought about that for a minute or so. "Sometimes I does, sometimes I doesn't."

"When are the times you do?"

The girl began turning the knob that rolled the window up and down, first right, then left. "When you tol' me I could come along with you and your mama. I believed then."

Dorie was touched. "I think I believed then, too,"she said quietly.

Lily Dawn glanced up. "An' when we seen this ol' truck settin' there by the road, and them robbers out in the field where they couldn't ketch us, I figgered Jesus watchin' out fer us, an' fer your mama, too. He didn't let the bad folks hurt her."

"I see what you mean," Dorie said, then paused. "When are the times you don't believe?"

"When I seen that little baby in that dirty ol' place.

Jesus not watchin' over him!"

Dorie's heart leaped to her throat. "What little baby, Lily Dawn? What little baby you talkin' about, girl?"

"Little baby Loyal found back there in that building, where the dog run in."

"Loyal found a baby?" Dorie cried. "Where is it? Why didn't you tell me?"

"Couldn't tell you 'cause you was so mean mad. Loyal, he jus' wropped her in his coat and took her in the back with him and Petunia."

Dorie felt the blood rush to her head. "You tellin' me there's a baby in the back of this truck?"

"Less'n Loyal chucked it over the side."

"It'll freeze back there!" Dorie whipped off at an approaching exit and slammed on the brakes. "A baby! My glory, what next? Are we all kidnapers now?"

* * * * * * *

The sudden stop aroused Loyal Bunce, and he was awake to meet Dorie's fury. "Where's that child?" She demanded. "It could've died back here in the cold! And without milk! Why did you bring it? Why didn't you tell me so's we could take it to the police or a hospital or somewhere?"

"You din't gimme no chanct t' tell you. It was git outta there quick and tell about lost babies later. B'sides, you take it to the p'lice an' they gonna ask a whole lotta questions 'bout why you transportin' a dead woman in a truck,

Minding Mama

not to mention a baby an' a girl who ain't your own and a tramp with a trombone and a broken down dog."

Loyal unbuttoned his jacket, and even in the darkness Dorie could tell that the baby was alive and only sleeping. Her heart softened the instant she saw it, but her fear sprang up. What should they do with the baby? How could they explain coming this far, even crossing state lines, without reporting it? Dorie felt sick inside. Loyal made a good point when he asked what he should have done when he saw the baby bundled up on an old car seat without the car in that warehouse. If he had left it, the baby would certainly have died. But I wouldn't have known about it, Dorie wailed silently. Well, she decided, we'll have to figure things out later. For now, diapers and bottles were top priority. She gave Lily Dawn the choice of holding the baby in the front or riding in the back with Petunia while Loyal held him in front. If it was a him. It might be a her. Nobody had checked. Lily Dawn elected to hold the baby.

At the next town likely to have an all-night convenience store, Dorie pulled off, praying to the gods of finance that her credit card would still clear purchases against it because her cash was dangerously low. While Loyal filled the tank and watched Ruetta, Dorie took the baby inside. There she bought Pampers and baby formula in disposable bottles. She was amazed that the baby hadn't put up a fuss when awakened by the bright lights. In the restroom, she unwrapped the child and changed his soaking diaper. Yes, it was a he, and she judged him to be no more than six weeks old. He gazed solemnly at her out of bright blue eyes. Surprisingly, the little fellow was dressed in a relatively clean undershirt, sweater, and baby blanket. As she finished securing the clean Pamper, Dorie noticed a piece of paper tucked between the baby's shirt and sweater. There, in thick pencil, in letters that resembled the work of an early gradeschooler, were these words:

TO WHO FINDS THIS BABBI
PLEZ KEP HIM
I CANT KEP HIM
HIS NAM IS MOZUS

Well, Dorie said to herself, the modern Moses is found in a filthy abandoned warehouse instead of lovely green bulrushes, and the people who find him are hardly people of royal blood. She made the decision then and there to take the baby on to Jericho, even though the first Moses was forbidden. Ruetta had always held it against the Lord, just a little, that after all the trouble Moses went to with the children of Israel, he never got to enter the Promised Land. So, Mama, Dorie said under her breath, you're righting an old wrong. You'll sleep better now. As for herself, Dorie knew she wouldn't sleep peacefully until she had her mother safely in the mortician's hands. If then. Mortician or no mortician, she still had to face the law and the bureaucrats. But at the moment? At the moment, she had no time to lose. She had to drive, and drive hard.

Minding Mama

Back in the Toyota, the baby cried a little until Lily Dawn gave him his bottle, the way Dorie showed her. Then he settled into her arms and went to sleep. Soon the girl was asleep, too. For some reason, Dorie felt less tired and anxious than before she discovered the baby. Then, too, maybe in passing through Albuquerque she crossed an invisible hurdle. The goal actually seemed attainable now. The first light of morning was breaking all strawberry gold in the sky behind the little red pickup when Dorie pulled into Flagstaff. A pothole she hadn't seen jarred the baby and the girl awake. The baby began whimpering and the girl comforted him, cuddling and bouncing him a little. She looked over at Dorie, and Dorie smiled at her.

"You know what?" the girl said, "Jesus lookin' out fer this baby after all. He took us to him, didn' he?"

"Yes," Dorie said. "Jesus took us to him. He sure enough did."

Five

Flagstaff, Arizona, was the real West to Dorie June Grimes. Texas had always seemed like a pretender West to her. Except for the cows, it was too much South ever to be genuine West. New Mexico and the bottom half of Arizona, on the other hand, went all out to be southwestern, which meant they couldn't settle on which folks to copy, the Native Americans or the Mexicans, so they copied both. But Flagstaff was different. It was a mountain town, with big evergreens and high country smells and people in cowboy hats, flannel shirts, and leather boots. Dorie liked it, and so she bypassed the cutoff in order to gas up and perhaps take a catnap in Flagstaff. Now why couldn't Mama and Papa have settled here instead of in the dry ditch desert that Jericho sits in the middle of? she wondered. And how could they have been contented there in the sand and cactus, with rattlers and coyotes for neighbors?

Ruetta always said Dorie needed to open her eyes to the

Minding Mama

gorgeous sandstone bluffs and sculptured canyons and the blue, blue sky before she criticized the vicinity. It must have had something or Hollywood wouldn't have grabbed it. Ruetta admitted that Jericho could be hot in the summer, but she regularly pointed out that its heat was the dry kind, where Atlanta's was the wet. That statement always reminded Dorie of a cartoon she saw once that showed two parched skeletons in cowboy hats lazing in front of a splintery frontier tavern. One of them was saying, "Well, at least our heat is dry."

But Flagstaff, Dorie argued silently, was both dry and cool, the best of both worlds. She could almost hear her mother's well-rehearsed rebuttal on Flagstaff winters. "Why, I know people who got snowed in there days at a time, maybe weeks! Why, it snows in April and May, too!" Ruetta used to say. Dorie never tried to verify or discredit her mother's claims. What would be the point? Ruetta was a woman who knew what she knew, regardless of the facts. Facts only confused an issue she had already settled to her complete satisfaction in her head.

The road map said Flagstaff was in the San Francisco Mountains, but that didn't make sense because San Francisco was on the California coast and nowhere near Arizona. Dorie and her mother had discussed the matter when they were laying out the course for their overland voyage. Ruetta argued that because Arizona was more easterly than California, and settlement of the US of A had gone from east to west, Arizona's places had been named first. When California heard the name San Francisco, it liked the sound of it and stole it from Arizona, knowing full well that one day California's city would be more famous than Arizona's mountains. Therefore, everybody would assume California thought up the name first and Arizona stole it from them. It wasn't often that Dorie agreed with her mother's explanations for things, but she had always admired the older woman's creativity. Dorie chose not to mention that New Mexico had the Sacramento Mountains and a city called Las Vegas.

Dorie picked up a few things at the convenience store where she bought gas and changed the baby. The air was downright nippy here, and the thickening clouds overhead looked heavy enough to portend snow. A stretch of winter weather had not figured into Dorie's plans. We southerners live in a cocoon, Dorie told herself. It never occurs to us that roads in other parts of the country could experience a foot or two of snow in March. Little Moses started fussing while she changed his diaper in the restroom, and he showed no signs of letting up. Dorie figured it meant he was getting his strength back after his tenancy in the warehouse. She smiled weakly at the clerk and prayed that the frumpy woman in a straggly brown ponytail and yellow Grand Canyon sweatshirt would just naturally assume that she was the child's grandmother and not its abductor.

Dorie tried to act grandmotherly as she balanced Moses on one arm and searched her handbag for a credit card with the other. Since Clarence Ross and Mona Fay hadn't gone into production before their separation, Dorie's primary

Minding Mama

guide to grandmothering was the older women she saw on the Lifetime movie channel, and frankly they were few and far between. Apparently there was too little romance in their lives to qualify them for leading roles on Lifetime. They were relegated to the Golden Girls. Occasionally, one of Dorie's customers at the beauty shop brought a grandchild along to her weekly shampoo-set, which gave Dorie an opportunity to gain some negative experience in the business of grandmothering.

As it turned out, the clouds looming overhead indeed held snow, and chose to unload their frosty burden on northern Arizona. Loyal Bunce and the more or less loyal Petunia were probably already shivering in the back at this altitude—6910 feet, the map said. Snow would add to their misery. Dorie didn't know what to do. There was certainly no room for an additional man and a dog in the cab, or even a trombone. Maybe they could crawl under the tarp that had sheltered Mama, at least until the road dropped off the high plateau into the Painted Desert. When she put it to Loyal, he said cold didn't bother him as much as heat, but he'd try the tarp. The trombone, he added, was his main worry since he and Petunia were accustomed to hardship.

Snow began in earnest as the pilgrims left the outskirts of Flagstaff on US 89 going north. Small pellets, then flakes bigger than quarters, plastered the windshield. It was the first snow Lily Dawn had ever seen, and she suggested that Jesus had sent it for her special pleasure, another sign that he was looking out for them. Dorie had her own take on the storm, but elected not to disenchant Lily Dawn. At least Moses had stopped crying and finished his bottle.

The snow drove at the little pickup with a fury, and within a few miles Dorie could feel the pavement growing slippery beneath the tires. A road sign indicated that the turnoff to Sunset Crater National Monument was coming up soon, and she thought maybe she'd pull off there and lock the hubs in 4-wheel drive. In the newer models, and even some not-so-new ones, a person could just click into 4-wheel drive inside the cab, on the fly no less. But this vehicle required a person to stop, exit the cab's shelter, and manually turn the hubs on both front wheels from "free" to "lock." They weren't easy to turn, either. Dorie had broken more than one fingernail on that little maneuver. What did manufacturers in those days care if you were stuck in a mud hole or caught in a blizzard at 40 below when you needed 4-wheel drive? It was no skin off their noses.

* * * * * * *

Squinting against the thickening snow, Dorie said half aloud that she'd sell her soul for a shower and clean underwear, and that she'd sell it a second time to give Lily Dawn a good scrubbing. Lily Dawn only looked at her and said huh? Suddenly, the junction sprang out of the falling snow, and Dorie reflexively stomped the brake pedal, sending the pickup into a textbook skid. As luck would have it—bad luck, that is—a white monstrosity resembling a school bus

Minding Mama

was pulling onto the highway from the monument road when the sliding pickup arrived at the intersection. The impact sent the pickup spinning off the shoulder, nose first into a fallen log.

Badly shaken, Dorie sat gripping the wheel and staring into space for most of a minute before she could speak. At that point, the baby began howling to beat the band; and Ruetta, askew in her seatbelt, was pinning a speechless Lily Dawn against the door. Clutching the baby to her, the girl stared at Dorie with frightened brown eyes. Then, finding her voice, though not her full vocabulary, she kept repeating, "Glory be, praise the Lamb!" over and over. Then she started to cry.

Finally, Dorie spoke. "Don't cry, girl. We're all alive. Leastways, them that started alive have stayed alive," she added, glancing at her mother. "Here, help me get Mama back where she belongs."

Then Dorie thought of Loyal. She released her own seatbelt and twisted toward the rear window. Through the snow she saw a tousled head emerge from the far end of the tarp. It appeared that Mama's tarp had saved him from being thrown out and over the cab. Dorie supposed that Petunia and the trombone had fared as well. When she turned back and reached for the door handle, her eye caught the hoary face of a man she didn't know from Adam outside her window. She screamed and Lily Dawn followed her lead, an octave higher.

It turned out that Dorie's initial impression was in error.

Marilyn Arnold

The man at the window was not the Abominable Snowman, but merely the bearded driver of the reborn school bus that Dorie had slammed into from behind. After the collision, he had managed to pull onto the shoulder and engage his flashing emergency lights. Then he ran back to see about the occupants of the small pickup that struck him.

"We can't sort things out here," he said when Dorie finally regained her composure and got her door open. "Come over to the bus, and we'll talk there. We have plenty of room."

"All of us?" Dorie asked. "There's a man and a dog and a trombone in the back. And this girl and a baby and me up here." She paused. "And Mama. We got Mama here in the middle." Dorie paused again. "Mama's dead." Another pause. "Nobody killed her; she died of natural causes."

The man didn't seem astonished at the news, but merely nodded. "You say she's dead? Well then, we can leave her here for now. The cold will be good for her. The rest of you follow me. Wear your coats."

"Ain't got no coat," Lily Dawn said, her face in a pout. "Where I come frum, who needs a coat?"

"I've got a light jacket in a bag in the back," Dorie said, "but it won't keep you very warm or dry."

"Wait here," the man said. "We have some ponchos I'll bring you."

"We're dirty and smelly," Dorie said. "You won't want us in your bus."

The man smiled. "We don't mind, we're used to dirt."

Minding Mama

* * * * * * *

What could she do but go with him? At least Mama
would be refrigerated while they parleyed. The fellow
seemed nice enough, but Dorie was wary. She didn't know
there were any flower children left. She thought they went
out with LSD. When the man left on his poncho errand,
Dorie instructed Lily Dawn. "Keep your lips buttoned, girl,
and follow my lead. Agree with anything I say, even if it
stretches the truth or leaves it altogether. I hope Loyal's
smart enough to do the same. I'll take the baby, you carry
my handbag and the baby's things. Snow's slippery. Be
careful you don't fall."

"I don't see no bus," Lily Dawn grumbled.

"You can't see it because it's painted white and blends
in with the snow. Now smile and be grateful."

Dorie was all confidence in speaking to Lily Dawn, but
in her heart she was worried sick. She turned the key in the
ignition, just to test it. Nothing. They were stuck here a
good seven or eight hours from Jericho and no way to get
Mama home. They couldn't leave her in the truck, and it
looked like the truck would have to be towed back to
Flagstaff and fixed somehow. But in this weather? And
how would she pay for it? So here she was, Dorie Grimes,
certified cosmetician, responsible for this whole sorry
bunch—a man, a girl, a baby, a dog, and a trombone with
a name. Plus herself and a dead woman to whom she was
closely related and to whom she had made an irrevocable

promise. Was it possible that scarcely two days ago—less than two days—Dorie had left Atlanta, grieving, yes, but feeling oddly unburdened? At the time, she was doing right by her mother, and she was focused on her mission. Proof that even Ruetta Flatray couldn't deny.

And now? Now she could only wonder what on earth had gone wrong. How did all this happen? How come all these strangers were depending on her? Cleve and Clarence Ross would say she brought it on herself, but then they said that about everything bad that happened to her except themselves. They saw themselves as God's own gift to her. As she thought back to her life in Atlanta, it all seemed simple, even easy, by comparison with the present. At least she was used to Cleve and Clarence Ross, and they didn't need any protecting. She could see what people meant when they talked about gaining perspective. Yesterday can seem pretty grim when you're in it, but when you set it against today it might not look so bad.

Dorie's interior monologue was interrupted by a tapping on the window. This time it was Loyal, out of the truck bed, jacket collar turned up against the storm and rubbing a few sore spots. Dorie was relieved to see him on his feet. The poor fellow certainly got more than he bargained for when he sneaked into the back of this particular pickup with his dog and his trombone. Then she grew almost angry with him for his lack of horse sense. Anybody with half a brain would think twice before bedding down in a smelly, beat-up truck bed like this one. Who invited him,

Minding Mama

anyhow? Besides, he's free to leave any time he wants. Which is more than I can say for myself, Dorie added silently.

"Here's Loyal," she said to Lily Dawn. "Gimme the baby and get out soon's the man from the bus comes with a poncho. We'll leave Mama here, like he said. Snow won't hurt you 'long as you don't slip and fall in it."

Dorie opened the door a crack. "We're goin' to their bus to talk things over," she told Loyal. "Petunia can stay here under the tarp." She paused. "Here's the man now with jackets for me and Lily Dawn. You've got your own jacket. C'mon."

By the time she got the poncho over her collapsing hairdo, and over Baby Moses too, Dorie was so wet she wondered why she had bothered with protective covering at all. And now, how was she to get the baby, a squalling bundle of protest, safely from point A to point B? What if she slipped and fell, crushing Moses? Dorie hadn't realized until this minute that ponchos had no front opening and no arms. They were, in fact, nothing more than glorified pup tents with a hole in the ceiling for the face and slits in the sides for arms. They were designed exclusively for the wearer who was not transporting a baby in a snowstorm. Well, at least the thirty slippery yards Dorie had to traverse against wildly blowing snow gave her a new appreciation for the sport of football. She knew now that thirty yards could seem like a mile. Cleve would be pleased to hear it since, as far as she could tell, football was his only passion.

Marilyn Arnold

When she and the others arrived at the bus—Lily Dawn fell only once and whined only three times—Dorie could see that the aged vehicle was not plain white, but had art work on its side, a mural of sorts. In her absorption in the baby and the treacherous footing, she forgot to look for the dent she had undoubtedly made somewhere in the metal canvas. As if by magic, the door opened the instant she arrived, and two strong hands grasped her waist from behind and boosted her onto the first step. They belonged to the man with the beard. "Give me the baby," a kindly female voice said from inside even as the woman's hands lifted the poncho to free Moses. Then another strong hand belonging to a third party grabbed Dorie's right forearm and pulled her to floor level.

"Thanks kindly," Dorie gasped, blinking snow from her eyes, but seeing nothing clearly. "We're in big trouble. My truck won't start, and here I've crashed into you, and I've got this baby an' this girl an' this old man—I mean my daughter here an' her grandpapa an' his dog—an' my mama who died on the way to the reunion who's still in the truck and so's the dog and trombone, and if we're not in Jericho by this afternoon there'll be hell to pay."

Dorie stopped for breath, and Lily Dawn, who had arrived stomping and dripping, filled the hiatus. "Her mama will start to stink!" she cried, shaking snow off herself like a wet dog.

Dorie turned and glared at her. "Well, it's the truth, ain't it?" Lily Dawn said, thrusting her lower lip into a pout. "An'

Minding Mama

she ain't my mama neither. My mama's part white an' part black, an' Dorie Grimes she's all white."

Dorie sank into one of the bus seats while Lily Dawn stood accusingly above her. Dorie assumed the girl had finished with her litany of disclosures, but she hadn't. Loyal arrived in time to trigger another volley.

"An' that ol' man, he ain't her daddy, neither. He's a tramp that clumb into our truck when we wasn't lookin'." Lily Dawn stopped, wide-eyed, and looked scared about what she had just done. "There ain't no reunion, neither," she whimpered, "an' that ol' lady was dead to start with an' some robbers stole our truck an' we found that baby in a ol' building where its mama left it with a note."

Dorie fully expected the three of them—four, if you counted the baby, five if you counted Mama—to be turned out into the storm as raving lunatics. Some people had a low tolerance, constitutionally, for lies, and Lily Dawn was one of those. It was just Dorie's luck that when a few harmless fictions might have saved the lot of them, including her mother, Lily Dawn reached her volume limit for falsehood and hemorrhaged truth at the mouth. Dorie shook her head and dropped her chin to her chest. Then, to her surprise, she heard laughter. She looked up to see a fellow with a shaved head and two rings in his right ear throw his hands in the air and his head back. His guffaw split the air as he dropped limply into the driver's seat. Opposite him, on the lower step, the bearded fellow slapped his leg and laughed merrily while the woman who held the baby took

97

a seat across from Dorie and began giggling.

Lily Dawn looked from one face to another with an expression that said here I've wound up on this ol' bus with a bunch of crazies and now what do I do? Loyal, who had taken a seat behind Dorie, began to snicker, and at last Dorie was gathered into the rollicking pool of infectious delight. Her face broke into a smile as the absurdity of her circumstances washed over her, and she surrendered to the healing power of laughter. Lily Dawn, still uncertain, tried on a puzzled little grin before venturing tentatively into full-fledged laughter. It was obvious that the girl was a stranger to mirth. Dorie laughed until she cried, then pulled Lily Dawn awkwardly to her lap, wet poncho and all.

"C'mere girl," Dorie said, cradling and rocking her. "You're mine 'til we get you to your grandmama's, anyway. And who knows, maybe I won't let her have you a'tall. Appears I need somebody to keep me on the straight an' narrow. You can take over Mama's job."

For just an instant, the March sun broke through the snow's dense curtain and encircled the small band of strangers. It seemed to flash a halo of light through the window where Dorie sat assuring the girl that she, and therefore all of them, had a very bright future.

* * * * * * *

At last, one of the "hosts" of this extraordinary little gathering spoke. It was the man sitting sideways in the dri-

Minding Mama

ver's seat, the one with the shaved head and earrings. Dorie could see now that the three of them—the two men and the woman—were young, at least by her standards. She guessed them to be in their middle thirties. Children, she told herself. Age, like many other things, was relative, depending on where you yourself were positioned on life's highway. Dorie had heard that we start dying the minute we're born, and she didn't like the sound of that. She had never fancied one-way streets with U-turns prohibited. A quick glance to the far end of the bus revealed no additional passengers, and confirmed that the rear half of the vehicle had been converted to living space. Ethan Allen it wasn't. Even Winnebago wouldn't claim it. Well, Dorie thought, it's not the Marriott, but it beats the back of a truck by a mile.

Welcome, the fellow was saying, welcome to our little island of peace. He went on to introduce himself and the others, by first name only. The three, he explained, had decided that last names were superfluous and had abandoned theirs. After all, he continued, did Abraham need a surname, or Joseph, or Jacob? And yet we all know who they were, don't we? Dorie could have disputed his logic, but she saw his point. Call me Ishmael, he said, and her Rachel, and the poncho bearer Jonah. Following Ishmael's lead, Dorie introduced her contingent, including little Moses, whose name won instant approval with this crowd.

Ishmael said that fate had brought them together, and that now they had to work out their combined destiny, even though it be short-term. Dorie squirmed a bit. Philosophy wasn't exactly her line. She had heard of Transcend-something-or-other in high school English, and wondered if these three were practitioners of whatever it was. The only destiny she cared about at the moment was getting Ruetta Flatray to Jericho fast. Traveling with a corpse, she realized now, was a persuasive argument for the immortal soul because the minute that soul departed, decay was just around the corner. At least when the soul was present, the aging process went slower.

Since Lily Dawn had already let every cat in ten counties out of the bag, Dorie could see no advantage to inventing a plausible explanation for why she was on the road with this motley assortment of fellow travelers. Also, it was action that was needed now, not words. She had no time to spare even if it was cold outside and her mother wouldn't spoil so fast. And she was tired enough to sleep standing up. Maybe it *was* fate that put them all here, she said, but she couldn't leave it to fate to get her mother to Jericho by this afternoon. The problem was she couldn't transport her dearly beloved in a truck that wouldn't start and that at present was stuck off the road with its nose against a big log. Ishmael looked at his companions.

Jonah spoke up and said it was clear that they had to get the dead woman to Jericho, but that they should tow the pickup back to Flagstaff first. Otherwise, the highway patrol would find it and complicate matters. They could leave the vehicle in the parking lot of a twenty-four hour supermarket, and no one would notice, at least for a few days.

"You mean to take all of us to Jericho?" Dorie was incredulous. She cleared her throat. "Uh, did I mention that there's a dog, too? A big one."

"It wouldn't be the first time we've taken on passengers, two-legged and four-legged both," Jonah said. "There are just the three of us. We have room."

He was a rather tall, lean man, with a quiet manner and gray eyes pocketed deep beneath heavy brows and high cheek bones. He fit Dorie's idea of a prophet perfectly, except he was rather youngish and wore pants instead of a robe. The beaded maroon tunic and the neck chain helped the image, however. Then again, Dorie realized, some prophets were younger than others. She had seen pictures of Joseph Smith in her mother's things, and had once, unwisely, remarked to her mother that he didn't look much like a prophet to her. Not only did he lack the distinguishing facial hair, she said, but he was far too young and wore the same clothes everybody wore.

Dorie realized her mistake at once. A person shouldn't mess uninvited with somebody else's religious beliefs. Ruetta had bristled and stayed bristled for two whole days. Her words still hung in Dorie's memory. "Well, what's wrong with that?" Ruetta had demanded. "What rule says a prophet has to be old, wear a beard, and dress funny?" Dorie, again unwisely, had countered by pointing to John the Baptist, conceding that although she guessed he was pretty young, he sure enough looked like a prophet and acted the way we expect prophets to act, living like a wild man and eating disgusting things like insects. "He ate honey," too, Ruetta had replied. "Don't forget that. And how about Jesus? How old was he?" Well, Jesus was young, too, Dorie admitted, but he had long hair and a beard, and wore a robe and sandals. All the pictures show him that way. "He dressed like folks in his day, and Joseph dressed like folks in his," Ruetta snapped, and walked away.

Knowing she was licked before she started, Dorie had backed off, calling to her mother's retreating figure that she was only suggesting that since a prophet had a fairly hard go in what was a tough business at best, he could do himself a favor by trying to look the part. Model himself after Abraham or somebody like that. Or Jonah, as this fellow did, although taking up residence in a school bus seemed to Dorie an unwarranted extreme even for a self-styled prophet.

As for the woman—Rachel, Dorie remembered—well, Dorie thought a woman traveling with two men might be what the Bible called a harlot. Unless, of course, she was married to one of the men, which Dorie dearly hoped to be the case. For Lily Dawn's sake. Luckily, Ruetta was in no condition to object, though in life she would have been appalled at what she called cohabitation of the sexes. Prophets or not, harlot or not, these people had appeared out of nowhere, and Dorie had crashed into their bus. She wasn't sure who was at fault, but in any case she was in their hands. "Thanks kindly," she said in a belated answer to Jonah's offer, "I regret bein' such a bother."

Minding Mama

In light of the circumstances, "bother" was hardly an adequate word, but Dorie didn't know what else to say. The men, joined by Loyal, went to work immediately, in the ponchos Dorie and Lily Dawn had shed, hooking a tow chain to the pickup's rear axle and maneuvering the bus into a position to pull the pickup out. Luckily, they could work from the vacant monument road. The Rachel woman still held Moses and seemed easier with him than Dorie ever had. Her long black hair was pulled back and clipped together with a silver and turquoise ornament. Dorie noticed how fine her features were, her eyes a striking blue in her olive complexion. By any measure, Rachel was beautiful, though seemingly unaware of her beauty. She assured Dorie that the bus had excellent traction and that they would soon be on their way back to Flagstaff.

She was right, but it took some doing, first to get the pickup onto the road, then to turn it around so it could be towed nose first. Ishmael rode in the truck with Ruetta, to steer and brake, while Petunia paced nervously in the truck bed. Finally, she crawled under the tarp and took up residence. It was a perilous trip to Flagstaff, but the snow had begun to abate when the pickup was deposited in the sparsely populated lot of a large supermarket. There were no visible witnesses to the transfer of Ruetta Flatray from truck to bus, for which Dorie was mightily grateful.

Within minutes, Ruetta was stowed in a rear seat of the bus, one that had been turned sideways to accommodate conversation, which purpose was of no interest to her just now. There was a time, however, when she would have appreciated it. There she sat, anchored by Dorie's manure-scented travel bag and secured to the arm rest with a detached luggage strap. She appeared ready and eager for the next adventure while Dorie sincerely hoped there would be no next adventure. Lily Dawn insisted on sharing Dorie's seat, but she wanted by the window. Dorie was too tired to argue with the girl and stood to let her pass.

"Lookee there," Lily Dawn said, her face against the glass. "That ol' mutt won't come."

It was true. There was Loyal, on hands and knees in the truck bed, tugging and coaxing Petunia who had apparently decided she was not about to leave the pickup and its protective tarp. Finally Loyal crawled off the pickup and, after a few words with Ishmael who had joined him, came to the door of the bus. Inside, he addressed the group rather formally.

"Petunia," he said, "aims to stay with her ship. She's scairt a' this here bus, and I cain't force her to come aboard. Maybe it's them whale eyes and teeth on the sides."

Dorie's jaw dropped. "Whale?" she sputtered. "You mean this here bus looks like a big white whale?"

"Hog-tie me and drag me through p'ison ivy if it don't." Loyal saluted. "Anyways, I cain't leave Petunia, so I'm stayin' with her. I thank y'all kindly."

"Wait!" Dorie cried. "You can't stay here. What'll you do?"

Loyal smiled indulgently. "Why, jus' what we been

Minding Mama

doin' fer years. Me 'n Petunia, we take care of each other. Besides, we still got Matilda. She'll keep us fed."

"Don't leave yet!" Dorie insisted, digging in her handbag. "I'm sure I've got an extra key in here somewhere. You can get inside the truck out of the weather 'til I decide what to do with it. I've got the baby's things with me, but there's some food in a bag on the floor. Sell the spare tire if you need to; I would've."

Ishmael, Jonah, and Rachel remained respectfully silent while Dorie and Loyal resolved their dilemma and said their goodbyes. The trio of wanderers were not the sort to interfere in such things. Dorie found the key and approached Loyal. She embraced him for a long silent moment, then returned to her seat. Lily Dawn was facing the window, iron-stiff, but Dorie could hear the girl's sniffles and feel her silent tears.

Dorie sat down heavily, patted Lily Dawn's dirt-streaked knee, looked around at her rescuers through tear-filled eyes and said, "Let's go home to Jericho!"

Six

And so here they were, the six of them, strangers on a train, Dorie Grimes told herself. Only they weren't on a train. Still, except for the clackety-clack, a modified bus was probably the nearest thing on wheels to a Pullman car. This particular bus had enough of its own noises to more than compensate. Take the windshield wipers, for starters, currently in motion thanks to the snow. They swept in jerky parallel rhythm, dragging Dorie's eyes with them, groaning and scraping across the windshield, leaving streaks and blobs in their wake. It registered in some corner of Dorie's mind that the blades needed replacing and weren't likely to get it any time soon, from the looks of things. The thought triggered an unexpected stab of homesickness. Dorie was astonished to discover that she missed Cleve. He would have groused about those wiper blades from now 'til Christmas, but nothing would have happened 'til she up and did it.

Minding Mama

Cleve was sloppy and lazy all right, but then she wasn't exactly a model of perfection herself. One thing was certain, she'd never have to worry about him waltzing off in a school bus decked out in maroon tunic and earrings. And even if he didn't shave every day, you'd never catch him sporting a long, unruly beard. What's more, to her knowledge, he wasn't fooling around with some other woman. Credit bone idleness and inertia more than fidelity, Dorie told herself. Cleve didn't have the energy of cold toast. Just the same, maybe it was a good sign that she was missing him. Maybe she'd keep him after all. Come to think of it, who else would have him? Clarence Ross, however, was something else entirely. He was Mona Fay's problem, not hers, and Dorie intended to put her foot down and his out the door as soon as she got back to Atlanta. For his own good. It was time he started supporting himself. Past time.

Although Dorie wasn't the religious person her mother was, she recognized that the names of her rescuers all came from the Bible. Personally, she doubted that those were their real first names; but if people wanted to go and rename themselves, it was all right with her. And they could leave off the last name, too, if they wanted; she couldn't care less. Dorie liked to think of herself as broad-minded about most things even though Cleve maintained she wasn't. In any case, she was glad the names these people chose were relatively easy to pronounce and not too far off the wall. After all, they could have picked

Nebuchadnezzar or some mouthful like that. Besides, Rachel was a godsend. She more or less took over the care of little Moses once she learned how long Dorie had gone without sleep. More for the baby's sake than mine, Dorie supposed.

Dorie had a whole lot of questions she wanted to ask these people—questions like, where did they come from and did they have jobs and where were their families and how did they put food on the table and who painted the bus? Oh, yes, she had questions, but she was in no position to be asking them, since she was the one on charity here and not the other way around. So far, they hadn't volunteered the information. And now, completely at their mercy and only a few miles out of Flagstaff, Dorie could feel her head growing too heavy for her neck. She didn't like to sleep among strangers and felt for her handbag. There it was, on the floor between herself and Lily Dawn, who was already, as Ruetta would say, in the Land of Nod. Of course, now she thought of it, what did she have that anybody would want to steal? A few dollars at most. Besides, these people didn't seem like the stealing kind. And they didn't seem to mind traveling with a dead person, which in Dorie's view said a lot for them. In fact, Ishmael and Jonah had carried Ruetta to the rear of the bus and turned off the heater back there.

As Dorie began tilting toward oblivion, she realized that it couldn't be much more than two hundred miles to Jericho. They were going to make it. She almost dared to

Minding Mama

think that they were going to make it. Ruetta Flatray was less than five hours from home. Under normal conditions. On the instant, Dorie wondered what had possessed her to assume for even a moment that normal conditions would prevail on any segment of this journey, least of all the last one. Then she let go, and time passed that was no time to Dorie Grimes.

* * * * * *

Subconsciously aware that the bus was slowing to a stop, Dorie crawled out of a dream in which she was dashing about in a surreal cemetery, searching for a grave for her mother. Everywhere she turned, headstones toppled over and vicious dogs resembling Petunia chased her away. She was frantic. A huge hourglass appeared in front of her, and she could see the sand shooting through the narrow aperture at record speed. She heard herself cry out, "No, no, stop!" Then she woke up.

Outside her window the sky was gray, but no snow was falling. What Dorie saw was not a ponderosa covered plateau but a broad desert landscape. The Painted Desert. It took her a moment to remember where she was, and where her mother was, and why she was in this whale on wheels instead of her Toyota pickup. Instinctively, she felt for her handbag. It was there, its strap tangled in the feet of the sleeping Lily Dawn. Then it hit her. The baby. Where was Moses? Twisting around, Dorie saw a yellow plastic clothes basket secured in the aisle between the rows of seats. A custom-made baby bed, lined and padded with sweatshirts and a pillow. Then she realized that the bus had stopped, and that its owners had vacated the premises.

A twinge of panic raked up Dorie's spine. Had she been deserted? Had the bus conked out? Serves you right for celebrating too soon, her husband Cleve would have said. Cleve prided himself on never counting his chickens before they hatched. He was an I-told-you-so sort of person who took pleasure in other people's misfortunes, which explains why Ruetta Flatray and her son-in-law Cleve didn't see eye to eye on a number of things. She enjoyed other people's good luck right along with them, and her favorite saying was, "Hope springs eternal in the human breast." Ruetta and her sayings used to drive Cleve crazy. And it drove him crazy that Dorie didn't mind them. Ruetta had her quirks, yes, but her goodness more than offset her little oddities. Dorie used to tell Cleve that she wished she could say the same for him and Clarence Ross. If that's what it takes to be good, then who wants it? he'd retort.

Grunting noisily, Dorie raised herself to her feet by grabbing the back of the seat in front of her. Lily Dawn sighed in her sleep and brushed something imaginary away from her face; Moses was out for the count. Unable to see much from the aisle, Dorie stumbled to the open door. The air was less frosty than on the plateau, but, as her mother would have observed, it was still nothing to shout about. Ruetta Flatray had been sensitive to cold all her life and

Minding Mama

wasn't afraid to say so. "Cold-prone," she called it. Dorie knew no one else who used the expression. In some ways, her mother was an original. In other ways she was a rubber stamp.

Dorie stepped gingerly to the highway's gravel shoulder, alternately patting her hair and tugging at her blouse in a futile effort to make it cover her hips. She squinted toward the rear of the bus where she made out an odd-shaped vehicle parked along the road about fifty yards back. In front of its raised hood she counted five people, two of them bent into the gaping mouth that housed what she presumed was the vehicle's engine and the other three taking supervisory roles. As Dorie approached the group, Rachel waved, but the two people with her didn't. A man and a woman Dorie didn't recognize. The woman towered above the man.

Even from a distance, Dorie could tell that these were not your down-home, everyday travelers. For one thing, the woman was fitted out in a dress—a long, extra full dress, mind you—out here in the middle of nowhere. You'd never find it in the window at Dillard's, or even Sears or J.C. Penney. With its puffy sleeves and ruffled yoke and hem, the dress was more like something you'd see at a square dance or in a rerun of *Gunsmoke*. And there, dangling behind her back, attached by a bow under her chin, was what had to be a bonnet. The man, whose bones made knobs in his ill-fitting black suit, wore a misshapen black hat that had probably been sat on more than once. He looked like a folded up bat. As Dorie drew closer, she could see that he also wore a crooked black string tie and that he gestured every which way when he talked. Or maybe it was when he listened. From her vantage point, she couldn't tell.

Even before Dorie arrived she had sized up these people and their car. "Judge not that ye be not judged," Ruetta would have prompted, and then gone on to make what she called "an accurate assessment." In Ruetta's moral universe, an accurate assessment was different from a judgment and therefore acceptable to the Lord. The more Dorie looked at the vehicle, the more she thought that "car" was the wrong word for it. Maybe "rolling duplex" was a better term. What it looked like was a car's front end with a prairie schooner hooked on behind. Where car and schooner met was the joining of two centuries. Her mother would have called the thing a covered wagon with a motor transplant. Closer now, Dorie could see that somebody had cut down an old Buick and made a crude pickup out of it. Then a canvas had been rigged across high curved ribs to span the open part. Dorie braced herself for the worst.

* * * * * * *

Not that it made any difference, as Dorie was to discover. On arrival, Dorie could see that Ishmael and Jonah were performing an autopsy on the Buick, apparently trying to determine what killed it and if the body could be resuscitated.

Minding Mama

"Dorie, come meet the Pococks. They're having some car trouble," Rachel said, stressing the second syllable, Po-*cock*.

The woman, a rather imposing figure with a crooked nose and ringlets whom Dorie guessed to be sixty or so, stepped forward and looked Dorie over. "Pleasured, I'm sure," she said. "The name's *Poh*-cock, with th' accent at the front. Christened Brightness Louise. You can call me Brighty Lu, for short. This here's m' husband, Bertram Levi Pocock. We call him Bertie. He's a preacher, but he sings better'n he talks. I always say he sings like a Bertie in the treetops." She punctuated the comment with a hearty chortle, as though it was the first time she had heard it herself and could scarcely believe her own extraordinary wit.

Bertram Pocock extended his bony, freckled hand; and Dorie, helpless to do otherwise, took it. He looked her in the eye. "Have you been saved?" he demanded.

Brighty Lu interrupted. "Ain't that sweet?" she cooed. "He always asks people that right off. He's focused!"

"I'm so happy for you," Dorie mumbled, then repented of her sarcasm. "You say he's a preacher?" she asked, with as much false interest as she could generate. "What church?"

"Why, the Last Chance Holy Doom's Day Church," Brighty Lu responded. "You ever hear of it?"

"Can't say as I have," Dorie responded, without enthusiasm. She was wondering how long the delay would last. She didn't need this, what with Ruetta approaching the spoiling point in the rear of the bus.

Rachel interrupted. "The Pococks are headed for Zion National Park," she said, putting the accent in the right place this time.

"Oh?" Dorie asked, with labored civility.

"Yup, we want to be in Zion when the end comes!" Brighty Lu cried. "At the Great White Throne."

"What end is that?" Dorie asked nicely. Too nicely. In her head she was thinking, first the Great White Whale, now the Great White Throne. What next?

Brighty Lu looked at Dorie with an expression that said she couldn't believe the utter ignorance of some people. "What end? Why the end of the world, a' course! The Apocalypse!"

"The end of the world? You know when it's coming?"

"The Lord has revealed the date to his servants of the Last Chance Holy Doom's Day Church." Brighty Lu turned to Bertram Levi. "Ain't that right, Bertie?"

"Right as rain," he replied, raising both hands and lowering them while he wiggled his fingers to indicate rainfall.

"And what date is that?" Dorie asked blandly.

Brighty Lu answered before Bertram could free his dog-eared pocket calendar from the lining of his inside coat pocket. "It's Saturday, day after tomorrow. We're goin' to be transported directly to heaven by legions of angels. By Saturday night we'll be in glory."

Bertram nodded glumly at his composite vehicle. "That is, if'n we can get to where them angels will be arriving."

Minding Mama

He raised his right hand in supplication to heaven.

Dorie suppressed a wicked grin and responded in her most innocent voice. "Ummm . . . you don't suppose those angels might head for Angels' Landing in the park 'stead of the Great White Throne, do you?"

Brighty Lu turned to Bertram, clearly alarmed at Dorie's suggestion. "You mean there's a actual place for angels to land in Zion Park? Set aside for the purpose?"

Rachel looked at Dorie as if to say, where are you going with this? "Why, yes," Dorie replied. "Isn't that right Rachel?"

"Well, there's an Angels' Landing, but . . ."

Brighty Lu interrupted. "Then that's where we've got to go. No if's, and's, or but's about it. That's where they'll come. Right, Bertie?"

"Right as rain," he replied, then thought a minute. "Question is, how we goin' t' get there?" He pointed north.

Brighty Lu folded her arms across her ample bosom and smiled a smug little smile. "The Lord will provide," she said.

* * * * * * *

And that is how the Great White Bus acquired two more passengers and an assortment of prayer books, pamphlets, and holy writ. The Pococks were not to be caught unprepared when the call came. As Brighty Lu Pocock put it, they would be clothed in the whole armor of God. Dorie questioned the effectiveness of paper armor, but kept her comments to herself. She had more pressing matters to occupy her than the mere ending of the world. The covered Buick, as Dorie called it, was being abandoned, more to Dorie's dismay than the dismay of the Pococks. After all, Brighty Lu said, come Saturday they'd have no use for it anyhow. The angels sure wouldn't want to bother with it. She and Bertie had the promise of reliable transportation to Zion, and that's all they needed. Privately, Dorie gave thanks that Jericho came before Zion on the map.

The Pococks bustled onto the bus with their bags and Doom's Day literature, staking out the two front seats. Jonah carried their bags to the rear, stepping over a sleeping Moses as he went. Brighty Lu stood and watched him, then followed him as far as the baby. At that point she espied Lily Dawn, who was awake now and rubbing her eyes. Brighty Lu looked from one to the other, Moses to Lily Dawn and back. She addressed the girl.

"Hello there, girl, is this here your child? How come it's white and you're brownish? You been breakin' the commandments, girl? Lookee here, Bertie." He was right on her heels.

Lily Dawn eyed her accuser and yawned. "I ain't broke no big commandments, none that count anyways."

Bertram Levi spread both arms. "They all count, girl," he said, "ever' last one."

In the meantime, Brighty Lu's sharp little eye had traveled to the back of the bus where Ruetta was partially visible.

Minding Mama

Immediately interested, Brighty Lu stretched to see around the returning Jonah. "Who's that back there?" she demanded. "And why's she back there by herself, if it is a her?"

Dorie entered the bus in time to hear the question and respond to it. "It's a her, all right, and she's back there because she prefers it. She's no concern of yours." Dorie caught Lily Dawn's eye and silently warned her. She could tell the girl was busting to let fly with all she knew. She could also tell that the bus and its occupants would be a fertile field for the inquisitive evangelist. A woman like her wouldn't leave much for the gleaners. Dorie decided that she could tolerate anything for three hours. What she couldn't tolerate was sitting here stock still while the clock ticked away. She turned to Rachel who had boarded the bus behind her. "We've got to get Mama home fast," she whispered.

"We'll make it," Rachel assured her. "I'd better change the baby and feed him, unless you'd like to."

Dorie waved Rachel off. "No, no, you go right ahead. I hereby deed Moses over to you, for the time being. Between Lily Dawn and Mama and the Pococks, I'll have my hands full. All we're missin' is the circus tent," she added, with a nod toward the preacher and his wife.

Rachel smiled. "Yes, it's getting a little populated here in the belly of the whale, isn't it? But I guess it takes all kinds to make a world."

Dorie shook her head. "In a story I read once by this southern lady, one person says to the other that it don't *take* all kinds, there just *is* all kinds."

Marilyn Arnold

Rachel chuckled. "Here's Ishmael. We're on our way."

Ishmael's customary seat having been usurped by a bonnet and a black hat, he took the seat behind the baby. On his return trip from the rear, Jonah squeezed by the Pococks who were still busily surveying their new kingdom. Rachel and Dorie waited for him in the stairwell. Brighty Lu seemed to be mentally measuring the length of the makeshift bassinet, wondering whether a trip to the far end of the bus would yield enough information to offset the risk of tripping over the basket, since the basket occupied the entire width of the aisle and wasn't a short basket either. Her long skirt with the ruffled bottom greatly increased the risk.

"All aboard," Jonah cried, starting the bus engine, and the Pococks reluctantly returned to their seats, allowing Rachel and Dorie to do the same.

* * * * * * *

The unlikely band of nomads hadn't gone far when the strain of data deficit became too much for Brightness Louise Pocock. She broke the silence by addressing Jonah, her nearest victim. In a loud voice she asked who owned this here bus, and who everybody was—not just their names—and why they were traveling in a bunch like this, and why they didn't travel in normal cars like normal people. Dorie almost swallowed her gum at Brighty Lu's allusion to normal cars and normal people. As if the woman thought the revised and recently abandoned Buick and its occupants qualified.

Minding Mama

Jonah, a man of infinite patience it seemed, smiled and called back to Ishmael. "You're the storyteller, Ishmael, what do you say?"

"Well," Ishmael began, "do you want the long story or the short story?"

Brighty Lu, who kept staring suspiciously at Ishmael's shaved dome and multiple earrings, said she wanted the short one so's she could get in more comments herself. Dorie was dying for sleep, but she didn't want to miss what Ishmael said. Lily Dawn had returned to dreamland. As far as Dorie could tell, sleep was what the girl did best. She had perfected the art.

Ishmael began his tale with how things were a year ago, when he and Jonah were employed by a large advertising firm in Chicago and fast-tracking upward. Jonah was already in charge of the art division, Ishmael himself was a vice president, and Rachel was the wife of the owner, the head honcho. Ishmael paused to ask Rachel if she wanted to tell this part. She shook her head. Ishmael then explained that they had all been friends, socially as well as at work. Then one day they discovered that Rachel's husband was sleeping with both Ishmael's and Jonah's wives. The yuppy dream was shattered. So the three friends who had been betrayed by their spouses teamed up and sallied forth in search of a new dream, and here they were. Their children, one apiece, were in boarding schools and had prudently elected to stay close to the money.

The Pococks were appalled. Dorie was fascinated. She

had heard of people who opted out of the mad dash, but she'd never met any until now. People who turned their backs on good jobs, financial security, and nice homes in search of a simpler, more fulfilling life. Dorie didn't exactly have what she would call a terrific job, but even so, she'd be scared to leave it and the meager security it provided. Let's face it, Dorie told herself, you're not adventuresome. Then again, crossing the country in a very tired pickup with a dead woman and an exhausted line of credit wasn't exactly playing it safe, was it?

But, she argued, I was driven by necessity, by a promise. It isn't the course I would typically choose. What makes me feel bound to honor that promise? Dorie's mind halted. The answer came with the shock of a bullet to the brain. Love. Something that goes far beyond duty. Mothers and daughters don't always agree on things, but they are linked by bonds of blood and memory, indefinable but stronger than bands of steel. Dorie surprised herself again. I think I love Mama more than comfort, more than safety, more than home, more than anything money can buy, Dorie uttered silently. Why, I think maybe I love her more than I love myself. Dorie caught her breath. And Mama loved— maybe still loves—me the same. Dorie sat there in a bus full of strangers, in a barren landscape, struck by the thought, and by the lateness of its arrival. How come I'm only learning this now, now that it's too late to tell Mama? she cried in mute agony, then stopped. "I love you, Mama," Dorie whispered. "Please be listening, somewhere."

Minding Mama

Brighty Lu interrupted Dorie's revery. "I declare," she said, "I never heard of such a thing, have you Bertie?"

What such thing haven't you heard of? Dorie's mind asked as she wrenched it back to present concerns.

As if on cue, Bertram Levi stood and raised both arms. "We're on a bus headed for Hell," he declared, looking straight ahead. "No two ways about it." Then he looked out the window across the sand to the rusty bluffs in the distance. "We're crossin' a spiritual desert with a company of the damned."

"Now wait a minute, dear," Brighty Lu said, pulling Bertram back into his seat. "These ain't the transgressors. These is the ones what was transgressed against."

"It's all the same. It's no difference," he muttered.

"These is the ones takin' us to Zion!" she exclaimed. "These is the ones takin' us to catch that heaven-bound train!" She thought a minute. "I ain't sayin' it's right for them three to be travelin' together outside the bonds of blood or wedlock. I ain't sayin' that. I'm just sayin' they was more sinned against than sinning." Abruptly she turned in her seat to face Dorie. "Whatta you think, lady?"

"What do I think? Why, I . . ."

Brighty Lu's attention shifted to Lily Dawn. "And who's that girl, anyhow? Don't seem likely she's yours, 'less you got friendly with somebody you shouldn't of."

Dorie was not comfortable with this turn in the conversation. She had no intention of justifying any aspect of her past or present to this woman, nor of condoning her bigotry.

She looked out the window and said nothing. The sky was still gray, and Dorie found herself hoping for rain here, too, for the sake of the plants and animals in this vast empty land. The threatening clouds brought Loyal Bunce to mind. Was he warm and dry somewhere? She felt dreadful about leaving him, but getting Mama home had to be her first priority.

Coming up empty in her overture to Dorie, Brighty Lu Pocock took her case to the girl, whose head snapped forward, waking her.

"Who are you, girl? Where's your mama? How old are you?"

"Huh?" was all Lily Dawn could say at the moment.

Then a light seemed to switch on in Brighty Lu's head. Here was a potential convert to the fold of the Last Chance Holy Doom's Day Church. Here was a soul to be saved and taken up in a concourse of angels. The others hereabouts may or may not be lost causes, but here was a fresh soul as yet unsullied by the world. A perfect candidate for Doom's Day salvation.

Dorie should have guessed what the woman was thinking, but she was distracted by her own thoughts and by the movement of the clouds and how far she could see with nothing blocking her vision. It felt like a new kind of freedom to her. Even the crows seemed freer than any she'd seen east of here. The colors of the desert floor appeared constant, and yet if she looked away for an instant, they had changed when she looked back. She realized, as her mother had insisted, that it was beautiful. What she saw

Minding Mama

was beautiful. For the first time, she understood why Ruetta loved this part of the world, why she wanted to be buried beneath the ever shifting and blowing sands.

It wasn't just that her husband was here, sleeping in the little cemetery, waiting for her, though that was reason enough. It was that this was home. Her spirit could be at rest if her body was where it belonged, deep in the parched desert earth. None of that loamy black soil for her, none of that damp, heavy air, none of that moist, penetrating smell of thick foliage. Much of this landscape was horizontal, at rest. Even the high mesas were shaved flat on top. But the towering distant cliffs and pinnacles gave the desert lift, carried one into the sky on the light, dry wings of the everlasting wind. Dorie nearly wept with the revelation.

"Come with us to Zion, girl, and catch that golden chariot. Confess to me and Bertie, here, and be saved!"

Once again, shrill, discordant words sliced into Dorie's consciousness. The woman was going after Lily Dawn! Just then Dorie heard Moses cry and Rachel murmur comfort.

Seven

"There's somethin' fishy goin' on around here, and I aim to get to the bottom of it," Brightness Louise Pocock declared, planting herself in the aisle by her seat and facing her commandeered congregation.

In the driver's seat Jonah stifled a snicker. "You're right," he said, "if you consider the whale to be a member of the fish family."

Brighty Lu snapped her head in his direction. "Huh? What's that got to do with anything?" She grabbed her husband's arm and yanked him to his feet. "Bertie, you hop over that there baby basket and check out that old woman in the sideways seat. I've seen plenty a' stories on the TV about abuse of the elderly, and I ain't about to stand by and watch it happen right under my nose. I bet they got the poor soul drugged. Look there, she ain't budged an inch since we came aboard."

Minding Mama

Bertram Pocock shook his head. "You go," he said, "you're a heap better at talkin' to the ladies than I am."

Brighty Lu smiled indulgently, then went on about how he was talkative enough with the *young* ladies, mind you, and how she had her hands full at the moment with the new communicant (she gazed knowingly at Lily Dawn, who slumped farther down in her seat), not to mention the baby and a whole passel of people more'n likely livin' in sin. She had her work cut out for her and only a few hours to do it in. "Maybe the Lord blew out our engine," she said, "so's we could save these souls before Doom's Day." She raised her hands in front of her, just above shoulder level, and closed her eyes. "I'm here, Lord," she sang out, adding a lot of mumbo jumbo that only she, and possibly the Lord, understood. Then she gathered herself up and started down the aisle.

Dorie allowed as how it was a good thing Ruetta Flatray was dead and didn't have to witness this display of grandstand piety or be subjected to the Pococks' last ditch efforts to save a few more of the ungodly from the flames. On the other hand, Ruetta dearly loved spectacle, so long as it didn't insult Jesus. Her mother, Dorie prayed silently, was at this very moment dancing with angels and paying no heed whatsoever to the abuse being visited upon her mortal shell. Ruetta firmly believed that come Resurrection Day her now lifeless remains would rise up, join her immortal soul, and the two of them live happily ever after as one. But until that day, it was up to her bumbling daughter to get those remains appropriately tended to and buried where the soul could find them when the trumpets sounded. Dorie wished she were as sure of a Resurrection Day reunion as her mother was.

She realized now that she and her mother might well have talked less about the relative merits of rhubarb pie over peach pie, and more about life eternal. After all, it was no news to anybody with ears that Ruetta preferred rhubarb pie over all others. And to accommodate that preference, she cultivated the principal ingredient for it herself, behind the house in Jericho. "Ru-etta" and "rhu-barb." The words even did what Dorie's high school English teacher called "allitification," or something like that. Dorie, who favored peach pie—and not just because she was a registered voter in Georgia, the peach state—wondered why little snippets of useless information like that attached themselves permanently to her brain, while some days she could hardly remember her own telephone number. She also wondered if anybody had been watering the rhubarb in Ruetta's long absence.

Just as Brighty Lu reached the baby basket, Ishmael came to the rescue, leaping to his feet, flailing his arms, and spouting gibberish. Seconds later, he was in the aisle, hopping and skipping wildly. Then, staggering to the rear section of the bus, he created a roadblock with his body and commenced to roll his eyes, wag his head, and flop his tongue—all to the accompaniment of hysterical laughter. Ruetta sat unmoved by his performance, but Brighty Lu gasped and fell back a step, grabbing her throat, her eyes

Minding Mama

very nearly popping out of her head. Rachel looked up from the baby, who didn't seem to mind the outburst at all. Moses only gave a tired little yawn as if to say what a pity that the fellow with the shaved head has gone off his nut again. You folks can wake me when it's over.

Dorie, sensing that Lily Dawn was about to participate with a frightened outburst of her own, clamped a strong right hand on the girl's left knee, a hand that said if you value your life don't you so much as move a muscle. Lily Dawn stayed put. Dorie was pretty certain Ishmael was faking a demonic seizure to distract Brighty Lu, who had likely been itching to cast out an evil spirit or expose a witch for years. And now she had her opportunity, in the nick of time, before the world went up in smoke. Since burning at the stake was no longer in vogue, she would have to resort to other means. Dorie's curiosity overpowered her need for sleep; the ensuing show, she figured, would be worth staying awake for. In the large rear view mirror, which was cracked from top to bottom, she could see Jonah glancing back, a pleased grin on his face.

Brighty Lu looked frantically at Bertram and then at Dorie and Rachel. "There's a madman on this bus!" she screamed. "The devil's got him. We got to cast him out!"

The man or the devil? Dorie mumbled to herself, gazing back blandly as if to say this was the Pococks' department, not hers. She had nary a toad nor the juice of three spiders in her pocket.

Rachel, who had been watching the various performances in bemused silence, addressed the evangelist with studied calm. "This happens only when someone tries to remove his earrings or interfere with his grandmother," she explained. "He's very protective of her. It's quite sweet, really. I recommend that you stay away from that part of the bus for the rest of the trip. What you've seen is actually quite a mild spell, by comparison."

"Mild!" Brighty Lu shrieked. Then, as if she had merely exchanged one mask for another, peace spread slowly over her face, like hot caramel sauce over ice cream. Dorie could see that the woman was fully awaking to her extraordinary opportunity. She retreated to the front seat and began digging through her large handbag while Bertram sat across the aisle, solemn as a headstone and twice as still. "C'mon, Bertie, we're goin' to exorcise a demon and save a soul. We got to do this right. The girl and the old woman can wait." She dug around some more. "Where's that preacher manual a' yours? Maybe it tells how to go about it."

"I dunno," Bertram said finally. "I ain't never had call to use the manual b'fore. Always worked by direct inspiration."

* * * * * * *

Eager as she was to reach Jericho, Dorie half hoped they wouldn't arrive before this little drama played itself out. It was what Cleve would call gen-yoo-wine entertainment. Anything that insulted the intelligence and was free of charge was Cleve's idea of a good time. In this case, Ruetta would have a front row seat, but she wouldn't be conscious of the fact. Dorie felt a little sorry about that. On the other hand, Lily Dawn would be present with eyes and ears fully engaged. The trick was to keep her from becoming an active participant. Sitting next to Lily Dawn just now was like clutching a live nerve. The girl's agitation was building to the point that Dorie wouldn't have been at all surprised to see her fly through the roof of the bus. Suddenly, the girl was on her feet.

"Ma'am," she cried, "can you raise the dead?"

Brighty Lu jumped as though stabbed in the posterior region with a yucca cactus spike. Temporarily incapable of speech, she stared dumbly at her inquisitor. Bertram, suddenly animated, answered for her, springing to his feet and waving his arms. "O' course she can, if'n she puts her mind to it, although I'm the preacher, the one officially called to perform such. I could do it, I just ain't never cared to. Who's the dead you want raised?"

Defeated, Dorie buried her face in her hands and surrendered. You can't smother an exploding hand grenade with a tea towel. All you can do is pick up the pieces after it's over. "What will be will be," Dorie chanted under her breath. The phrase was one of her mother's sayings, borrowed from an old Doris Day film. Ruetta wasn't one to attend a great many movies, except the ones shot around Jericho which she attended in order to see herself in pioneer dress as one of the townspeople. But the ones she did see stuck with her. For example, she knew *The African Queen* forwards and backwards. She always thought she resembled Katherine Hepburn, just a little. Ruetta did have prominent cheek bones, Dorie had to admit whenever the subject came up. It pleased Ruetta to hear it, so she looked for opportunities to elicit the comment from her daughter, who had watched the film with her on the Classic Movie Channel to verify the resemblance. Dorie was also required to affirm that it was the best movie ever made.

* * * * * * *

It has to be said that when Jonah swerved the bus at that auspicious moment, he took advantage of the fact that both Pococks were on their feet in the aisle and vulnerable. Happily, the other members of the party were more firmly entrenched. Moses lay safe in Rachel's arms, Dorie was seated, Ishmael was braced for heavy artillery coming in his direction, and Lily Dawn had the seat in front of her to grab onto. "Lookout!" Jonah yelled, too late, of course. "Big coyote! Nearly hit him!"

Brighty Lu pitched forward in the bus, then lurched to the right with the lower half of her coming to rest on the top step, facing the door. Bertram landed there just after she did, spread-eagled across her shoulders. The very picture of innocent remorse, Jonah pulled off the pavement and brought the bus to an easy stop. Then Rachel handed a frightened, howling Moses to Dorie and went to help the

Minding Mama

badly shaken Pococks. Ishmael, miraculously "cured" on the instant, arrived seconds later. The jolt dropped Lily Dawn back into her seat, astonishment stamped across her face, her unspoken words a logjam behind her tongue. Dorie's first thoughts were not for the Pococks, but for Moses and for her mother. Hoisting the baby to her left shoulder and patting his back gently, Dorie stood and surveyed the rear section of the bus. Ruetta Flatray was no longer visible.

That worried Dorie. She didn't want her mother injured even if she was dead and couldn't feel it. Furthermore, she didn't want to deliver a damaged corpse to the mortician in Jericho. What if a bone or two broke, or a crack appeared in the skull? Can a dead body bruise? Dorie couldn't bear the thought of it. And besides, anything suspicious and the mortician would summon the coroner, putting her on the spot to explain a lot more than collateral damage. As she stood there, rocking back and forth to soothe Moses, Dorie asked herself how she had wound up in this mess anyway.

When she set out for Jericho two days ago, with only her mother and the pickup to worry about, it was mainly a race against the clock. A bit tight, perhaps, but certainly do-able. Even Cleve, who was anything but positive in his attitude about most things except football and his son and heir in idleness, and who took great pleasure in foretelling disaster, had to admit it was probably do-able. Hare-brained, but do-able. Maybe she should have thrown in the towel at Flagstaff while her mother was still in one piece. Let a mortician and the police sort it out. She was too tired to think straight. A jail cell didn't look so bad right now.

I feel like a strip of fly paper, Dorie confided silently to Moses, a strip of fly paper attracting every piece of unattached life that comes within spittin' distance. Except Loyal didn't stick. I've let him kick loose. Do I need any of these people? Well, she conceded, I may need the throwback hippies and their bus just now, but I sure as sin don't need the zealots. Moses offered no opinion, so Dorie started toward Ruetta's quarters. Here is this good woman, she told herself, suffering every kind of indignity, and whose fault is it but mine? Her own daughter's. Dorie sighed miserably.

What began as a sigh turned into a groan. It was too late for Flagstaff now, and too late for regrets. Preoccupied, Dorie nearly tripped over the baby basket, clearing it by the slimmest of margins. Moses, thanks be, had quieted to an occasional whimper. Her arms felt almost too weak to hold him, but his look said he'd complain to high heaven if she put him down. Moreover, in Lily Dawn's agitated state, Dorie couldn't trust her to hold the baby. Why, flighty under the best of conditions, just now the girl could throw Moses out the window and then wonder ten seconds later where he'd gone to.

If only Loyal Bunce were here. He'd be a rock in these extreme circumstances. The thought of Loyal, abandoned there in Flagstaff in the cold, with a broken down truck, *her* truck, triggered a new wave of guilt, even lonesomeness. The three bus people were nice enough, Dorie supposed,

Minding Mama

but they weren't the sort you could get personal with or introduce to your neighbors. Several bricks short of a load, Cleve would have said of the trio, taking comfort in his own proven superiority. Dorie didn't doubt their good intentions, but she was in a huge hurry, and these hippy retreads seemed determined never to hurry again as long as they lived. Then, too, she herself was always leery of strangers, while these folks took in any Tom, Dick, or Susie they ran onto, herself being a prime example. You make do with what you have, her mother would have said, and the bus was headed in the right direction. It just wasn't headed fast enough to suit her.

Dorie thought maybe she would have been more comfortable with the hippies if they still had full-time jobs and full-time worries like other people. What if everybody did what they did? Nothing would get done in this world. We'd still be living in caves. Then she remembered that Cleve had initiated his freedom from work program before Jonah, Ishmael, and Rachel launched (she recognized her pun and let it go) theirs. Dorie had always thought of Cleve as a special case, not to be compared with normal people. But then, maybe there was no such thing as normal people any more. Who was she to say? Did normal people pack their dead mothers into pickups and head across the country on a wing and a prayer?

When Dorie arrived at her mother's seat—which faced the aisle—she saw that Ruetta had tipped over on her side, still bent, but had been held in place by Dorie's bag and the luggage strap stretched across her. She seemed intact, though one of her slippers was missing. Dorie wondered if it came off in the pickup, or in the transfer from truck to bus. In any case, the ankle stockings would have to suffice. It wasn't as if Ruetta had to walk anywhere, or might take a chill. As Dorie stood there, bouncing Moses, she felt an overpowering need to talk with her mother, and to find comfort by giving comfort.

With the baby on her left hip, Dorie gently raised the stiff little bundle cushioned in quilt and pajamas to an upright position, carefully straightening the coverings and then smoothing the white hair. In her exhaustion, it almost seemed to Dorie that she heard her mother say thank you as she had so many times in the past. It occurred to Dorie that those were not empty words to the woman who uttered them, even though at the time they might have been next to meaningless to the woman who received them. Dorie moved her bag and dropped wearily onto the seat beside her mother, the side show in progress at the front of the bus seeming like a farce being enacted on a stage, a production bearing no resemblance to real life, especially her life. Even Moses in her lap was a shadow baby who might disappear if she blinked.

* * * * * * *

Dorie awoke with a start. She wasn't even sure she had been asleep, or for how long if she had. The bus was rolling again, for which she was grateful. Her mother was there, next to her, as she had been in the pickup. Moses was wide awake, working his arms and legs like little pistons, and on the brink of a tumble. In grabbing him, Dorie scared him and he began to cry. Swift as a genie from a bottle, Rachel appeared in the aisle, holding out her hands for Moses. He seemed to recognize her and grew quiet the moment she lifted him to her shoulder. I'll feed him, she said, and disappeared. Dorie could only nod her head. She felt drugged.

The next thing Dorie knew, there was Lily Dawn, pointing triumphantly at Ruetta Flatray. In tandem behind her were Brighty Lu and Bertram Levi Pocock, in that order, fired with righteous indignation and apparently recovered from their adventure in the stairwell. Ishmael's having been miraculously released from his demons by the very presence of the sanctified meant the Pococks could turn their spiritual energies to other projects. Predictably, Lily Dawn had been happy to fill the void created by Ishmael's cure with news of Ruetta Flatray. Crossing her heart and hoping to die if she were telling a single lie, Lily Dawn had brought the pair back to prove that the old woman was not abused but only dead. Dorie figured that Jonah and the others had given up trying to protect anybody from the Pococks. Go with the flow was their usual *modus operandi* anyway. Maybe that's why they traveled in a whale, to symbolize their motto.

As for Lily Dawn, Dorie realized that it was well-nigh impossible for the girl, constitutionally, to let a fabrication of this magnitude go unmolested. Where it had been the lie that was intolerable at first, now it was the injustice the girl couldn't bear, the false presumption of abuse. Oh, Lily Dawn could run off to another planet without telling a soul, and sleep in somebody's empty car, and abet a little petty theft, and who knows what all. But could she out and out lie? Not on your life, nor on hers either. Nor could she tell any less than all she knew. The girl was a truth machine, and therefore a danger to herself and everybody else in a society that depends on the well-intentioned lie to keep the peace. The police ought to hire her and send her out to walk the streets and witness crimes. She'd always return with the straight story, and she couldn't be bought off. Then again, Dorie thought, maybe the police didn't necessarily want the iron-rod straight story every time. Maybe Lily Dawn would be a liability.

Fatigue had always affected Dorie's cognitive abilities, and she knew that every passing hour without significant sleep left her that much more vulnerable to twisted turns of thought. And now here she was, off in la la land just when she needed all her faculties in order to deal with the Pocock conundrum. And speaking of la la land, where did she get that word "conundrum"? Then she remembered. It was her father's word. Demont Ralph Flatray was a man who, when he encountered an attractive but unfamiliar word, looked it up, tucked it away, and pulled it out to use and admire when the occasion called for it. She had forgotten that quirk, and, she admitted, practically everything else about

Minding Mama

her father. And now Dorie knew that she had forgotten too many things, dragging her mother into her own present in Atlanta and virtually shutting the door on the past, almost denying its reality. When Ruetta talked about Jericho and Demont Ralph, Dorie nodded her head but didn't listen. She had left home so early and moved so far away that she could hardly remember what it was like to have a father.

Aware that the Pococks were now attacking on more than one front, Dorie shifted instinctively to shield her mother. Brighty Lu approached from the right, craning her neck to get a good look at Ruetta; Bertram came in from the left on his reconnaissance mission, and Lily Dawn directed traffic.

"If'n she's dead, how come she don't smell?" Bertram demanded, reaching as if to touch Ruetta's head, then withdrawing his hand.

"She will, soon enough," Dorie responded. "Lazarus she isn't. You notice, however, that the bus is cooler back here."

Brighty Lu broke in. "Oh, we know all about Lazarus, don't we, Bertie? You can't tell us nothin' about Lazarus."

"Lazarus raised from the dead!" Lily Dawn chimed in. "I learnt about him an' some others in Bible school."

Brighty Lu pushed Lily Dawn aside and bent forward, tilting first right and then left, giving Ruetta the once over. "You sure she's dead? Light's so poor back here, she could fool me."

"You touch her, you know she's dead," Lily Dawn assured the woman. "Whyn't you try to raise her?"

Dorie stood up, blood, as they say, in her eye. Brighty Lu retreated a step. "You just back off," Dorie said, glaring at the Doom's Day woman. "You hear me? You just back off. Nobody's foolin' with my mother!"

Brighty Lu leaned away from Dorie. "*Your* mother! I thought she was the madman's grandmother! What's the harm anyways? Just a simple little raisin' of the dead."

Lily Dawn broke in. "Jesus th' on'y one raised folks from the dead. Nobody else! I learnt that, too, on'y I forgot it 'til now." She paused. "People can't do it less'n he tells 'em to."

"Well!" Brighty Lu exclaimed, shuffling around Dorie. "I guess I know when I'm not wanted. C'mon, Bertie." She hesitated. "'Course, now I think about it, there ain't much point in bringin' somebody to life for two days. Maybe we oughtn't to strain ourselves, Bertie. Save our strength for liftoff at Angels' Landing."

Brighty Lu stopped and looked hard at Dorie, one eyebrow arched menacingly. "It's a mighty curious thing, travelin' with a dead person, assumin' she is dead and that she died of natural causes." Then she looked knowingly at Bertram. "I suspect foul play, m'self," she sniffed. "Looks like what we got here is a dead person smuggling ring, killin' people and hauling 'em off so's ever'body thinks they're just passengers on a bus. Mighty sneaky." Brighty Lu pushed Bertram along ahead of her, then turned back to Dorie, damnation in her voice. "You're lucky it's almost Doom's Day. Too late for earthly justice, but not too late

Minding Mama

for the other kind."

"Never too late for that," Bertram added cheerfully. "Why I . . ."

A yank on his arm interrupted the man's discourse, a discourse his spouse apparently had no interest in hearing.

* * * * * * *

As the pair made their way to the front, crossing the makeshift bassinet with considerable difficulty, Dorie felt the bus slowing. She grabbed Lily Dawn's arm and informed her that they were returning to their seats and leaving Ruetta in peace. Dorie wondered why the bus was stopping and hoped it was only an intersection or some such. One thing she knew for sure: whatever happened, her mother was less likely to need watching than was Lily Dawn.

Eight

Reaching her seat, Dorie Grimes pushed Lily Dawn into it, then walked toward the front to determine why the bus was stopping yet again. They had gassed up at Flagstaff, so that wasn't it. Dorie's heart sank as she saw an old yellow Volkswagen van off to the side of the road and a woman in a head wrap and shawl waving frantically at the white whale. What does she think this is, a Greyhound? Dorie wondered. She has her animals mixed up. Naturally, they were stopping. Jonah couldn't pass anyone in need, even if it meant putting one of his passengers in serious jeopardy, the deceased one who couldn't protest verbally, though soon enough she would have more persuasive ways to apprise him of her objections. He had taken the Good Samaritan story all too seriously, in Dorie's view. Even Ruetta Flatray, who applauded Good Samaritanism as a principle and practiced it herself, might have taken exception to it on this occasion.

Minding Mama

The closer they got to the woman, the less Dorie liked it. What was she doing out here by herself, miles from anywhere, in strange garb and a vehicle that was a candidate for the salvage yard ten years ago? Dorie pitied the woman, stranded as she was, and resented her at the same time. One more passenger, especially one decked out like a gypsy, would put a strain on Dorie's already depleted reservoir of good will. Of course, had Ruetta been alive and not at risk, she would have welcomed the diversion with open arms. That was Ruetta for you. And now, here was Brighty Lu Pocock, bouncing in her seat, pounding Bertram's knee. She was obviously pleased at the prospect of a potential convert, perhaps one more receptive to the holy word than the likes of her current batch of fellow travelers. It was with great effort that Dorie held her tongue.

Jonah pulled up behind the van and stepped out to meet the woman rushing toward him. All we need on this bus is one more fruitcake, Dorie said to herself, bending to get a better look. Are the highways filled with candidates for the nut house, or do I simply have a gift for smoking them out? She felt a bump from behind.

"Lemme see! Lemme see!" cried Lily Dawn, trying to squeeze by.

Dorie turned. "Go on back to your seat, girl, this is no concern of yours."

"Is she a crazy? She looks like a crazy, don't she?"

"No more'n the rest of us," Dorie muttered.

"Is she comin' on our bus?"

"I wouldn't be surprised, and it's not *our* bus."

Dorie put both hands on Lily Dawn's shoulders. "About face, girl. You're not leavin' this bus." Dorie marched the girl back to her seat. "You stay put, y' hear? I'll go light a fire under these folks. Mama can't last much longer and neither can I."

First, however, Dorie went back to cover her mother's face, hoping Ruetta might pass for a pile of bedding. Not that physical concealment would do any good, what with Lily Dawn and Brighty Lu all primed for public speaking before a fresh audience. Ishmael followed Jonah outside, but Rachel remained where she was, seemingly unconcerned, reading *Sierra* magazine, rocking the clothes basket with her foot, and softly humming a lullaby. Brighty Lu stood the suspense as long as she could then she, too, was up and out. Bertram wasn't far behind her and Lily Dawn wasn't far behind him. By the time Dorie stepped off the bus at the end of the line, the woman was surrounded by a small congregation.

Dorie sized the woman up. What she had taken for a shawl was one of those drapy affairs with a hole in the middle for the head. Dorie didn't know what to call it, but it looked for all the world like a glorified poncho, a purple one no less, and fringed to boot. Beneath it was at least one brown skirt, and maybe more, of a loose weave that hung almost to the ankles above high beaded suede moccasins. The woman's head with its red and purple wrap looked African, though her face and jewelry looked more Middle

Minding Mama

Eastern, her torso Latin American, and her feet Native American. Except for maybe Japan and China, it appeared that she had covered her bases pretty well. She looked like an equal opportunity mystic. Traveling as she was, however, in a German-made vehicle, she could also have been a living advertisement for the United Nations. Dorie's was not a charitable assessment, she knew, and she felt the sting of her mother's reproach; but by now she was long past feeling charitable toward anybody.

"What's the trouble?" she asked, approaching Ishmael.

"VW bus seems to have thrown a rod," he said.

"Well, I can relate to that. I'm about to throw a fit myself." Dorie had no idea what a rod was or what it meant to throw one.

Ishmael laughed. "I guess we're taking on another passenger."

"Time's running out for Mama. When can we leave?"

"As soon as we load the lady's things into the whale."

"How much is there?"

"I don't know yet."

* * * * * * *

The woman's "things" turned out to be a small multi-colored tent with a canopy, a crystal ball, a stool, several decks of cards, a box of bottled potions, and a trunk reputed to be full of colored scarves, silky blouses, shawls, and long, loose skirts. The trunk was useful in that it created

143

another barrier between the bus's breathing occupants and Dorie's mother who was sitting obediently in the back. The new passenger turned out to be an independent fortune teller who made her living following carnivals and circuses. In the slow season, she hired out for parties and festivals of various kinds. Or she just showed up wherever the action was and took her chances. Dorie wondered privately if she ever did funerals.

Confronted with this disturbing information, Brighty Lu had to reel in her earlier enthusiasm and take exception to the intrusion of what she called a "gypsy soothsayer" in their midst. And she didn't hesitate to pull Dorie aside and give her an earful while Jonah and Ishmael finished transferring the contents of the VW to the big bus. Brighty Lu said the woman was headed for Turner, Arizona, where there was an outdoor rock concert scheduled for tonight, as close to the Pebble Canyon Dam as the police would allow. The woman intended to work the crowd—reading palms and inventing the future and looking mysterious in her multi-colored tent behind her crystal ball, which ball Brighty Lu said was nothing more than an upside-down light fixture from Wal-Mart. What she would do after the concert was anybody's guess. The woman hadn't thought that far ahead. In Brighty's view, she was very likely an emissary of Satan, sent to compete for men's souls with God's chosen prophets and prophetesses. Meaning Bertram and Brighty Lu herself.

Minding Mama

* * * * * * *

Gathering her skirts about her, the woman mounted the bus steps and took a moment to survey the territory, swaying to keep her balance as Jonah set the bus in motion. She nodded in a proprietary way at Rachel and Moses, and assumed the pose of a commander of a conquering army. Dorie wouldn't have been surprised to see Madame Taji Mahi (that's what she called herself) hoist a flag and claim the vehicle as sovereign territory for soothsayers. Brighty Lu said the name was a fake, like its owner. From all appearances, Brighty Lu Pocock had met her match in the department of prophecy and hocus pocus. In the meantime, Lily Dawn decided that her seat by the window was a disadvantage when the real action was inside, not outside, the bus. She begged Dorie to switch places, and Dorie was tempted to oblige. But only for a moment. If Dorie's body were no longer wedged between Lily Dawn and whatever was transpiring in the aisle, the girl would be wholly unrestrainable, instead of just partly.

"You just set there, girl, and don't give me any trouble, y'hear? Eat those Cheetos an' be still." Dorie lowered her voice and glanced around. "Don't you be volunteerin' any information to this woman, neither. For all we know, she's a witch."

"A witch!" Lily Dawn sang out before Dorie could muzzle the girl with her hand.

"Huh? What's that?" Instead of taking a seat, Madame

145

Mahi jerked her head toward Lily Dawn and marched to the seat where Dorie and the girl sat, locked hand to mouth. "Who's a witch?" she demanded.

"Uh . . . nobody, nobody at all," Dorie sputtered. "I mean, we were only talking about *which seat* the girl wanted, on the aisle or by the window. What we said only sounded like *witch*. Actually, it was *which*."

Madame Mahi leaned forward, ignoring Dorie. "You think I'm a witch, girl? You see any black pointed hat and broom around here?"

Lily Dawn wriggled free of Dorie's grip. "Wa'nt me what said it," the girl cried. "It was her, Dorie Grimes. An' you ain't the on'y witch on this here bus neither. See that lady up there? She c'n bring down hellfire an' damnation an' maybe raise the dead besides."

Madame Mahi stretched her head in the direction Lily Dawn indicated. "So she can raise the dead, can she? Well, we'll see about that." Her gaze returned to Lily Dawn and she adopted a superior tone. "On a scale of one to ten, raising the dead's nothing compared to foretelling the future. And that's what I do. I can see into the future like it's a big mural somebody painted on the wall." She spread her hands out to indicate a large mural. "All I have to do is look at it and tell what's there. How many people you know can do that?"

Lily Dawn wasn't impressed. "Bible's fulla people told the future. Isaiah an' all them folks. On'y Jesus raised the dead. Nobody else. I learnt that in Bible School."

Minding Mama

By this time, curiosity had brought Brighty Lu Pocock out of her seat and into the aisle behind Madame Taji Mahi. "Did I hear somebody call up the Bible? Nobody can tell me nuthin' I don't know about the Bible."

The madame turned and glared at the evangelist. "Not from me, you didn't hear it. I don't believe in the Bible, or in God either, for that matter."

Brighty Lu gasped and nearly lost her footing in the moving bus. It wasn't often she heard somebody blaspheme right out loud, in front of chosen witnesses like herself and Bertram. When she located her voice, she asked what the Madame believed in if she didn't believe in God and the Bible. Madame Mahi eyed Brighty Lu and pulled a deck of cards from her skirt pocket. She said she believed in these and that they contained more information than a hundred Bibles; then she sat in the seat immediately in front of Dorie and her young charge. Lily Dawn was shocked into silence while Brighty Lu gasped again and appeared to be searching her brain for a suitable reply. Dorie found the little theatrical quite amusing. It was the first time she had seen Brighty Lu speechless, and now she had seen it twice in a row.

Finally, Brighty Lu recovered herself enough to challenge the woman she had earlier realized was no convert-in-embryo, but was in fact already converted in the wrong direction. Bracing herself against the seat across the aisle from the madame, she ordered Bertram to bring her a Bible so she could defend herself with the ammunition of righteousness. It appeared that the holy wars were about to begin. Dorie glanced around at Rachel and Ishmael, both of whom were grinning broadly. Ishmael winked at her, and she decided to sit back and enjoy the show. She noticed that Lily Dawn, for whom sleep had been a major occupation over the last thirty-plus hours, was wide awake, and that worried her. Except when asleep, the girl was not the kind to be satisfied with the role of spectator.

Dorie found herself wishing that her mother could watch the battle between what the evangelist saw as the powers of righteousness and the forces of evil. As a practicing Mormon, Ruetta would not have swallowed the card business, or the crystal ball; but chances are she'd have asked the madame to tell her fortune just for the fun of it, just to see if any of it might come true. As a practicing skeptic, Dorie wanted nothing to do with fortune tellers or self-proclaimed seers. A palm reader at a carnival once told Ruetta that she had a long lifeline and would bear many loving and brilliant children. The long life part of it panned out, but Dorie couldn't see that the other had to any degree. Only one of Ruetta's two children, Dorie herself, could by any stretch be called loving, and she was too late showing the trait for her mother to get any benefit from it. Furthermore, neither child could be called very smart, much less brilliant. In marrying Cleve, Dorie had proved that she didn't qualify, and Marva Grace had flunked out of college. Business college, mind you, which takes some doing.

Minding Mama

* * * * * * *

Madame Taji Mahi did not seem particularly interested in mortal combat, especially with someone she deemed an obvious inferior, and she only looked at Brighty Lu with scorn in her eyes. Instead of answering Brighty Lu's challenge, she stood and regarded the evangelist with one raised eyebrow for a few seconds. Then she changed her whole demeanor, as if donning a mask. She became instantly mysterious, turning the pack of cards over and over in her hand and speaking in an exaggerated accent apparently intended to suggest faraway eastern cultures.

"Who wants the fortune told? I tell it while we ride," she said, wooing her audience with her eyes and a husky voice.

No one responded, though Dorie could feel Lily Dawn stirring next to her. Brighty Lu turned and stomped back to her seat next to Bertram at the front of the bus.

"Come, have no fear," Madame Mahi encouraged. "Forget the cards. I read the palm and tell the future." She paused and gazed around.

"Read mine! Read mine the first!" Lily Dawn cried, leaping to her feet.

The madame smiled a fake mysterious smile. "Ah," she said, "the young one believes. Come, my pretty. Sit beside me."

But Brighty Lu would not be upstaged. There she was in the aisle again, defending the innocence of youth, insisting that she herself, not Lily Dawn, be the devil's first victim.

"I aim to defuse the power of the wicked one," she said bravely, "sacrificin' myself for the good of this here child who is not fortified to be so tested."

"No, no!" Lily Dawn cried, pounding the back of the seat in front of her. "I'm fortified. I been to Bible school. Ask Dorie. Ain't nobody more fortified than me!"

Dorie no longer had the energy to interfere in whatever was going to happen. If Lily Dawn wanted her fortune told, she could have her fortune told. Herself, Dorie was much more interested in what the fortune teller would say to Brighty Lu Pocock, the dispenser of Doom's Day doctrine who knew already that whatever mortal future she had was on the brink of expiring. For Brighty Lu and others of the saved, said mortal future was sufficiently short to be past worrying about.

Dorie gently tugged at the girl's arm. "Let Miz Pocock go first, so's you can see how it's done." Lily Dawn plopped back into her seat, a pout on her lips.

"I can't see good," the girl complained.

"You just stand up there and look over the seatback You'll see plenty," Dorie avowed. "As for me, hearin' is the most I can tolerate." Even that might be too much, she added under her breath.

* * * * * * *

By this time, Brighty Lu had planted herself across the aisle from Madame Mahi. To facilitate a palm reading, she

Minding Mama

raised the arm rest and twisted sideways in the seat, elbows resting on knees, hands palms up. Madame Mahi likewise turned in her seat and prepared herself to receive enlightenment from the cosmos by tilting her head back, closing her eyes, reciting some gobbledygook Dorie couldn't for the life of her understand, raising her hands to the sky (in this case, the ceiling of the bus), and spreading her fingers. Then, reaching toward Brighty Lu's extended palms, she took them in her hands, chanting something that sounded to Dorie like a recipe for upside-down cake. Lily Dawn was straining to see, leaning first over the seat in front of her and then hanging over Dorie's shoulder. Finally Dorie surrendered and gave her the aisle seat.

When the main feature began after the lengthy preliminaries, Dorie had no trouble at all hearing, even from the window seat. Madame Mahi, well aware of her larger audience, practiced elocution with gusto. She warmed to the task by studying the evangelist's hands and moving her own head in a deliberate circle while she hummed—or wailed—an incantation; then she began to speak in a slow, knowing voice, punctuating her words with inflected ooo's and ohhh's and ahhh's.

"Ahhh, yes, here the lifeline. I see, I see. Ooo. And now this line. Ohhh, is so sad. And the swirl here, and the zigzag there. Ahhh, so sorry."

"Whatya mean, ooo and ohhh and so sorry?" Brighty Lu interrupted. "Whatya see? I already know it's the end of the world day after tomorrow. That ain't bad news, that's good

151

news! The Lord has informed his special messengers, and we're prepared to greet him in glory without sufferin' death."

"Ooo, no end of world. I see beautiful young woman walking hand in hand with man. Yes, is Meester Pocock! They very happy."

"That's me! Transformed in the afterlife into the image of my gorgeous inner self, glidin' through Elysium fields. I'm saved! I'm saved! The Lord has confirmed it!" Brighty Lu was ecstatic. She seemed to have forgotten that the receptacle for this stunning piece of divine intelligence was in league with the devil.

Madame Mahi closed her eyes and shook her head sadly. "So sorry, is not you. Is someone else."

Brighty Lu jerked her hands loose. "Whatya mean it's not me? O' course it is. Who else would it be?" She got to her feet, shaking her hands to rid them of uncleanness. "I've had enough. This is bunk. Don't you listen to a word, Bertie, you hear?"

Madame Mahi remained calm. She looked up at Brighty Lu, her face full of mock sympathy. "Is more. I learn more. You want to hear more?"

Brighty Lu allowed as how she had heard all the drivel she cared to be subjected to in one day. But then a look of doubt traversed her round face and she glanced about the bus. "What else?" she asked in a broken voice and sat down again.

The madame swallowed a smile and took Brighty Lu's hands a second time, studying them for a long minute. "I see baby, newborn baby . . ."

Minding Mama

"The Christ Child!" Brighty Lu cried.

The fortune teller didn't miss a beat. ". . . is older now, is riding a . . . how you say it? . . . tricycle."

"Huh? How can the Christ Child be riding a tricycle?"

"Wa'nt no tricycles in Jesus' day!" Lily Dawn cried out. "Jesus, he rode a donkey." The girl started to elaborate, but went mum when the madame shot her a disapproving look. Dorie, of course, bought none of this monkey business, but she regretted again that her mother and Cleve were missing the show. Perhaps Loyal Bunce would have enjoyed it, too, though he might have been inclined to take it seriously, he was such a trusting soul. As for his dog Petunia, well, if Petunia were here maybe Madame Mahi would read her paw. Dorie snickered out loud at the thought.

Madame Mahi chose to ignore Dorie and to continue with her analysis. "Is not Christ Child," she said solemnly, "is your child."

"*My* child!" Brighty Lu shrieked, leaping to her feet. "How can it be my child? I've been barren for sixty-three years!"

A loud chortle sounded from Ishmael's direction, and Jonah called out from the driver's seat, "Rest stop ahead. You can grab a bite here and use the facilities. Next stop is Turner, Arizona." Then he broke out laughing.

Lily Dawn, apparently unsure as to what to do, giggled nervously, then jumped into the aisle and grabbed Brighty Lu's hand. "Lemme see the tricycle! I wanna see the baby on the tricycle!"

Brighty Lu snatched the hand away as Jonah pulled to a stop. "Go ahead and laugh, ever' last jack one a' you," she cried. "Him what laughs last laughs best."

Off balance, she staggered backward toward the front of the bus as it slowed, falling heavily into her seat beside Bertram. He patted her knee, then put his right hand over his heart. "The Lord works in mysterious ways his wonders to perform," he said.

"Well, I know one wonder he's not about to perform," she replied. "My name ain't Sarah, nor Elizabeth neither! And you're no Abraham nor Zacharias."

* * * * * * *

The various occupants of the bus had trooped back after the break, and the front section where the Pococks sat was unusually quiet. The reforming dooms-dayers had withdrawn into their shell of virtue, apparently intending it to shield them from the tainted company with which they were currently forced to travel. It's possible that, while Bertram Pocock was impervious to thought, his companion was thinking. Actually thinking. It would be rather a new experience for her, since she had assumed for years that she had all the answers that were to be had and was therefore shielded from the hazards of an original thought.

As the bus rolled down the highway, Lily Dawn grew more agitated. At last, she reached around the seat in front of her and tugged at Madam Mahi's clothing. "It's my turn,

Minding Mama

ain't it?" she asked in a meek voice. "I waited, and now it's my turn . . . ain't it?"

"Let it go, girl," Dorie whispered loudly. "Maybe later."

"But when, Dorie, when? We almost to my grandmama's by the dam. Then I got to leave this here bus. For good! An' you soon be gone, too."

"Listen here, girl. We've got no time to find your grandmama 'til we get Mama buried. Then's when we worry about your grandmama, after Mama's safe in the ground. You just hold your horses."

The fortune teller's head appeared around the corner of her seat. "Madame Mahi has time to read girl's palm. Let her come."

Lily Dawn was not one to wait for a second invitation, or to seek a second opinion. She was out of her seat and into the seat Brighty Lu had vacated before Dorie could assemble further opposition. Madame Mahi went through the same ritual she had followed with Brighty Lu—the rolling head, the raised arms, the chanting—except that she condensed it somewhat. Privately, Dorie wondered if the lines in Lily Dawn's hands were so obliterated by dirt as to be indecipherable. She should have inspected them when the girl left the restroom. Lily Dawn sat very still with her right hand outstretched, awed by the rites being performed in her behalf. Dorie slid toward the aisle for a better view.

Tracing a long diagonal line across the girl's palm, Madame Mahi smiled. "Ahhh," she said knowingly, "is good, is good."

Lily Dawn emerged from her trance. "What's good? What's good? Am I gonna be rich? Is my grandmama where I'm goin' gonna be rich, too?"

"Ah," the fortune teller crooned, "I see girl . . . girl looking for home. And . . . wait . . . yes, I see girl find home. Happy. Much love."

"With my grandmama?"

The madame closed her eyes in an attitude of exploring the ineffable future. "I see woman, yes, but is mystery who woman is. Maybe grandmother, maybe not. Maybe other woman. I see other woman . . . blonde hair."

Dorie jerked to attention. What was the fortune teller up to, sowing ideas in the child's mind? Curiosity, however, kept Dorie from speaking out. She realized that the madame's line of work had trained her to pick up hints and clues, inklings of truth among her clientele that she could use in her so-called analysis. She gleaned enough from a quick eye and ear to make educated guesses about people at a first encounter. She read people all right, but not through their palms. Dorie couldn't help wondering what the woman might have seen in her. More to the point, what did she think she saw? Ruetta always used to say that half-truths were more dangerous than out-and-out lies. Dorie was beginning to realize that her mother was a whole lot smarter than her daughters ever gave her credit for.

"My grandmama by the dam has black hair, less'n it's gone white by now. I ain't never seen her. On'y pitchers my daddy shown me. So that there woman you seen in my

Minding Mama

palm ain't her. She somebody else." Lily Dawn thrust out her left hand. "Here, what's this'n say?"

Madame Mahi examined the hand, then closed her eyes and tilted her head back. Then she spoke. "I see school. Much books. Much happiness."

"On'y school I ever found tolerable was Bible school, an' I can't go back there to it." She looked skeptically at the madame. "Did you jus' make that up, that school part?"

Obviously, the fortune teller was accustomed to being challenged. She had a ready answer. "See the palm?" she invited, pointing to lines near the palm's outer edge. "Here two buildings. One has pointed end, other has square. One Bible school, or maybe church, other regular school."

Dorie approved of this particular line of falderal, so she held her peace. But she also decided to have her own palm "read," to learn, not the future, but the madame's take on her and the manipulative advice she would spout in the guise of prophecy. Not that Dorie would give any of it a minute's consideration, of course, but because it would make a good story to take home to Cleve and Clarence Ross. Besides, it would fill the time between here and Turner, and maybe keep Brighty Lu quiet. Dorie relieved that she didn't have to worry about baby Moses at the moment, that Rachel was seeing to him pretty much full time. What they'd ultimately do with the child, how-ever, was anybody's guess. A bridge still to be crossed.

* * * * * * *

157

When the fortune teller finished with Lily Dawn, Dorie traded seats with the girl and stretched her right hand toward the stranger. Madame Mahi looked surprised, but didn't object. Probably assuming that the preliminaries would be wasted on Dorie, she began examining the palm in her grasp at once.

"Ah," she said, "I see death nearby . . . burial of relative."

"It's her mama," Lily Dawn cried from her seat. "She's dead, and we're haulin' her to the graveyard!"

Dorie leaped to her feet. "You hush up, Lily Dawn. You just hush up."

"Well, it's true," Lily Dawn whimpered. "She's right back there, under them things." The girl gestured toward the back of the bus. "You c'n ask Rachel. You c'n go to the funeral!"

Dorie slumped back to the seat. What was the use of trying to keep anything under wraps when your traveling companion had an automatic spring in her tongue? "Just get on with the reading," she sighed. "We're not *goin'* to a funeral, we're bringin' it with us, body and all." She paused. "I promised my mama, is what I did, and that's why I'm in this bus at the moment when I should be back in Atlanta curling hair and it's too long a story to tell and who'd want to hear it anyway? I'm sure I wouldn't."

Just then, Brighty Lu Pocock popped up in the aisle, seemingly having found little satisfaction in silent indignation. "I coulda raised the old woman from the dead, but was prevented by infidels," she cried.

Minding Mama

Again Jonah came to the rescue. "Here we are, Turner, Arizona. Everyone to their seats," he called. "Where should we take you, Madame Mahi?"

The fortune teller dropped Dorie's hand and became again the woman who had first boarded the bus. "Get me as close to the dam as you can. With the help of my genie I'll manage just fine." She turned and winked at Lily Dawn when she said that.

"You got a genie?! Lemme see, lemme see!" the girl cried. She was halfway out of her seat when Dorie arrived. Within seconds, Lily Dawn was reinstated in her seat, this time next to the window. Again, Dorie blocked her exit.

"If she had a genie, she wouldn't be travelin' with the likes of us," Dorie said.

Nine

"Don't worry about me, I can take care of myself," Madame Taji Mahi called to Ishmael as he deposited the last of her belongings on the curb just outside the Pebble Canyon Dam parking area. "And don't worry about my van either. If I never see it again it'll be too soon. I hereby bequeath it to the state of Arizona." With a good deal of flourish, she blew a kiss south.

"But . . ." Ishmael protested.

"Listen, I'm going to make me a killing here tonight. Tomorrow I buy another vehicle and run it until it dies, too." She waved him on his way. "You have an appointment with the undertaker. Get going."

As the Great White Bus left Turner heading west, Dorie realized that not once had she heard the fortune teller thank her rescuers or offer to buy gasoline. A line from something her teacher had read in a high school English class came into her mind. It wasn't even a sentence, but just a phrase:

Minding Mama

"When gratitude is no more. . . ." The world would be a sorry place indeed if nobody felt or expressed gratitude any more. If Ruetta Flatray had taught her daughter anything, she had taught her that.

The more Dorie thought about it, the more it dawned on her that she had hit on one of the chief bones of long-buried contention between herself and her husband Cleve, and maybe her son Clarence Ross, too. They never thanked her for anything. She didn't thank them either, but then they never did much to warrant thanks, at least not that she could see. The lack of gratitude in the Grimes household became especially apparent when Dorie's mother moved in with her and Cleve. Ruetta may have been fussy and opinionated, but she was grateful. Dorie could certainly say that for her.

At that moment, Brighty Lu apparently felt moved upon to stand and address the group. "Well, it's goodbye, good riddance, and one less heretic to stain the atmosphere in this here bus." She paused, but receiving no response, she continued her sermon. It mainly concerned the evils of soothsaying and the tools of the devil that soothsayers employed in their trade. The evangelist concluded by inviting all to join in a prayer designed to cleanse the vessel in which they journeyed to their appointed ends. Her audience could not seem to generate much enthusiasm for the proposal. Lily Dawn, asleep now with her head against the hard glass window, gave out a fitful little snore. Ishmael sat with his head back and his eyes closed, and Rachel was totally absorbed in feeding Moses. Jonah cleared his throat, but kept his eyes on the road while Dorie succumbed to the irresistible seduction of sleep. The vast stark beauty of the mammoth lake sending long blue fingers into the humps of bare red sandstone was apparently lost on all the travelers but Jonah.

* * * * * *

"Here we are, Jericho, the Promised Land," Jonah called.

Dorie's head jerked, popping her neck. "Ouch! Mama! Where's Mama?" she cried out of a dark wild dream of gypsies and forests. There outside the windows were anything but forests. The very opposite, in fact. Filling half the sky stood great bluffs that literally leaped from the ground, redder and rougher, and yes, more beautiful than she remembered. And beneath them stretched acres of sand and brush punctuated by a few frame buildings. Within minutes, the little troop made the right, then the big left turn into the center of town. Jonah coasted to a stop across from the Center Street Plaza, giving passers-by ample opportunity to look the bus over without craning their necks and wrenching their spinal columns. Dorie couldn't believe her eyes. They were here. They had made it! Her mother was home! Dorie found herself laughing and crying at the same time.

Jonah turned, smiling. "Where to?" he asked.

Dorie tried to collect herself. "The mortuary," she said.

Minding Mama

"We've got to go to the mortuary." She stopped. "I can't remember where it is. Please, ask somebody. Anybody."

"You and me ain't goin' to no mortuary, nor no cemetery neither, are we Bertie? Not never." Brighty Lu Pocock made the announcement from her seat. "We're goin' to bypass them places on the morrow and go straight to glory. No dirt and worms for us. Right, Bertie?"

"Right as rain," he chanted. His customary mantra. It was the first Dorie had heard from him in some time.

"We here?" Lily Dawn asked sleepily. "What place is this? Lookit all them big orange rocks. Where'd they come frum? I wanted to find my grandmama by the dam, but we din't do it. We still got to do it."

"Hush girl. Like I told you, it's first things first, and my mama is first. She's why we came."

"Well, she ain't why I come. I come to find my grandmama by the dam, an' we up and lef' the dam."

On cue, little Moses awoke and began to cry. Rachel picked him up and began swaying back and forth. It occurred to Dorie that quite miraculously this helpless little fellow had accomplished what his namesake had been unable to do. He had crossed over into Jericho. Ruetta would have said that an old wrong had been righted at last. Dorie wondered if that was why Moses had joined her and the others. Providence. Ruetta would have called it Providence. Dorie herself was more inclined to call it coincidence, but she couldn't entirely rule out Providence. Not any more.

163

Dorie had been grateful to discover that the new mortuary was less than a mile from her mother's house. She could walk that, though a house that had sat vacant for eight years wasn't likely to offer much in the way of amenities. She only hoped the extra key was still hanging on a nail under the back stoop, and that there was a broom handy. The experience at the mortuary hadn't exactly been pleasant, especially when the sheriff arrived and threatened to arrest her for illegally transporting a dead body across state lines. Luckily, he was an old classmate of hers and knew the family.

She pled ignorance and begged him to hold off until her mother was buried, and he said okay, but don't go running off. How would I run off, even if I wanted to, she had asked. My truck's back in Flagstaff, dead as a pre-cooked goose. Her arrival at her hometown in a bus painted like a whale had not inspired confidence, he said, and she had assured him that the bus would be leaving right away, while she herself would be staying for the burial at the very least. The bus people had helped her out, is all. She chose not to mention the baby Moses and held her breath that Lily Dawn wouldn't feel impressed to tell all she knew first chance she got. Dorie was glad she had left the girl outside with the others while she handled the mortuary business.

The mortician, a slender quiet man with the thinnest of moustaches, had apologized for calling the law, but said he was required to. He remembered Ruetta Flatray, he said, and would do the best he could by her, though he preferred his

Minding Mama

clients a little fresher. He hoped she would fit in a regular coffin, bent as she was in the shape of a car seat. Dorie said she could only afford a nice pine box anyway, and maybe it could be made to fit her mother in her current shape. (This, of course, was a deliberate falsehood because just now Dorie couldn't afford any box, except maybe a cardboard refrigerator box. She crossed her fingers when she said it and was glad that Lily Dawn was out of earshot.) The mortician said he'd do what he could. In any case, they couldn't bury her until Monday. Dorie said okay, she'd have to manage until then. Just make sure you dig the hole next to Demont Ralph because Ruetta promised him and I promised her, Dorie insisted. It would have been a lot easier to bury her in Atlanta, she added. The mortician said he knew it would.

Once her business was finished with the mortician, Dorie went out to where Ishmael, Jonah, Rachel, Lily Dawn, and the baby relaxed on the grass in front of the mortuary. The questions to be answered now centered around Lily Dawn and little Moses. The evangelical Pococks were nowhere to be seen. When Dorie asked after them, Ishmael explained that the pair had cased the convenience stores and fast-food joints in the area, looking for bumper stickers that said things like "Jesus Saves But Don't Push It," or "Repent Before Your Neighbor Beats You to It," or "The World Ends Tomorrow or the Next Day." Brighty Lu and Bertram apparently found a suitable sticker and joined forces with whoever owned the vehicle it was attached to. They had disappeared with their luggage and religious books and artifacts while the others were getting milkshakes.

"I think I'll even miss them a little," Rachel laughed. "Very little."

Dorie sank to the grass. "I could sleep for a week," she said. "But we got Mama home." She looked at the others. "Thanks to you." She opened her bag and pulled out her last crumpled bill. "I want you to take this for gas. It's not much, but I can send more when I get it, to fix the dent in the bus."

Jonah shook his head. "The accident was more our fault than yours. Forget the gas and the dent. What can we do for you? How about your pickup? Where will you stay?"

Dorie reached over and pressed the bill into his hand. "I'm not a charity case yet," she said, then yawned and rubbed her eyes. "Just take me to my Mama's house. I'll figger somethin' out."

Ishmael objected. "Even if the place is still standing and is habitable, you'll have no water or power or heat. You can't stay there. And what about Lily Dawn and the baby?"

"My head's too tired to think. Leave Lily Dawn with me. We'll work it out."

"I got to go back to my grandmama's! That's what I come all this ways for!" Lily Dawn cried out. She was on the verge of tears.

Rachel reached over and patted Lily Dawn's knee. Looking at Jonah and Ishmael, she spoke. "We'll take you back to Turner and find your grandmother, won't we boys?"

Jonah and Ishmael looked at each other. "Sure,"

Minding Mama

Ishmael said. "Sure we will. We're in no hurry."

"Oh, please, please, pretty please!" Lily Dawn begged.

Dorie wasn't sure how she felt about that. Lily Dawn had been appended to her for what seemed months, and she didn't like to entrust her to strangers. On the other hand, Rachel would look out for her; and besides, Dorie was in no position to take care of the girl, being homeless herself, not to mention carless, bathless, and broke. Finally, she consented, wondering whether she'd ever see Lily Dawn, truth-teller without rival, again. It made her ache inside to think of it, which astonished her more than a little. Lily Dawn, however, was ecstatic, hugging and kissing Dorie and Rachel to show her happiness.

Once the matter of Lily Dawn's future was settled, for the moment, anyway, the group turned its attention to baby Moses. They agreed that authorities somewhere would have to be notified. In all likelihood, the baby would not have been reported missing. Its mother must have assumed that either he died or he was found by somebody or other. She could be prosecuted.

"She's not the only one," Dorie wailed. "I've carried Moses from Texas to here, in addition to Mama and Lily Dawn. There's some would call me a kidnaper and a body-snatcher."

"No, no, Dorie!" Lily Dawn cried. "You saved Moses. You never hurt 'im! He'd of died in that smelly ol' place where we found 'im!"

Dorie had to agree that the baby's chances had been

167

slim. Who on earth would have discovered him in an abandoned warehouse? Furthermore, she herself had neither the
strength nor the will to solve that problem at the moment,
nor the time, energy, and resources to care for a baby just
now. She had a mother to bury and a rundown house to
clean up and dispose of. Rachel, on the other hand, was
well-equipped for the job. And so, since Moses was accustomed to Rachel and Lily Dawn and the bus, the three
friends volunteered to take him along on the return trip to
Turner. Rachel confessed to having grown quite attached to
the little fellow.

"We'll work it out later," she promised. "One of my
brothers is a lawyer."

"Just don't let the local sheriff see Moses yet," Dorie
warned. "I'm in enough trouble with the law as it is. I might
wind up in jail on account of Mama." She paused and smiled
wearily. "Which might solve two of my most worrisome
problems, where to sleep and how to eat." Dorie dragged
herself to her feet, stretching her arms above her head. "It's
gettin' on. You'd best hustle on back to Turner. It's easier to
find people b'fore they go to bed, especially grandmamas."

* * * * * * *

The parting with Lily Dawn had been teary on both
sides. Once the girl was past her immediate jubilation, she
seemed to realize that she might be leaving Dorie forever.
At least she has *some* feelings for me, Dorie mused as she

Minding Mama

stood in the gravel in front of her mother's house. The vagabond trio had, at Dorie's insistence, left her and her worn travel bag and handbag there and departed for Turner. The lawn had died years ago, and been replaced by enterprising weeds. Everything about the pinkish frame house sagged, from its peeling white shutters to its drooping porch and galvanized rain gutters.

Dorie made her way to the back of the house, past dead bushes and overgrown vines. There she knelt and scratched through the cobwebs and dead leaves under the warped plank stoop until she found the house key, right where her mother had always kept it. Whether it would turn the lock was another matter. As she stood at the back door wiggling the tarnished key in the rusty lock, a small elderly woman, waving a stick and yelling at the top of her lungs, burst through the weeds and tall dead grass along the ditch that separated the Flatray yard from its neighbor to the west.

"You there! Git away from that door! I'll call the p'lice on you! You ain't gonna burgle this here house if I have anything to say about it! Now scat!" She arrived at the bottom of the stoop, squinting up the two steps at Dorie through gold-rimmed eyeglasses that hung crookedly on her thin wrinkled face. "If you was a man, I'd a' called the p'lice already."

The woman looked slightly familiar. Dorie held up the key. "I'm not breaking in, I have a key. See?"

"Not to that there door, you don't."

"I don't?"

"I had them locks changed, just in case somebody turned up with a key, or found where Mrs. Flatray had it hid."

"You knew my mother?"

"You say Mrs. Flatray was your mother?" The woman looked skeptical. "Hmmph. A likely story. One a' her daughters is clear out to Georgia somewheres, and the other'n wouldn' trouble herself to visit her mama, much less break in her house. Come down here an' lemme get a closer look."

Dorie stepped to the ground, but she still towered above her accuser. "Well, I'm the Georgia daughter, believe it or don't, and I've brought Mama home."

The woman perked up and swiveled her head from left to right. "Mrs. Flatray here? Where is she? Ruetta Flatray was my dearest friend in all the world, and then that Georgia daughter come and hauled her off after Mr. Flatray died." She paused. "Was that you what done that? You look differ'nt. Ruetta promised me she'd come back, soon's she could convince her daughter t' bring her." The woman lowered herself with some effort and sat on the stoop, grunting as she did so. "She's as good as her word. She's done come home." The woman looked around again. "If she's here, where in tarnation is she? Is she hidin' t' surprise me? She's such a tease, she is."

Dorie sat beside the woman on the rickety old stoop. Her eyes traveled to the horizon that glowed below the darkening sky. "She's at the mortuary." Dorie blinked back a tear. "Mama died. I promised to bring her home and bury

Minding Mama

her next to Papa because she promised him." Dorie folded her arms tightly against the evening chill. "I kept my promise, and she'll keep hers," she said quietly.

The aged neighbor sat silent for a long minute. "Mrs. Flatray was always one to keep her promises," she said finally.

* * * * * * *

Once she was convinced that Dorie Grimes was indeed Dorie Flatray before she was Grimes, Mrs. Eckersell wouldn't hear of Dorie's staying in that rundown eyesore of a house without light or heat or water or anything. That was the neighbor's name, Mrs. Eckersell. She was one of those women of an earlier generation who lost their first names in their forties and never found them again. She was also one of those women who believed in hospitality and practiced it like a religion. As such, she made Dorie promise to board with her until after the burial Monday, and longer if she wanted. She said that why, land, she was glad for the company. Besides, it was the least she could do for her old neighbor who had now gone to her reward. Dorie had to admit she had been worried about where she'd sleep until Monday. And her worries wouldn't be over then, either, because she was flat broke until the house sold, *if* it sold— a big if, given its current state of disrepair. Somebody would have to take it on as a project, or tear it down and start over. There was also the matter of her pickup sitting in

Flagstaff. Who knows what it would cost to get it running? Her auto insurance was the $500 deductible type.

As for Marva Grace, Dorie's only sister, Dorie figured she'd show up Monday about ten minutes before the burial services, fresh from the pool at the luxury motel, if there was one, where she would no doubt be staying once she arrived. Naturally, her husband and children would not trouble themselves to come. Furthermore, Marva Grace wouldn't offer to share quarters with Dorie, not in a million years, and Dorie wouldn't ask. She still had her pride. What was left of it. Dorie had to call Marva collect to give her the details. It's a wonder she accepted the charges. Marva Grace was going to have to advance the money for the mortuary, too, to be repaid when the house sold, though Dorie hadn't delivered that piece of news on the phone. She decided to hold onto it until Ruetta was safe in the ground. Dorie assured the mortician that her sister would be paying him in full on Monday. In the meantime, he had the body as collateral.

When Dorie awoke Saturday morning, after sleeping for thirteen hours straight, she couldn't remember where she was. The room was unfamiliar with its dated floral wallpaper, grim faded portraits, and embroidered religious sayings in gold-painted frames. The borders of the ceiling and doorway were a heavily carved dark wood, and from the pale pink light fixture in the ceiling hung a curled, yellowing piece of flypaper. The place even smelled old, emitting a faint scent of gardenia. Then it came to her. Mrs.

Minding Mama

Eckersell. She was at Mrs. Eckersell's. Wait a minute, Dorie told herself. Is that her name? Ruetta had mentioned her old neighbor on several occasions, but Dorie hadn't paid much attention, even when Mrs. Eckersell introduced herself yesterday.

* * * * * * *

It took most of Saturday to make the necessary arrangements for the burial. Somebody had to be in charge, and Mrs. Eckersell knew who. The bishop, she said. He'll be at home on a Saturday. You just tell him Ruetta Flatray was in his ward for many years, and now it's up to him to get her properly beneath the ground. When Dorie protested, Mrs. Eckersell said it was what bishops were for. And the Relief Society, they'll dress Ruetta properly and bring repast for the mourners. What mourners besides the two of us and Marva Grace, assuming she turns up? Dorie had asked, and Mrs. Eckersell said Dorie might be surprised. Then Mrs. Eckersell had marched to the phone, dialed a number (yes, her phone was the old rotary type), and handed Dorie the receiver. Dorie was not a Latter-day Saint, as her mother called herself, and corrected others who called her a "Mormon," but she knew the terms "bishop" and "ward" and "Relief Society" from living with Ruetta for the past eight years.

When Dorie awoke Sunday, Mrs. Eckersell was nowhere to be found. Then Dorie realized that she would be attending church services. The house seemed hollow without its busy little owner scurrying about. Dorie regretted not having made plans to attend herself. It's the least she could have done to acknowledge her appreciation to those who would see to things tomorrow. There would be tributes, and a musical number, and a dedicatory prayer, with the bishop conducting. All would be in order. Then it occurred to Dorie that she had made no arrangements for flowers, nor did she have the wherewithal to make any. And Marva Grace certainly wouldn't think of it. Ruetta's coffin would be bare. Aunt Lola's Flowers would be closed today anyway, but maybe she could get a few flowers at the grocery store Monday morning. Something, anything. Maybe there was enough loose change in her handbag to buy a little bouquet.

Groaning, Dorie raised to an elbow and swung her legs stiffly over the bed's edge. The mere rustling of the spread unleashed a nostalgic fragrance, a *potpourri* smell reminiscent of Ruetta's old Sunday dress with the browning lace collar. Dorie staggered over to where she had deposited her handbag on the green needlepoint seat of the room's only chair, a mahogany piece of indeterminate age. Returning to the bed, she upended the bag, grasping it from the corners. A good many coins and a great deal of paraphernalia tumbled onto the quilt's multi-colored stitched squares. Dorie shook the bag, dislodging the crumpled twenty-dollar bill she had given Jonah for gas, and with it, paper-clipped in a tight fold, three one hundred-dollar bills. Dorie sat on the

Minding Mama

bed, buried her face in her hands, and let the tears come.

It was a cleansing in many ways, and perhaps long overdue. Strangers, whom she had silently questioned and impatiently prodded, had seen her need and quietly answered it. They were what Ruetta was talking about when she spoke of the good Samaritan, or the father of the prodigal son, and used the phrase "pure religion and undefiled." Dorie remembered hearing her mother read to her as a child, "When saw we thee a hungred, and fed thee? or thirsty, and gave thee drink? When saw we thee a stranger, and took thee in? or naked, and clothed thee?" Dorie also remembered Jesus' reply: "Inasmuch as ye have done it unto one of the least of these my brethren, ye have done it unto me."

Dorie had never had very much in the way of the world's goods, but she had always managed to make ends meet. Until now. This was the first time she had been wholly needful, entirely without resources, completely dependent on the generosity of others. It gave her a new perspective on poverty and homelessness. And on desperation. Desperation such as the frightened young mother of the baby Moses must have felt when she wrapped her child and left him in a warehouse (or in bulrushes long ago—was it so very different, really?), desperation such as Lily Dawn must have felt when she ran away from the evil advances of boys she feared, desperation such as Loyal Bunce might have felt when he crawled into the back of an old pickup looking for a new reason to hope.

Marilyn Arnold

And now that Dorie thought about it, what was it but desperation that was driving Brighty Lu and Bertram Pocock toward what they wanted to believe was instant redemption instead of mortal death? Were they so afraid of death and sin that they abolished both—for themselves and their converts—by inventing a theology that allowed them to sidestep death and judgment? Then, too, how about Madame Taji Mahi, or whoever she was? She seemed so confident, so self-satisfied, so ready to meddle in other people's lives—so sure of "making a killing" by preying on her fellow mortals. But wasn't she desperate and needy like the rest of them? Driving that old VW van, carrying all her earthly possessions with her, living from hand to mouth, what reason had she to act so superior? Dorie realized now that Jonah and Ishmael and Rachel had seen past the various facades of their passengers to the deep-down need. And with each of them it was a human need, a human need for human caring. Having worked through their own disappointments and desperation, they were equipped to lift the burdens of others.

Then Dorie remembered the bank robbers, and how she had left them stranded and even taken delight in doing so. What would the three companions of the bus have done about those drunk young bank robbers? Now there was a moral dilemma of real magnitude. Are we required to extend charity to reckless criminals? Dorie asked herself. Well, Ruetta might have reminded her that Jesus forgave the woman taken in adultery, and adultery was against the

Minding Mama

law in his day (at least for women, though apparently not for men!). But when push came to shove, Dorie was pretty sure Ruetta would have enjoyed getting the best of Bonnie and Clyde. "We didn't hurt 'em any," she'd have said. "We only fixed their wagon, but good, so's we could make a clean getaway." And then she would have chuckled with delight.

Ten

Early spring in the desert could sometimes play winter tricks, and Monday morning turned blustery, blowing up swirls of last year's brittle leaves and silencing returning songbirds. The burial service for Ruetta Flatray was scheduled for two o'clock, which would give her daughter Marva Grace time to arrive and check into her motel and get beautiful. Dorie Grimes knew her sister would appear at the cemetery in either a BMW convertible or a Lincoln Continental, depending on which impression she wanted to leave with the local folks—that of wealthy playgirl, or that of sophisticated rich woman. And she'd be dressed fit to kill. Dorie herself would be wearing her one dress that fit, a pink polyester with a V neck, which would be acceptable by Jericho standards and considered poverty level by Marva's standards. Dorie hadn't bothered to buy pantyhose for the occasion, and her feet would be shod in the sandals she had worn across the country, Mona Fay's.

Minding Mama

That morning Dorie donned her better slacks and her only jacket, squeezed her size ten feet into a pair of sneakers (whose?) she found in a box in her mother's closet, and walked to the cemetery. She wanted to make sure the grave had been dug, and dug properly. But first, for old time's sake, she walked up Center Street. Some of the homes and commercial buildings she passed looked familiar, though it had been many years since she traveled Jericho's streets on foot.

The Trail's End Café was still there, but now it was called Houston's instead of Peach's. She remembered eating in that very building when her mother's college-educated aunt came to visit. Ruetta wanted to make an impression by going "out" to dinner, even if they couldn't afford it. Dorie wondered what had happened to the little clothing boutique across the street—was it called The Pink Poodle? The college kids who worked summers at the north rim of the Grand Canyon used to blow their paychecks at that place on their days off.

Jericho was a small town by any standard of measurement, though in recent years people had moved there in search of a simpler life in a reasonable climate. Then, too, some fast-food places and a new Crescent Moon Theater had been added on the highway south from the central business block. Those establishments sprang up in deference to the tourist trade, Dorie supposed, since Jericho was the last bastion of anything resembling civilization before Arizona and the Grand Canyon. As Ruetta regularly reminded her,

Marilyn Arnold

Hollywood had discovered Jericho a long time ago and filmed a good many westerns in the vicinity. Dorie would reply that native Georgians wouldn't think it good for much else, except maybe breathing dry air and committing suicide. Native Georgians had their biases like everybody else.

Following the mortician's directions, Dorie found her father's grave and the rather large squarish hole next to it. Seeing it now, Dorie was glad that when her father died, Ruetta had arranged for her own name and birth date to be engraved on the headstone alongside the statistics for Demont Ralph. All that had to be added was Ruetta's death date. Unfortunately, Dorie noted, the hole was dug on the Demont Ralph side of the headstone, but she wasn't about to request a transfer or a new headstone. Who'd know the difference but the worms? On earth, Ruetta might have raised a small ruckus, but Dorie figured that where her mother was now, she see'd it as a joke. One she could enjoy while she was up there cavorting merrily in the clouds.

In her folded condition Ruetta Flatray hadn't fit in a normal rectangular coffin, but the mortician had tracked down an oversized pine wood coffin at a mortuary in Smithville, some ninety miles away. It was to have been brought over yesterday. There would, of course, be no "viewing," as the locals called the opportunity for people to come to the mortuary before funerals, assess the quality of the mortician's work, and say to each other that the deceased looked as if she were only sleeping. Dorie didn't want Ruetta's friends to see her bent in the shape of a pick-

Minding Mama

up seat and lying on her side instead of her back.

As for the mortician's work, Dorie couldn't see that her mother looked much different than she had on the trip west, except she was dressed better and had her hair fixed. Through every adventure, her mother had never lost her calm or looked anything but peaceful, which state in death Dorie attributed to a good life and peace of conscience. The mortician had succeeded in maintaining that look. And speaking of the mortician, Dorie truly hoped Marva Grace was bringing her checkbook. What mortuary was going to take an IOU from a dead client? In the undertaking business Dorie supposed that it was strictly cash and bury. You wouldn't care to repossess your product.

Dorie sat on the grass next to her father's grave. She was tempted to talk to him, to tell him she was sorry she had left home so young and stayed away so long. But then she realized that if she were going to talk to anyone, she should address the two of them, Demont Ralph and Ruetta, father and mother, because if Ruetta was right, the two were already a pair again and had been for several days. And never the twain shall part, Ruetta used to say. She had "had his work done," she used to say also, and Dorie took that to mean some ceremonies had occurred that guaranteed the marriage beyond the grave, so long as he agreed to it. Dorie figured that with his broader, post-mortal perspective, he probably had agreed to it. She vowed then and there never to have Cleve's work done, since the main benefit she could see to her own death would be getting shut of Cleve. The last thing she wanted was forever with him. Or was it? Sometimes she wasn't entirely sure.

* * * * * *

"Practically the whole ward's here," Mrs. Eckersell said proudly as she and Dorie approached the open grave and coffin of Ruetta Flatray some minutes before two o'clock. Dorie knew that the term "ward" meant the same thing as "congregation" or "parish" in regular churches. So far as she could tell, there wasn't much that was regular in the Mormon Church. Her mother used to say that was one reason she liked it, because it didn't copy everybody else but got its instructions straight from the Lord. And whatever the Lord wanted to call a thing was all right with her.

It was a bit warmer now, and less windy, but Dorie was still surprised to see how many friends her mother had, and how loyal they were to her after all these years. They came out in force, even on this raw March day. Naturally, Mrs. Eckersell wasn't surprised at all. She knew her people, and she knew their affection for Mrs. Flatray. The graveside service was announced in church Sunday, she said, and people volunteered left and right to bring food for the gathering afterward.

Dorie was surprised again to see the coffin covered with flowers. She herself had forgotten, but her mother's friends hadn't. The whole scene was a revelation to Dorie. No wonder her mother liked living here. No wonder she

Minding Mama

wanted to be buried here. No wonder she was glad to be a Mormon. She was loved. In Atlanta, who'd come to see me buried? Dorie asked herself. Her fellow beauticians, a few clients, and a neighbor or two, and that would be it. She almost felt envious. To be honored and mourned by friends is high tribute. Who could ask for more?

The ward bishop, who had come to Mrs. Eckersell's and met with Dorie on Saturday, moved to the grave and signaled that the service was about to begin. Just then, a red BMW convertible screeched to a halt beside the hearse on the narrow cemetery roadway, blocking traffic. Dorie didn't have to look. She knew who it was. Marva Grace, making her grand entry. She had elected the wealthy playgirl option. Everyone turned as a woman dressed elegantly in a white leather suit and lavender blouse with matching high heels rushed across the grass and pushed through the crowd to the front. Dorie reached out and pulled her sister next to her. Marva Grace began protesting.

"Hush," Dorie said, "the service is beginning. Can't you ever be on time for anything?"

"Well, I like that! Here I've gone to all this trouble to get here, and all I get is criticism."

"Yeah, some trouble. You don't know what trouble is. Hush now."

The bishop waited patiently, then began the service. Three women sang, *a cappella*, "*Jesus, Savior, Pilot Me*," and Dorie thought it the most beautiful song she had ever heard. Then a man played a flute solo, and four shivering little children sang "I Am a Child of God" while an older boy accompanied them on a guitar. Dorie was deeply touched, but she sensed that Marva Grace was impatient to have it over with. She wasn't what you'd call the sentimental type. Dorie hadn't thought that she herself was either, until lately. The trip with Ruetta had changed a lot of things, and that was one of them. She feared she was in danger of becoming what her mother called a "softie," and it couldn't be blamed on exhaustion because she wasn't all that tired any more. She had caught up on her sleep.

Next, a woman who looked to be in her mid-thirties stepped forward, pulling her sweater close against the wind. She was to give a personal tribute to the dead woman. The bishop had suggested her, and Dorie had gladly agreed because she herself did not want to speak. The young woman said that Sister Flatray—all these people called each other "brother" and "sister"—had been her Mutual teacher some years ago. (Dorie assumed that meant her mother had taught in the Church's youth organization.) The speaker went on to describe how Sister Flatray had taken a keen interest in the girls in her class, listening to them, counseling with them, even going canoeing and water skiing with them when most women her age would have sat on shore and watched. "More than that," the speaker continued, "she tracked me down at a party one night, a rowdy party, where drugs and drink were flowing freely."

"My parents were out of town," the woman said, "but Sister Flatray heard where I was. She came and dragged me

Minding Mama

out and took me home with her. I was furious at the time, but ever so grateful later. Two of my friends got pregnant that night, and another was killed in a car wreck after the party. Several others spent the night in jail for drunk and disorderly conduct. If Sister Flatray had known the others, she'd have hauled them out of there, too. That experience changed the course of my life. She made me see where I was headed, and she kept watch over me from then on. I didn't dare do anything wrong because I knew she'd find out about it. I'm eternally grateful to her."

The young woman then walked over and placed a white rose on the coffin. The only sound that broke the stillness was the sweet warble of a house finch that was entertaining from a tall headstone in the next row of graves. At last the bishop stepped forward, thanked the young woman and the others, then delivered a short message of comfort and assurance. Ruetta Flatray had lived a godly life, and she was secure in a blessed place. The speaker said that Sister Flatray would have wanted her daughters, both of whom were present today, to know that she loved them and was proud of them. He spoke of Christ's redemptive mission so powerfully that Dorie found herself hungering for that kind of faith. She sensed that something important was missing from her own life, something that Ruetta had and would gladly have shared with her daughters if they hadn't thrown up a barrier against it.

Well, my father didn't go along with it, and he was living with Ruetta, Dorie told herself. If he didn't accept it, he must have seen something wrong with it. Or, she added silently, maybe he was stubborn like his daughters, or perhaps he was unwilling to commit his time and energy to something as demanding as religion the way the Mormons practiced it. Who'd want to get up in the middle of the night and drag a teenager kicking and screaming from a drunken orgy? And I'll just bet, Dorie added, that this was only one instance of many where Mama sacrificed her own convenience and comfort for the sake of someone else. Why, she saved that girl's life. It's as simple as that. Refused to let her throw it away. Dorie learned more about her mother, the person she was in addition to being a mother, in that hour in the cemetery than she had learned in eighteen years at her parents' home and another eight in her own home with her mother in the next bedroom. The difference, Dorie knew now, is that this time she was listening.

* * * * * *

Dorie thanked the bishop—Wardle, his name was Bishop Wardle—and the others who participated. He had announced that everyone was invited over to the meetinghouse for a lunch which the Relief Society sisters had prepared, but Dorie wasn't sure she wanted to go. Marva Grace said wild horses couldn't drag her there, so Dorie decided she'd better represent the family. She didn't want to seem ungrateful.

"All right, Marva Grace," Dorie said to the departing figure, "you go pay the mortician and I'll go to the church."

Minding Mama

Dorie wondered where she got the courage to say it outright, the part about Marva Grace paying the mortician.

Marva spun in her tracks. "*Me* pay the mortician! I'll do no such thing! Whatever gave you that idea? I'm not made of money, you know."

Dorie's ire was up. "You did! You're the one gave me that idea, drivin' up here on a solemn occasion like you were the Queen of the May! You an' your fancy cars and fancy clothes. Mama would've been ashamed to see it."

Marva Grace only sneered. "Thou shalt not covet. Isn't that one of the commandments? You're just jealous because I *could* pay the mortician and you can't. If you're so smart, Dorie June, you figure it out. I'm going for a swim in the motel's covered pool, and then I'm going home. Nobody forced you to marry a pauper." With that, she turned and resumed her march toward the waiting BMW. Ruetta always said Marva Grace was a girl who could stop traffic, and Marva had proved her mother right today. Everybody was pretty much stuck until she moved her vehicle. Dorie figured her sister had planned it that way, to call attention to the sports car and thereby make an unspoken but unmistakable announcement that although she and Dorie came off the same vine, they were different fruits entirely.

Dorie's first impulse was to stomp across the grass after Marva Grace and make her shoulder some of the responsibility. Then she thought better of it. How could she make Marva Grace do anything when she had never won an argument with her sister in her entire life, or with anybody else for that matter? And besides, there was something sacred about ground that held the dead. She could feel it. A cemetery was not a place where sisters should argue about money, even if one of the sisters was rich and selfish and the other was on the brink of poverty.

Thinking it over, Dorie concluded that she and her mother should have planned better. She herself should not have waltzed merrily along as though Ruetta would last indefinitely. And she should never for a moment have expected a miraculous transformation of character in her sister, or even hoped that over time her sister had become constitutionally capable of feeling guilt. Marva Grace was the kind of person who never doubted that she was in the right, though it meant the rest of the world was in the wrong. She had always been like that. Nothing was ever her fault. Dorie was just the opposite. She grew up thinking that most things were her fault, and Cleve had been only too happy to continue the tradition.

Chances are the mortician wouldn't expect his money until tomorrow, this being the day of the burial and all. But tomorrow will come and I'll have to face the music, Dorie worried silently. She felt very alone, maybe more alone than she had ever felt in her life. Mrs. Eckersell and the others had gone over to the meetinghouse to get the lunch spread out—funeral potatoes, she said, along with baked ham, cooked carrots, and lime jello with pineapple and shredded cabbage in it—leaving Dorie to contemplate her mother's coffin and the symbolic significance of funeral

Minding Mama

potatoes and green jello. The coffin was large indeed, big enough for two Ruettas. Dorie wondered if people ever doubled up in coffins, the way children did in beds when their cousins came to visit. It occurred to her that a bigger coffin probably meant a larger hole. Maybe that's why the grave diggers made the hole on the wrong side, to protest the extra work.

Dorie hugged her jacket against a sudden wind gust and gazed intently at the coffin, marveling that her wiry little mother could be so still and so disinterested in her confinement. Ruetta always liked wide open spaces and had never been one to take anything lying down. "Goodbye, Mama," Dorie said, sniffling a little. "I got you home all right, like I promised. You tell Papa I got you home." Then she took a step closer and patted the coffin gently. "You take care now, and . . . and save a place for me up there in heaven, if you can." She paused. "If you can't, it's okay. I'll understand. I haven't been as good as you. But maybe you could put in a word for me and tell 'em I'll try to do better so's I can see you again. There's lots I need to tell you. Stuff I never said that I should've." Dorie shivered and picked up a white lily that had fallen off the coffin. "If it's okay with you, I'm keepin' this here lily to remind me that I love you, and . . . to remind me that you love me." She stopped. "You do love me, don't you? . . . and you forgive me?"

Dorie found a used tissue in her jacket pocket and blew her nose loudly. She would have to walk to the church. Marva Grace hadn't offered, and everyone else had disappeared.

189

Marilyn Arnold

Being stranded without a vehicle reminded Dorie that she had yet another matter to attend to, her pickup. Her transportation back to Atlanta. Helplessly, Dorie turned toward the cemetery road. There, a short distance away, she saw an ugly white school bus painted to look like a whale. Letting out a surprised little cry, she ran toward the bus and into Ishmael's outstretched arms. He held her while she sobbed her sorrow and her fear and her need. Her friends had come. Only now did she fully realize that they were her friends. She was more than a charity case to them. They cared about her and had come to give comfort. They came as family.

"The money," she said at last. "I can't pay it back yet, but I will. I promise. Thank you, thank you, my friends, my dear friends."

"It's not a loan," Jonah said quietly, "it's a gift. One doesn't repay a gift. One passes the gift on to another as one is able."

"Come inside," Rachel offered, "it's chilly out here. You're freezing."

"Maybe for a minute," Dorie agreed. "I have to go to the church."

Rachel nodded. "We'll take you, but first we want to report."

"Yes, yes," Dorie said, stepping into the bus. "Lily Dawn and Moses. Are they all right? I need to see to them, don't I?"

Ishmael responded. "There's little Moses, right where you left him, in his favorite laundry basket. We'll discuss

Minding Mama

Moses and Lily Dawn in a minute, but first, where are you staying? Can we take you back to Flagstaff?"

Gathering Moses into her arms, Dorie found comfort in his sweet, warm softness. As she rocked him, she explained that she had temporary quarters with her mother's next-door neighbor, and that she had many things to see to before she could even think about fixing her truck and returning to Atlanta. Jonah made a note of Mrs. Eckersell's name and address and promised to check on Dorie in a couple of days.

"In the meantime," Jonah chuckled, "we have an appointment at the Great White Throne, or thereabouts, to see about our friends, the Pococks. Call it curiosity."

"You're going to find those nutty Pococks?!" Dorie couldn't believe her ears. "I thought you were glad to be shut of them."

"Maybe so," Jonah replied, "but by this time they are powerfully disappointed and disillusioned. The world didn't end, and now they have to face life, life that has probably lost all purpose for them."

"Yes," Rachel added. "They're more needful now than ever before. Their faith has betrayed them. We thought it was the least we could do."

Dorie was astonished, but her spirits were lifted, momentarily, just by talking with this trio of kindly wanderers. They calmed her by their unassuming generosity and by their very presence, as did the baby Moses. Their news about Lily Dawn, however, was disturbing. The search for her grandmother ended when they learned from a neighbor that the woman bearing the name of the girl's grandmother had been moved to a nursing home not two months ago, after a stroke had left her partially paralyzed and unable to speak. Their only recourse, Rachel explained, had been to take the girl to Social Services, where someone would try to locate her parents.

Lily Dawn was not happy. She swore that she would not go back home, nor would she tell anyone her full name or who her parents were or where she came from. "We weren't much help at all," Ishmael confessed. "We told them only that we had picked the girl up on the highway, and that all she would give us was her first name and her grandmother's name in 'the town by the dam.'" He explained further that the twice-widowed grandmother went by her second husband's last name, so there was no link to Lily's father. Until her parents could be found, Lily Dawn would go to a youth facility in Turner.

Dorie's heart sank, and she vowed to do something, though she hadn't the vaguest idea what it might be. Rachel and the others were obviously troubled as well. They agreed that nothing could be done at the moment, and maybe never at all. Some things are out of the hands of even the best-intentioned people, they said, adding that sometimes they turn out for the better without interference. Dorie had responsibilities here and elsewhere that would take all her energy and resources. Maybe she would just have to let Lily Dawn go, trust the girl to a kind Providence. Dorie realized then that she could never do

Minding Mama

that, never leave the girl to fate—not willingly anyway.

As for Moses, Rachel said that she wanted to keep him, somehow, if that was all right with Dorie. Dorie was relieved to hear it. A minimum of two felonies, for transporting her mother and Lily Dawn across the country, plus a broken down house and a five thousand dollar bill with the mortuary were about all she could deal with right now. Besides, how could she ever explain Moses to anybody? Who would believe her? Then there was her escapade with the bank robbers, including the temporary theft of their car. How many actual crimes had she committed, anyhow? Perry Mason reruns had not brought her up to speed on the finer points of the law.

On top of all that was Marva Grace's impossible attitude, which Dorie chose not to mention, remembering that Ruetta had always said to hang your family's dirty laundry on an inside line. Nor did Dorie allude to the mortuary bill, for fear her rescuers would up and sell the bus to pay it. It would be just like them. Some people were so generous and principled you had to watch out so as not to send them to the poor house. What's more, there was the abandoned pickup down in Flagstaff which had probably been impounded by now. Well, if the police had it, at least it was safe from vandals and car thieves.

* * * * * *

Marilyn Arnold

Dorie felt just a little empty, some twenty minutes later, as she watched the Great White Bus drive away from the church. Inside, she sat at a long table covered with blank newsprint, half the time staring at the food on her paper plate and the other half trying to act interested in what the woman next to her was saying about the worsening drought and the grasshoppers that came with it. Dorie was in what Mrs. Eckersell called the cultural hall of the church, but to Dorie it looked for all the world like a basketball court with a small stage attached on one side as an afterthought.

Out of the blue, something occurred to her. Ruetta had a safe-deposit box in Jericho, and in the rush of things Dorie hadn't thought to bring the key from Atlanta. She remembered going to the bank with her mother after Demont Ralph's funeral, before they left for parts east. There she signed a card that made her a joint "owner" of the box, so she could get into it should the need arise. Ruetta had faithfully made the rental payments for eight years, over Dorie's objections, out of the minuscule amount she received from Social Security. You're never going back there, she told her mother. Just close that box and bring your papers out here. What's in there anyhow, besides the deed to your house and your will leaving the house to me after you die—not that I want it or would ever live in it?

But Ruetta had insisted. She's given up everything else, Cleve had argued. Let the old lady hang onto the silly box. There ain't many people you can keep happy for forty-five bucks a year. Dorie had to agree, and so Ruetta kept her

194

Minding Mama

box and her key. Now where did we put that key? Dorie asked herself, squeezing her eyes shut to assist memory. Then it came to her. The key was taped to the underside of the top drawer of the little bureau in Ruetta's room. Cleve could find it and mail it to her express, overnight. If he would, that is, and if he found enough money to pay the postage, and if she promised to pay him back. Not that it wasn't all her money anyhow. She'd call him the minute she got back to Mrs. Eckersell's. Collect. At least she'd try collect. It would be just like him to refuse to accept the charges, even though she was the one who paid the bills. The only time he was tight with her money was when she herself wanted to spend some of it for something besides food and video rentals.

Mrs. Eckersell hovered about while Dorie attempted to eat. She didn't seem to have much appetite these days. When Mrs. Eckersell was not hovering, she was bringing ward members one by one to meet Dorie, though Dorie remembered none of them three seconds later. Her mind was elsewhere, a dozen elsewheres. It was a relief when Mrs. Eckersell was finally ready to go home and take Dorie with her. Dorie wanted to look in the classified ads to see if a 1989 Toyota pickup might sell for enough to embalm and bury somebody.

Then again, did mortuaries ever accept goods in kind, like used pickups, for payment? she wondered, but supposed they didn't. Not in this day and age. Maybe she could get a new VISA card from one of those outfits that send applications to anyone, living or dead, with an address, even if it's the wrong one. Their goal is to bury the whole populace in debt with their particular company instead of with somebody else. No matter. A new card would give her a new line of credit, wouldn't it? But then, what if mortuaries didn't accept credit cards anyway?

Home at last, Dorie sighed under her breath as Mrs. Eckersell rolled into the driveway alongside her house and stopped. Well, home in a manner of speaking. Dorie kicked off her sandals and asked Mrs. Eckersell if she could make a collect call on her telephone. Mrs. Eckersell clucked her tongue and shook her head. "Land, child," she said, "make your call, but don't bother none about the collect part. Ruetta Flatray was my best friend. It's the least I can do. Besides, you know what they say. You can't take it with you."

"I have a little money," Dorie said. "I'll pay you. But thanks."

"I never woulda paid Ruetta Flatray for such a thing. She wouldn't of allowed it. You go fight it out with her ghost." Mrs. Eckersell pointed to a little table in the kitchen, next to the living room door. "There's the phone, and don't let me hear another peep out of you about money. Land, what's this world comin' to?"

Dorie sank wearily onto the small wooden chair by the telephone table. Burial days are hard, just plain hard. She hoped the next burial service she attended would be her own. Lifting the old black receiver from its cradle, she dialed her house in Atlanta. There was no answer. She'd try

Minding Mama

again later, she told Mrs. Eckersell. Taking herself into the spare bedroom, her quarters for the moment, Dorie dropped her sandals to the floor and stretched out on the quilted spread that covered the old four-poster brass bed. The next thing she knew, Mrs. Eckersell was peeking in the door, her head silhouetted in the light behind her. Evening was coming on. Dorie had slept several hours.

"I say, dear, are you awake? I've stirred up a little barley soup. It'll stick to your ribs."

Dorie yawned and rotated to her back. "Ooo, how long have I slept? Too long. It's getting dark."

"You needed the rest. Your mother used to say an hour in the daytime was worth two at night."

Dorie sat up suddenly. "I've got to call Cleve—that's my husband—tonight, so's he can go to the post office first thing in the morning." She rushed to the phone and dialed her own number again, letting it ring several times. Still no answer. "Now where can those two be?" she asked no one in particular. "It's two hours later in Atlanta."

"Well, you come and eat a bite and then you can try again."

"No, I've got to track them down, Cleve and my son Clarence Ross. They're a bad influence on each other. Act like two boys sometimes, only I can't spank them."

Mrs. Eckersell chuckled. "Boys will be boys," she said indulgently.

But men shouldn't be boys, Dorie countered silently. Men should know better.

Marilyn Arnold

At last Dorie decided to try her next door neighbor in Atlanta. Maybe Marybell could watch for Cleve and Clarence Ross and have one of them call the minute they got home. This was not something that could wait. She remembered that when a man on her street in Atlanta died, his wife left him lying there on the floor while she dashed to the bank, cleared out their account, and emptied the safe-deposit box. Only then did she call the undertaker. The woman had heard that boxes were sometimes sealed when people died and stayed sealed until after probate. Dorie didn't know if the woman had it right or not, but she wasn't the gambling kind. Maybe the bank hadn't heard yet that Ruetta had passed on. It wasn't in the newspaper, and banks were closed most of the weekend. But she had to get that key fast. That she knew for certain. She couldn't sell her mother's house without the title.

Luckily, Dorie knew the neighbor's phone number. She's the one Dorie often called from work to see if Cleve had turned off the hose, or locked the door, or fed the dog, or brought in the garbage can. Which he usually hadn't. She answered after two rings.

"Hey, Marybell, is that you?" Dorie tried to sound as natural as possible.

Marybell said it was indeed her, and why on earth was Dorie calling, and this late, too. Wasn't she in Utah by now, and did she make it okay, you know, before Mrs. Flatray spoiled?

Minding Mama

Dorie wasn't about to go into any details. Marybell was such a gossip. "We made it fine," she lied, "and Mama is cozy in the ground. What I'm calling for is this. I've been tryin' t' call Cleve and nobody answers. I need to talk to him real bad. Something that can't wait. Could you go over and leave a note for him to call me at this number the minute he gets home? It's real urgent."

There was a long pause. "Why, honey," Marybell said, "didn't you know?"

"Didn't I know what?"

"Why, Cleve and the boy, Clarence Ross. They sold the house Saturday and left. I ain't seen 'em since. Didn't you know? I thought sure you knew. I figgered they were comin' to where you were. That you all decided to live out there in Utah." (She pronounced it Yooo-taw.)

Dorie felt faint. "No . . . no, I didn't know," she said and dropped the receiver in its cradle. All she knew was that she would be unable to walk to the bedroom door, it was so many miles away.

Eleven

"Is something wrong, Dorie?" Mrs. Eckersell asked. "You're looking pale-ish. You better go lay yourself down for a spell."

Dorie Grimes looked at Mrs. Eckersell as though she had never seen her mother's neighbor before in her life. Then she rose slowly and moved toward Mrs. Eckersell's spare bedroom, feeling her way along the wall as a blind person might do in an unfamiliar place. When she arrived at the bedroom, Dorie turned and nodded blankly at Mrs. Eckersell, then went inside and closed the door before collapsing on the borrowed bed. It was too much. She couldn't take it in. Maybe if she went to sleep she'd wake up and find it was only one installment of a crazy nightmare. Cleve wouldn't do this to her. Not after all these years. Not even though the house was solely in his name. Not even though it had belonged to his parents and he had inherited it when they died together a dozen years ago, of a gas leak in that very house. Dorie got the leak fixed before she and Cleve moved in. She said she wouldn't live in a gassy house even if her in-laws would.

Cleve was an only child, and it never occurred to Dorie that she ought to get her name put on the deed with his. She had always assumed that if anybody left, she would be the one to do it, not Cleve. Inertia was his middle name. Besides, he was the nearest thing to helpless without her, or so she thought. At least he created that impression by letting her do everything. Dorie couldn't help wondering if her son Clarence Ross had put Cleve up to selling the house and running off because Cleve had never shown that much creativity in his life. Somehow or other, in spite of her influence and training, Clarence Ross had grown up no more principled than his father. Maybe even less.

Dorie blamed it on the Grimes genes because it certainly didn't come from the Flatray side where principle was a fact of life. Then she remembered Marva Grace, who was nothing like her parents or her grandparents or her younger sister Dorie, who at times appeared to be ninety percent conscience and ten percent brains. A lop-sided split if there ever was one. Dorie allowed as how if she had been even sixty percent conscience and forty percent brains, she would not be in this predicament today.

Too stunned to cry, Dorie lay for more than an hour staring at the pattern Mrs. Eckersell's yard light made when its rays pierced the window and tracked through the room. The light got all its character from the window, which was cracked in a triangular pattern, creating a prism that cast a pale rainbow across the ivory colored ceiling. Her mother would not have believed this of Cleve, Dorie told herself. All in all, if Ruetta didn't out and out enjoy Cleve, at least she got used to him. But then, Ruetta could afford to be charitable. She wasn't married to the man, nor was she singlehandedly supporting him and his think-alike son.

Dorie figured that the two of them, Cleve and Clarence Ross, would go through the house money pretty fast and wished she could get her hands on just five thousand dollars of it before they blew it on who knows what. Cleve owed her that much, didn't he, for all the years she had curled hair so he could eat and watch television, and then had waited on him hand and foot when she got home from the beauty shop? Then she remembered. The key to Ruetta's safe-deposit box! It was probably still attached to that drawer, wherever the drawer was at the moment. She hadn't thought to ask Marybell if Cleve and Clarence Ross had taken the furniture, or sold the place as is, furnished and stocked. And what about her clothes and things? And her mother's? Not that either of them had a whole lot that was worth much.

Dorie supposed that she could put the police on Cleve's trail, for desertion, but then wondered what she'd do if they found him, except maybe sue him for some of the house money. She certainly didn't want to live with a man who would run out on her and leave her homeless and penniless the minute her back was turned, and with the phone still

Minding Mama

hooked up and the credit card debt to pay off. In what he characterized as a generous gesture, Cleve had let her have the card in her name, which in fact, she realized now, absolved him of any responsibility for it. Very likely, the box key was gone in any case. She'd have to plead negligence with the bank and hope they'd open the safe deposit box for her if she took her mother's death certificate and showed them her own signature on the form they kept in a little drawer.

No wonder Cleve didn't seriously object to her driving her mother home, Dorie thought. He scoffed at the idea, sure, but it was all an act. He knew she'd do it anyway. He was counting on it. Oh, yes, he knew how stubborn she was. Maybe he even had a buyer lined up ahead of time for when Ruetta Flatray died. Otherwise, how could he sell the house so fast? When she thought about it, hot tears burned down her cheeks. But they were not tears of grief any more. She was flat out angry. Jumping to her feet, Dorie paced from door to window, then finally marched into the kitchen where Mrs. Eckersell was asleep in her rocker, knitting needles poised across a sweater in the making. The old woman jumped, sending her knitting to the floor.

"I'm sorry to disturb you, Mrs. Eckersell," Dorie said, "but I need to get into Mama's house tonight. I haven't seen the inside yet, and it can't wait. Have you got a flashlight or a lantern or something? And I'll need the key again."

Mrs. Eckersell thought a minute. "There's a flashlight somewheres, but the batteries are prob'ly gone by now."

Then she brightened. "I've got me some big candles. How about a candle?" She hoisted herself slowly out of the rocker, shaking her head. "Why not wait till morning? It's cold and dirty over there besides bein' dark. Who knows what's crawlin' around?"

"Well, it can't be any worse than the vermin I've been livin' with for more years than I care to say."

* * * * * * *

With a squatty candle secured by wax melted in one of Mrs. Eckersell's pink cereal bowls, Dorie pushed through the creaky back door of her mother's house into what Ruetta called the laundry room. To Dorie it was always just the back porch. In the summer, her father used to take down the removable storm windows and replace them with screens, making a comfortable sleeping porch. Dorie set the candle on the old Bendix washer, extracted a crushed book of matches from her pocket, and lit the candle. The lines on which Ruetta hung clothes on stormy days sprang out of the darkness, punctuated by a few weathered clothes pins.

Most of the time, however, Ruetta carted newly washed clothes out to the yard lines and hung them there, to freshen them, she said. Indoor clothes dryers never interested her. She found comfort in the coarseness of cotton sheets dried by the wind instead of tumbled limp. In some ways, that little characteristic defined the woman, the woman her daughters hadn't taken the trouble to know. As Dorie made

Minding Mama

her way from room to musty room in the small house, tracing her mother's footsteps, she couldn't have told anyone what she was looking for, or why she felt an urgent desire to enter the old house tonight. Maybe she needed assurance that she wasn't lost after all, that here, at least, was a place she could call hers, that although she may have been abandoned, she wasn't homeless. Then too, maybe betrayal in the present made the past all the more precious. Maybe the past was all she had left, and she could find a fragment of it here if she searched hard enough. Maybe something from the past, something with permanence, would rescue her and make her feel whole again. Something that spoke of love and commitment and trust. Something to fill the void that had opened in her life like a huge maelstrom and was sucking her into its inky depths.

The furniture was still here, such as it was, most of it covered with old sheets and canvas. Dorie shuddered involuntarily at the grit scratching under her feet when she crossed the once bright linoleum floors. She was almost glad that in the dim light she couldn't see plainly the spider webs and the dead crickets and the mouse droppings, but she voiced a warning to all rodents and creeping or hopping things. The day of reckoning is at hand, she announced. Then she chuckled, in spite of herself, and observed that she was beginning to sound like the pious Pococks of the Doom's Day persuasion.

Before the transfer from Jericho to Atlanta eight years ago, Dorie and her mother had sifted through bureaus and closets in order to pack Ruetta's personal things, leaving intact the kitchen drawers and cabinets, plus the cellar and garage. Ruetta said she'd need that stuff when she returned to Jericho, so there was no point in throwing it out or moving it twice. What there was no point in, Dorie reflected, was arguing with Ruetta when her mind was made up.

In any event, Dorie wasn't about to venture into cellar or garage tonight, much less into shed or chicken coop. She was already pushing her dirt tolerance capacity to the breaking point. The garage, a frame affair at the end of the drive behind the house, was a little spooky any time, and a lot spookier after dark. The cellar beneath the house had a low ceiling and a dirt floor. Those places could wait for daylight and the return of courage. The shed and chicken coop could wait for the Millennium. Not that Dorie believed in the Millennium, understand.

Dorie remembered that her mother had used one drawer in the kitchen, the top drawer left of the sink, for miscellaneous papers, pencils, rubber bands, and notepads. There Ruetta could always find essentials like year-old grocery lists, expired prescriptions, yellowed newspaper clippings of obituaries and household hints, and decades-old letters from relatives and friends. Dorie and her mother had forgotten about that drawer in the flurry of packing Ruetta's things and closing up the house. In retrospect, Dorie wondered why the rush.

Oddly enough, that drawer had come to mind as she lay staring at Mrs. Eckersell's ceiling after she got the news about Cleve's departure. Her thought was that maybe, just maybe, the drawer harbored a spare safe-deposit box key. The more Dorie thought about it now, however, the less likely it seemed. She was more likely to find a recipe for corned beef and cabbage, or instructions for removing old floor wax. Well, since she was here, she might as well give that drawer a look-see. Removing the drawer, which clearly preferred to stay put, Dorie dumped its contents on the stained formica countertop.

Dust and crisp insect bodies and wings flew up, and Dorie involuntarily inhaled eight years of accumulated decay. Whatever the drawer used to contain, it now disgorged an assortment of advertisements, string, Scotch tape, long expired coupons for carpet cleaning and pizza, and scraps of paper with miscellaneous scribblings on them—pick up Bessie at 7, get cabbage for Friday, use Vaseline to remove grease, save hangers for the D.I. Dorie saw nothing very exciting. Then she remembered that things sometimes slipped off the back ends of drawers into the space behind and below them. Candle in hand, she bent down and peered into the gap left by the drawer she had removed. Nothing visible back there.

Risking her temperamental back, she dislodged the bottom drawer and set it on the floor, then warily dropped to a crouch, candle in hand, and scanned the dank cavern. There, near the back, she made out what looked to be a manila envelope, lying in dirt and old sawdust. By removing the other two drawers and stretching as far as she could,

Marilyn Arnold

Dorie was able to grab a corner of the envelope and slide it forward. She couldn't read the writing on it, but thought it more promising than the papers she had scattered across the countertop. Shaking off the worst of the dust, Dorie labored to her feet, tucked the envelope under her arm, and made for Mrs. Eckersell's clean home and electric lighting.

* * * * * * *

Mrs. Eckersell was in bed when Dorie returned, for which she was grateful. She was too weary to make explanations tonight. Dorie hadn't known what to expect when she opened the envelope, but she certainly hadn't expected to find what she did. A smaller envelope was folded around something with a little heft to it and tucked inside the larger envelope. On the front of the smaller envelope, in old-fashioned script, was the name of Dorie's maternal grandfather, Charles Ansell, who may have been the first owner of this house. As Dorie remembered it, her grandparents had moved to Jericho and bought the house when Charles worked on a government survey crew. Several years later, when they left for another assignment in Arizona, Dorie's parents bought the home from them and made it their permanent residence. Ruetta's brother and sister had died some years ago.

The envelope raised questions for Dorie. Had Charles forgotten to take it when he and his wife Minerva moved to Arizona, or had he given it to his daughter at some later

Minding Mama

date and then she had forgotten it? Or, did the envelope disappear behind the drawers, and no one thought to look below the drawers for it? The smaller envelope was sealed, and Dorie wasn't entirely comfortable opening it. But finally, curiosity triumphed over courtesy, and Ruetta wasn't present to recite the rules of privacy and decorum.

Carefully, Dorie loosened the seal and found inside a piece of white flannel wrapped around a few tarnished coins. One appeared to be a silver dollar, though Dorie couldn't make out the date. The others—three of them—were copper, and looked like thin pennies. Only one appeared to have Lincoln on the front, however. Dorie thought she'd ask Mrs. Eckersell for some silver polish in the morning. She could clean the coins and take them to the bank with her. If they turned out to be old, maybe they were worth something extra. When you're destitute, every little bit helps.

Dorie tossed and turned most of the night, agonizing over what Cleve, her husband of thirty-seven years, had done to her. How could he just up and walk away? If Ruetta were alive she'd probably offer the opinion that Dorie was upset mainly because he beat her to the punch. She wanted the satisfaction of leaving him rather than the other way around. Dorie had to admit that her mother would have been partly right, but only partly. Cleve was such a habit that Dorie most likely would have kept on with him. Loyalty was her weakness, what her father would have called her Achilles heel. Dorie once knew who Achilles was, but she had forgotten. Some Greek, she thought. Or was he Roman? Oh, what did it matter anyhow? The point was, he had a weak spot, and it brought him down.

As she wrestled with her thoughts, Dorie remembered Lily Dawn and wondered how the girl was doing. She, too, must feel abandoned. They had that in common. It was possible that the girl was already on her way back to wherever she came from, Florida or somewhere. If she were sent back, life would be even harder for her than it was before she left. And surely, she would leave again. There was Loyal Bunce, too, homeless for how many years? And how about baby Moses, and Bertram and Brighty Lu Pocock? Homeless all. And Madame Taji Mahi, and the travelers in the Great White Bus. Dorie realized that she had joined them, become one of them—the disconnected, the homeless, the castaways, and the runaways of the world. It was an odd feeling, to go from temporary companionship with such as they, superior in the knowledge that home awaited, to full fellowship in the world of the lost.

* * * * * * *

Mrs. Eckersell was interested in the coins Dorie had found, and rooted around among the bottles and cans under her kitchen sink until she came up with a white jar that said silver polish on its torn, water-stained wrapper.

"Here, Dorie, rub the coins with this. At least it'll clean the silver dollar up so's we can read the date." Mrs.

Minding Mama

Eckersell handed Dorie a piece of damp cloth. "Seth Johnson down the street here in Jericho collects old coins. I bet he can give you the lowdown on these, if you want. He's got lots of catalogues."

Dorie began rubbing, patiently working at the blackened dollar until she could make out some of the details on it. The date appeared to be 1895, and that was encouraging. Dorie figured that in the coin business, the older the better.

"See here, Dorie, 'pears this penny's got a Indian's head on it." Mrs. Eckersell had joined the enterprise with her own damp cloth.

"That's good. I think they're pretty rare. It oughta be worth a few dollars, anyhow." She paused and looked up. "Lunch money for a day or two."

"Look, 'pears this one's just like it. I'll work on it a minute."

"Can you see the dates? I think coin collectors are especially interested in the dates."

"Lemme see now." Mrs. Eckersell held two of the smaller coins up to catch the light better. "These is both Indian heads, I'd swear, and looks to me like the date on 'em is the same, 1877."

"Wow, that's even older than the dollar!"

Mrs. Eckersell chuckled. "It's even older'n me, child. 'Course Mrs. Flatray was older'n me, too. Leastways I think so. She wasn't one t' say, nor was she one to ask it of others."

"What about the other penny? Can you make it out?"

"Well, it's newer 'cause it's got Mr. Abe Lincoln on it. I can see him there, so dignified and all. Honest Abe. Lemme give him another rub." A couple of minutes later Mrs. Eckersell was ready to report. Looks like 1909 to me, and I can make out what looks like maybe an 'S,' too, and maybe a 'H.' Whoops. Nope, maybe that's a 'N,' and maybe not. It's got a 'D' by it, I think."

"You say you know somebody who knows coins?"

"Yep. Let's go see him. This's the most excitement I've had since the roof fell in on the Shumways' barn and killed two thoroughbred horses."

Dorie was hesitant. "I hate to bother anybody. Maybe we should call him first."

"No need of that. Dollars to doughnuts he's out on his front porch readin' the paper. He does that ever' morning the weather lets him, and sometimes even if it don't."

* * * * * * *

Seth Johnson, whom Mrs. Eckersell described to Dorie as an old bachelor, was not nearly so old as Mrs. Eckersell herself. Late fifties or early sixties, Dorie judged. He worked as a night watchman down at the electric substation, and he always made breakfast and read the paper before going to bed. Mrs. Eckersell also described him as a "little titched in the head, but harmless. Every town has one such, and he's ours," she explained.

"Good morning, ladies," Seth Johnson called as the two

Minding Mama

women pushed through his squeaky iron gate. "To what do I owe this most auspicious visit?"

"See what I mean?" Mrs. Eckersell whispered to Dorie. "He even talks funny." To Seth Johnson she said, approaching his porch stairs, "Mornin', Seth, this here's Mrs. Dorie Grimes, of Atlanta, Georgia. She's the youngest daughter of Mrs. Ruetta Flatray, who use to be my next door neighbor and sometimes brought you fresh bread when she baked." She paused. "'Cause you was a bachelor and all."

Seth Johnson sat behind *USA Today* in a blue-striped shirt and blue jeans held up by black suspenders. His peppered gray beard was neatly trimmed and his rather substantial nose easily supported a pair of wire-rimmed glasses. His bald head was ringed by a thick fringe of graying brownish hair that met his beard above both ears. He eyed his visitors over the top of his spectacles and invited them to sit in the two remaining wicker chairs. Seth may have been a bachelor, but he was prepared for a certain amount of socializing.

"She's come to bury her mother, which she did yesterday, may she rest in peace," Mrs. Eckersell said.

Seth looked at Dorie. "I hadn't heard," he said, "please accept my condolences." He tilted back in his chair until it leaned against his house, which was frame and badly in need of paint, Dorie noticed. "Ah, yes, so Mrs. Flatray has gone to that bourn from which no traveler returns."

Mrs. Eckersell was obviously not a woman with an ear for poetic language. "She's gone to heaven, if that's

213

whatcha mean," she said, "an' Mrs. Grimes here needs your help."

"Why anything for so lovely a lady. Your wish is my command."

Dorie knew full well she was no lovely lady, but she enjoyed hearing it said just the same. "I, uh . . . I understand you know something about old coins."

"Why yes, one might say so. It's a little hobby of mine. Everyone needs a hobby, don't you agree?"

Dorie honestly believed at the moment that she needed a hobby like she needed a hole in the head, but she wasn't about to disappoint Seth Johnson with that information. "Oh, yes. Hobbies can be very, uh . . . broadening. I've been meaning to take one up myself, when time allows."

Seth Johnson folded his newspaper. "But my dear, time flies on wings of lightning. It never *allows*. What we postpone often never gets done. Don't put off 'til tomorrow what you can do today."

Mrs. Eckersell broke in. "Mrs. Grimes here has some coins she'd like you to look at. They belonged to her mother. She wants to know if they're worth anything. I told her you had catalogues and things."

"Ah, yes, I do indeed have 'catalogues and things.'" He reached into his shirt pocket, extracted a small magnifying glass, and addressed Dorie. "You have the coins with you, I presume?"

"Yes, yes . . . here they are." Dorie removed the coins from the envelope that held them and unwrapped the flannel.

Minding Mama

"It looks like there's a dollar and three pennies."

"Ummm, yes, indeed, a dollar and three pennies, tarnished but unblemished." Seth paused. "Like me," he chortled, clearly delighted with his joke.

Dorie only smiled a thin smile. Indulge the man, she told herself. Don't rush him. "Can you tell me anything about them?" she asked, forcing a friendly, appreciative tone.

Turning the Indian head pennies over and over in his hand and looking at them from every angle through his magnifying glass, Seth finally said something. "Yes, I see. Indian head, 1877. On a good day, these might bring three or four hundred dollars apiece. Not much, but something. I have a few myself."

It sounded like a lot to Dorie. "How about the Lincoln penny?" she asked.

"The Lincoln penny, yes, how much might it garner? Yes, 1909 . . . SVD . . . San Francisco," Seth mumbled, then looked at Dorie. "Maybe five hundred dollars. I'd have to consult my catalogue. This is the first year for the Lincoln penny, you know."

"No, I didn't know that," Dorie said, "but I figured my grandfather must have saved it for a reason."

"Wise man, your grandfather. I'd like to have known him. We could have spent many a happy hour over my coin collection."

"Enough of this shilly-shallying," Mrs. Eckersell cried. "Get to the big one, the dollar. What's it worth?"

"Patience, my dear, patience. It's a virtue practiced by

too few, I fear." Seth Johnson sighed and raised his magnifying glass again. "Well, let us take the dollar in hand and see what we have."

"I think it says 1895," Dorie offered, "but the dollar looks rather plain to me."

"Well, I'll be . . . no, it can't be. There were only a thousand made . . . Philadelphia." After several minutes, Seth turned to Dorie. "Plain it is, this coin, yes, plain it is. There is no mint work on it. Every coin collector dreams of finding one."

Mrs. Eckersell jumped up. "What's it worth, Seth? How much can she get for it?"

Seth stroked the coin lovingly. "Yes, my little beauty, you'll bring a nice bit of cash."

"How much, how much?" Mrs. Eckersell was beside herself.

"Oh, no more than twenty or thirty thousand dollars, I'd imagine," Seth answered with studied calm.

Dorie nearly fell off her chair. "Twenty thousand dollars!" she cried. "Now I can pay the undertaker!"

What Dorie didn't know, of course, was how a person went about selling rare coins. Again, Seth Johnson was the man. He said he could go on the internet and sell the coins within a matter of hours, especially the silver dollar. People are begging for this coin, he said, adding that somebody over in Las Vegas was asking for one just the other day. Offered twenty grand for it. Seth was certain he could get twenty-five or more. Mrs. Eckersell told him not to take a

Minding Mama

penny under thirty. Dorie just stood there in a daze while Seth Johnson and Mrs. Eckersell bartered over a coin that didn't even belong to them. At last, Dorie broke in.

"Just get what you can, Mr. Johnson. I've never been a greedy person, but I do have some expenses just now." Dorie swallowed hard. "And I'm in a bit of trouble . . . home-wise."

Mrs. Eckersell glanced at Dorie, obviously not comprehending what Dorie meant, but certain that whatever it was, hard cash could fix it. "You just get in there and roust out that Las Vegas man, Seth. Tell him you've got the coin for him, but you want the cash pronto, else you'll sell that dollar to somebody else." She paused, but no one moved. "Well, don't just set there," she said, arising. "Get in that house and turn on that machine. We'll wait." She shooed him inside and made herself comfortable in the chair he had vacated. "Your troubles 're over, Dorie Grimes." she said smugly. "Aren't you glad I'm a woman with connections?"

Dorie didn't dare hope that the money would really materialize. Hard experience had taught her not to entertain great expectations because they seldom panned out. Even small expectations, such as that a person's husband and son would not sell her out if she left town for a few days, had a way of disappointing you. Dorie couldn't help wondering what would have happened if Ruetta had never come to live with her and Cleve in Atlanta. Would she have arrived home from the beauty shop one day and found her belongings in the street and strangers in her kitchen preparing supper?

Marilyn Arnold

Now that Dorie was out of shock and into despair, she wanted to call Marybell and get more information. Did Cleve leave a note, for example, or did he say where he might be going? Did he leave any of her things with Marybell? Did he seem jubilant, or sad, or just in-between? Dorie wanted to sit and think, plot out her next move, but Mrs. Eckersell wanted to talk. She was brim full of ideas for the money Dorie didn't have yet. She said Dorie could junk that pickup she'd left in Flagstaff and get something sensible, comfy but sensible. Or maybe she ought to go for racy. With the money Dorie would get for the coins and the house (meaning Ruetta's house), she'd be on easy street. All Dorie said was that twenty-five thousand dollars wouldn't put anybody, least of all her, on easy street these days, though it might keep her out of the poor house for the time being.

Dorie stood and announced that she was going to take a little walk. Mrs. Eckersell was invited to come along, but she declined. Said she didn't want to be somewhere else when Seth emerged with the good news. Dorie intentionally walked in the opposite direction from the mortuary. She didn't want to run into those folks and have to make excuses about their money. They'd be calling for it soon enough. Yes, indeed, life would be simpler if the coins happened to sell, for even half what Seth had said. Like her mother, Dorie hated to be beholden to anybody, and just now she was beholden to about everybody. And to think she once patted herself on the back for giving Lily Dawn a lift and

Minding Mama

buying her a few Cheetos and apples! Dorie laughed out loud at her naively grand view of her beneficence.

Twelve

"Well, my friends, I have jolly good news." Seth Johnson burst through his front door as Dorie came up the walk. Mrs. Eckersell, who had been dozing, jumped guiltily at being discovered in her host's customary chair. "The fellow in Las Vegas wants all four coins, though I suggest that you save at least one of the pennies. If some unforeseen emergency should arise, they're like money in the bank. And much less tempting to spend."

Mrs. Eckersell responded first. "Good! Now, how do we get the cash, how soon do we get it, and how much is he gonna pay?"

Dorie couldn't believe her ears. She was on the verge of being solvent. Her first impulse was to hug the man. "Oh, thank you," she cried. "What do we do next, and how much do I owe you?"

"Owe me, my dear? Why, what a novel idea. You owe me nothing, of course. The pleasure of holding this rare silver coin in my hand is payment enough."

"Words, words, words," Mrs. Eckersell complained. "How much, and when?"

"Patience, dear lady," Seth Johnson said, "I'm coming to that." He turned to Dorie. "The man will pay thirty thousand for the dollar and two pennies."

Dorie sank onto the top step. She couldn't believe her ears. Thirty thousand dollars. More than she made in a year, even with tips. Much more.

"In fact," Seth continued, "so eager is our client that he's driving over from Las Vegas today, if that meets with your approval."

"Does it ever!" Mrs. Eckersell exclaimed. "We'll take it!"

"There'll be taxes to pay on it, of course, but a tidy little sum will remain after."

"Taxes!" Mrs. Eckersell cried. "Wouldn't you know the gov'ment would jump in and spoil our fun. Taxes! I never heard of such a thing."

* * * * * * *

The Las Vegas buyer was as good as his word. At 3:15 that afternoon, he appeared at Mrs. Eckersell's door with a bank draft for thirty thousand dollars, which Dorie promptly took to the local bank where she opened an account and walked out with a cashier's check for five thousand dollars, made payable to the Delmose Mortuary. Then she returned to the bank, explained that her mother's key was lost, proved her own signature and her mother's decease, and removed her mother's will and the deed to her home from the box.

The will was short and simple. The home and all Ruetta Flatray's worldly possessions, with the exception of her grandmother's crystal set, went to her daughter, Dorie June Flatray Grimes. Dorie had expected something like this, yes, but seeing it in writing made her realize that, despite her failure to verbalize matters of the heart, her mother had somehow apprehended her love, even taken it for granted. It was perhaps Ruetta's acknowledgment that she knew Dorie could be counted on. The crystal, the closest thing the Flatrays had to an heirloom, went to Ruetta's daughter, Marva Grace Flatray Ashby.

Dorie assumed that the coins she had sold were included in the "all worldly possessions" clause, but she intended to take the document to a lawyer tomorrow, to make sure everything was on the up and up. The disposition of the will would not make Marva Grace happy, Dorie knew that only too well. And now she had to call Marva and break the news. She decided to put it off until morning. This evening she wanted to visit the cemetery and sincerely thank her mother, perhaps for the first time, for material gifts, yes, but especially for the gift of herself, the gift of example and principle and honor.

* * * * * *

Minding Mama

Never having been comfortable in cemeteries, but grateful that her mother's home was not far from the burial ground, Dorie walked slowly up the Avenue of Flags, the main road into the small cemetery. It seemed appropriate that the little plot sat at the base of a great red sandstone cliff. As Dorie approached her mother's grave, she felt a strange peace wash over her, a hush even, though the highway to Turner was just behind her. After visiting Ruetta's fresh mound, she found herself reluctant to leave. Wandering among the older headstones, she was touched especially by two small squarish rough hewn ones, no doubt shaped and then engraved by a family member, with a nail or pocket knife, in awkward letters. And then she noticed another, even smaller, square stone that bore only two letters, the initials S.L.

What struck Dorie especially, was the number of babies' and children's graves. She realized that the death of small children was a common fact of life in an earlier era, especially in pioneer Jericho and other remote towns and villages. She realized more fully what it meant to be isolated from the rest of the world. In sharp contrast to the infants' graves, however, was the grave of a woman born in August 1900 who lived until November 2000. A short cowboy poem engraved on the back of the headstone, which the woman shared with her mother, bore the woman's initials. Curiously, the father's headstone, unshared, was off to one side. Therein lies a tale, Dorie told herself.

Seeing the many sweet expressions, on the older headstones especially, Dorie wished that she had been more creative with the text on her father's and mother's. The children's headstones in particular bore touching phrases, such as "Our darling ones have gone before / To greet us on the blissful shore," and "Budded on earth to bloom in heaven." But the one that Dorie admired most, and took time to memorize, was a tribute to a woman who died in 1928, at age fifty-five. The inscription made Dorie wish that she herself had lived a different life, that something like this could be said of her—and truthfully—when she died. Is it too late? she wondered. She spoke the words aloud as she read them:

Amiable, she won all; intelligent, she charmed all;

fervent, she loved all; and dead, she saddened all. High praise, indeed. A simple, touching description of a successful life.

As Dorie left the cemetery, dusk was settling over Jericho, and she felt more hopeful than she had in a long time, maybe ever. She knew now that she could survive the hurt of Cleve's desertion. Tomorrow there would be Marva Grace to deal with, and the sheriff, and a hundred other things. But tonight, there was just mother, daughter, earth, and sky. The clouds flamed up from the West and flung bright banners of orange and red and yellow across the vast firmament, like a grand proclamation from heaven. The very air took on color, and not a single cloud escaped the sunset's brush. Somewhere nearby a mourning dove cast his soft lament abroad, like a promise, and it spoke comfort to Dorie's soul.

Minding Mama

When she reached her mother's modest frame house, she stopped and seemed to see it with new eyes. Even the faded paint and the peeling pillars that supported the sloping roof of the front porch looked less forbidding. As though in response to her awakened vision, the big tree near the street was showing plump buds of green. Its deep roots had kept it alive. (And therein lies yet another lesson, Dorie told herself.) An unexpected word popped into Dorie's head. *Home*, her inner voice said. Well, yes, she argued silently, Mama's home, and mine, too, I guess. At least her will says so.

As she contemplated the aging structure, the word persisted in her consciousness. Home. Dorie turned in and drifted toward the front steps. Home. She reached out and touched, almost caressed, the pillar next to the steps, feeling it solid and real beneath her hand. Home. Had Atlanta ever felt like this? Had Cleve's home ever really been hers? Was it ever more than just a house to her, or to him, for that matter? Backing away and walking slowly toward the lighted windows of Mrs. Eckersell's place, Dorie kept hearing in her mind a phrase from the inscription on the Statue of Liberty, an inscription set to music and once sung by her high school choir. Yes, she remembered, I used to sing a little, didn't I? "Give me your tired, your poor, your huddled masses yearning to breathe free. . . ."

* * * * * * *

Marilyn Arnold

Marva Grace didn't disappoint her. She wanted her share of the money from the coin sale, and from the house sale, too. She didn't care what the will said, and vowed she'd sue if she had to. Okay, Dorie responded, you can have half the coin money, after the mortuary and burial expenses and taxes, but what if I decide to live in the house? Dorie had actually said those words, as if saying them created, even confirmed, the possibility. Until last night, Dorie had never considered remaining in Jericho, much less living in her mother's house. What she had known was that she'd have to clean it up and paint it in order to sell it, and she didn't look forward to that in the slightest. Live in the house! Marva had literally screamed the words when Dorie spoke them. Marva followed them up by suggesting that if Dorie did that she'd be robbing her own sister, her own flesh and blood, of what was rightfully hers. Naturally, Marva Grace knew that Dorie could never buy out Marva's share, and that the only way Marva could "realize" on the house was by selling it to somebody.

The sheriff was much kinder than Dorie's sister. He told Dorie he had decided to drop the charges. She wouldn't be prosecuted for carrying her dead mother across state lines. Dorie was so grateful that she broke into tears and threw her arms around her old classmate. Embarrassed, he awkwardly patted her back and said he hoped she might stay in Jericho, maybe convince her husband to move west. The desert grows on you, he said, adding that she never gave it a chance before. It's something to think about, was all she said as she backed away, snuffling into a tissue. She couldn't help wondering what he'd do if he knew about Lily Dawn and Moses. Maybe he wouldn't be so generous. Anybody tallying up her offenses could conclude that she was practically a hardened criminal. She had a rap sheet longer than that of anybody she knew or ever cared to know.

* * * * * * *

Mrs. Eckersell, pretending to be cleaning in the vicinity of the telephone, had been all ears during Dorie's conversation with her sister. She heard Dorie suggest that maybe she'd live in the house. That made her smile. She also heard Dorie say that Marva Grace could have half the coin money. That made her frown. Mrs. Flatray had never spoken an unkind word about her older daughter, but Mrs. Eckersell knew that Marva's selfishness was a trial to her mother. Why, most Mother's Days went by without so much as a card or a call from anybody except Dorie back in Atlanta. It was a miracle Marva turned up for Mrs. Flatray's burial service. When she came for Mr. Flatray's funeral eight years ago, she scowled and complained the whole time about what she had sacrificed to come. Mrs. Eckersell could never understand how a good woman like her neighbor could have given birth to such a thankless child. Shakespeare was right when he said that such a child was sharper than a serpent's tooth. Mrs. Eckersell had always remembered that line, which she had underlined in her book of famous quotations.

Mrs. Eckersell held her peace until Dorie returned from her errands at the lawyer's and the sheriff's offices. But the more she thought about things, the madder she got. In her view, Marva Grace should be banished from the society of decent people, of whom she herself was one and Dorie Grimes was another. And Seth Johnson. He was a little odd, maybe, but he had a heart of gold. She decided that people with hearts of gold didn't concern themselves much with material gold. It was people whose hearts were made of stone that craved the precious metal. God spare me from a heart of stone, she prayed silently.

When Dorie appeared on the front walk, Mrs. Eckersell rushed to the door. She wanted to know what the sheriff said and what the lawyer said and if that greedy Marva Grace was going to get anything at all except the crystal. She also was dying to know if Dorie was serious when she said she might decide to live in Mrs. Flatray's house and be her next door neighbor.

"Quick, girl, set down there and tell me everything," she cried the minute Dorie walked in. "Did the sheriff let you off? Did the lawyer say Marva Grace won't get a red cent? Are you goin' to stay here in Jericho? You might's well, now that your faithless husband's gone and run off. I heard you say over the phone that he had and that you might stay—excuse my listenin' in—and I couldn't wait to ask. Why, I been hoppin' around here like a pregnant jaybird."

Dorie laughed. "Everything's all right, Mrs. Eckersell.

Minding Mama

Don't you worry about a thing. The sheriff's let me off, and the lawyer'll handle Marva Grace. I don't care about the money, except I need some to fix up the house and my truck and pay off the credit card. One way or another, if I stay in the house or sell it, I've got to fix it up. So that's where I aim to start. And I've got to get me some clothes and things. I didn't bring much, and I guess all my other stuff's gone. Maybe I should call Marybell in Atlanta and find out for sure."

"Leave it behind, girl. Start a new life. Cast off the old, I always say. Let the dead bury the dead."

"I keep askin' myself, what would Mama do in my shoes? She always wanted to come back here, always thought she could talk me'n Cleve into it. That's why she kept the house. Now Cleve's gone maybe I should stay here where I can at least visit her."

"Do it girl. I'm not able to do heavy cleanin', but I can still wash eight years of dirt off the dishes for you. And Seth, I bet he'd help. And there's men in the ward who can do the heavy stuff if'n I ask 'em. And the Relief Society, they'll step in."

"Hold on, Mrs. Eckersell. I'm not a charity case any more. Besides, the Mormons have got no call to help me. What've I ever done for them?"

"What's that got to do with anything? Service ain't done on a you scratch my back, I'll scratch yours basis."

Dorie smiled and stood. "Well, in any case, I've got to go over to Mama's house and look things over. I can start cleanin' today. Mama's got mops and buckets over there. Probably even soap. We didn't take much when we left for Atlanta eight years ago." Dorie sighed deeply. "No thanks to me. Anyhow, I guess tomorrow's soon enough to worry about my pickup truck. And there's some unfinished business in Turner I need to see to. A girl that might be in trouble over there."

Mrs. Eckersell stood also. "I been thinkin' about that truck of yours, and I've decided there's nothin' I'd enjoy more than a little road trip to Flagstaff, Arizona. Soon's you're ready, girl, we can drive my car down. It could use a little stretch of highway drivin' and so could I! And we can stop in Turner on the way, if you want. I've even got a cousin in Flagstaff we can stay with if we need to, if you can stand her parrot and pet snake. She's a person who loves company."

* * * * * *

That afternoon Dorie was at work in her mother's kitchen, removing dirt-caked dishes from bug-infested shelves. It was cool, almost cold, in the house, but working in an old sweater of her father's she was comfortable enough. She had found cleaning powder and rags where her mother always kept them, in a cabinet next to the washing machine. The city had allowed her to turn water into the house, so she had water, even though it was not heated. And she had the electricity turned on, though she was

Minding Mama

debating about the gas. There was no point paying the deposit unless she intended to stay. Water could always be heated on the kitchen stove.

Dorie had a little money, now, but she wasn't what anybody would consider flush. When she called the beauty salon in Atlanta to say she'd be a while yet, her boss wasn't exactly thrilled. She hinted that if Dorie couldn't get back fairly soon, they'd have to replace her. Dorie didn't tell the woman that at the moment she had no home in Atlanta to come back to, much less a husband and son. She decided not to burn the beauty shop bridge until she figured out what to do, or got fired—whichever came first.

In the meantime, it was a comfort to handle her mother's things. Ruetta had been attached to this house, and only now did Dorie realize how difficult it must have been for her mother to leave everything behind and move to a strange city. A "Gentile" city at that. It's not easy to make a go of living with someone else, even if it is a person's grown daughter. Dorie had thought only of the inconvenience to herself and Cleve, making space in their small house and making time in her already busy schedule. And it was an adjustment for Cleve, too, though he didn't complain much after the first two or three months. They'd have done better if Mona Fay hadn't sent Clarence Ross packing, only to wind up on the sofa sleeper in the Grimes living room. Four grown people sharing one bathroom gets a bit trying. Of course, Dorie was the only one who had to be anywhere at a specific time, so that helped.

Marilyn Arnold

A knock came at the front door as Dorie stood on a chair scrubbing the upper shelves of the cupboard above the stove. (Ruetta Flatray never had a microwave oven installed. She regarded such shortcuts as cheating, possibly even immoral. Moreover, she credited the microwave for the increased cancer rates in industrialized nations.) Who on earth? Dorie wondered. Probably somebody selling something. Mrs. Eckersell wouldn't come to the front door, nor would she knock. A yoohoo through a rear door she had already opened was more her style. Carefully lowering herself to the floor, Dorie wiped her hands down the sides of her capri style pants, which pants she intended to burn or bury at the first opportunity, once the house and yard cleaning were finished. There on the front porch to greet her were four women in work clothes, with buckets, sprays, polishes, brooms, and vacuums in hand. They introduced themselves as sisters in the ward, and ignored Dorie's protests. Your mother was the first to help anybody who needed it, they said. It's our chance to give a little something back to her. They added that their husbands and sons would come on Saturday to attack cellar, garage, and yard. They could paint the following Saturday if Dorie wanted them to, but she would have to choose the paint.

Dorie was overwhelmed. Tears filled her eyes as she stepped back and let the women in. Time flew, along with hands and feet. Curtains came down, rugs came up. The old house was transformed, its long empty rooms and halls filled once more with talk, laughter, and strains of song.

Minding Mama

Dorie could see again her mother as she was, moving about the place in busy contentment—now humming a favorite tune, now scolding Demont Ralph for tracking manure in from the chicken coop or leaving a tool from the shed on the kitchen table. By the time evening approached, softening the old house with long shadows, the place was shining. True, it needed paint, inside and out, and some minor repairs; but it was clean and livable. Dorie could hardly believe her eyes. She tried to pay the women, but they wouldn't hear of it. If you decide to stay, one of them said, you can join us for the next cleaning gig. Dorie gladly assented, adding that, who knows, she just might stay.

After the women hugged Dorie, each in turn, and left, she dropped into one of the newly scrubbed, though sorely faded, metal chairs on the front porch. It was the kind that had some give to it by virtue of bent hollow tubing that served as front legs and platform. From there she watched streaks of orange cloud in the West blend with the sky's bright robin egg blue. She had never seen sunsets like these. At least not when she had enough sense to appreciate them. The stillness was almost tangible. Dorie could hardly believe that there could be such peace, anywhere, and wondered why she hadn't noticed it when she had lived here as a youngster and thought only of getting away. Well, I got away all right, she chuckled softly, before I knew that the only thing I was escaping was myself.

Suddenly hungry, Dorie stood and stretched. Maybe Mrs. Eckersell will let me take her to dinner at the Trail's

End, or at Nedra's, she said half aloud. She decided to skip the Espresso Bar where, according to its billboard, the internet was served along with pastries, sandwiches, and ice cream. I'll need a shower first, though, and clean clothes.

* * * * * *

"I'm stuffed to my silly gills," Mrs. Eckersell sighed as she and Dorie left the restaurant and strolled toward the older woman's sedan. By then, night had set in. "Only thing missin' tonight is Mrs. Flatray. Oh, how she liked a good meal in a honest-to-goodness restaurant now and then. It had to be an occasion, mind you. She wasn't a woman to squander money on luxuries for herself. Basics. She was into the basics. Mr. Flatray was, too. Maybe that's why they got along so good."

"Did they get along?" Dorie asked. "I guess I never thought about it, one way or the other. They were just my parents. All I remember thinking about them was that they were old-fashioned and boring and wouldn't let me do half the things I wanted." Dorie shook her head. "I think I saw nothing but myself in those days. Parents weren't real people to me. They existed only to serve children. Since having babies was their idea, I thought it only fair." Dorie smiled. "Oh, the ignorance of youth!" she sighed.

"It's the way a' the world. Kids is kids. They ain't built to care about anything much but themselves. I don't know if

Minding Mama

the Lord planned it that way, or if it just happened that way."

"And with some of us it takes a long time, too long, to get over it," Dorie said, opening the car door. "Me, for instance. I think I'm just barely gettin' over it now. Guess I'm a slow learner."

"That ain't so, Dorie," Mrs. Eckersell said as she slid behind the wheel of her 1990 Chevy. "Why, Mrs. Flatray was always tellin' me about nice things you done for her. Presents and cards on birthdays and Christmas, flowers on Mother's Day. And sometimes a phone call. Such things mean a lot to a mother. B'lieve me, I know."

It struck Dorie then that Mrs. Eckersell must surely have had children, and a husband, and that she, Dorie, had not once asked about them. Maybe I'm not getting over it after all, she mused. I'm still acting as if I'm the only occupant of the planet. She resolved to ask Mrs. Eckersell about her husband and children that very night, even if it meant enduring a closet full of family photo albums.

"Say, Dorie, ain't that a car in front of your mother's house?" Mrs. Eckersell asked as her headlights swung around the corner onto 200 South Street.

Dorie leaned forward. "It sure looks like it . . . no wait, it's a pickup. . . . Hey, it's *my* pickup! Or one just like it! How'd it get here?"

"The p'lice didn't bring it, did they? They don't do such, do they?"

"I hardly think so. How would they find me even if they were inclined to deliver it and hand me the bill. Let me

235

out in front. I'll go see if it's mine for sure."

"Be careful, now. It might be somebody up t' no good. I'll keep m' lights trained on the truck."

As Dorie approached the pickup, the head of a large dog appeared over the tail gate, and she heard a low growl. Then a door opened and the figure of a man appeared. "Hush now, Petunia," the man said. "Don't you go causin' no trouble."

"Loyal!" Dorie cried, rushing forward. "Loyal, is that you? It's me, Dorie Grimes!" Half crying, she threw her arms around the man. "How'd you get here? How'd you find me? Is the truck running?"

"Hold on there, missy," Loyal Bunce said, chuckling and patting Dorie's back. "You don't wanna be huggin' such as me, I'm s' dirty an' all."

"What do I care? Are you all right?" Then Dorie remembered Mrs. Eckersell. "Come and meet my neighbor . . . I mean my Mama's neighbor. I've been stayin' with her. She's real nice."

"She won't wanna meet such as me, dirty as I am."

"C'mon, she won't care."

Loyal Bunce wouldn't allow Dorie to tow him over to the waiting Mrs. Eckersell, so Dorie had to explain his presence to her mother's neighbor, how she happened to know Loyal and how he happened to be driving her vehicle with a big dog in the back. All in abbreviated terms. Mrs. Eckersell was obviously curious, even wary, but she didn't say so. She wondered if Mrs. Flatray would approve

Minding Mama

of Dorie's choice of friends, but then decided that Mrs. Flatray would probably have invited the fellow in and fed him. Maybe even let him sleep in the laundry room, though she would have drawn the line at the dog. Mrs. Flatray never allowed a dog in the house. She said it wasn't sanitary, and that was that.

Introductions would have to wait, Dorie realized. Not only was Loyal reluctant, but the older woman was probably nervous about strangers, maybe smelly unkempt ones especially. Dorie decided to take Loyal to the nearby Sun and Sand Motel where he could get a hot shower and enjoy the benefits of Thomas Edison's genius. Petunia could stay in the truck. Tomorrow she'd buy clean clothes for him and for herself. Tomorrow would be soon enough to hear Loyal's story. Tonight she was tired. She could scarcely believe it had been little more than a week since she left Atlanta. It seemed like a lifetime. In some ways it was.

* * * * * * *

By noon the next day, both Loyal and Dorie had undergone total transformations, what people in the beauty shop business call make-overs. Give Loyal a shave and a haircut, put new jeans and chambray shirt on him, and he looked like any of the locals. Well, almost. Before taking him into the Trails End for lunch, Dorie found a beauty shop and bought a new outfit for herself—yellow slacks, plain white top, and new sandals. The old handbag

237

remained, however. Dorie was not one given to extravagance. Talking across chicken fried steak and mashed potatoes, the house specialty for more than fifty years, they brought each other up to date.

Loyal had found a nearby garage in Flagstaff that would allow him to work a couple of days in exchange for towing service and use of space and tools and a few parts in their shop. He knew cars, he said, and was able to fix Dorie's truck, except for the new bumper and grill it needed. He managed to pick up a little cash in the evenings by performing outside the movie theaters with Matilda. When he got to Jericho, the mortuary people eyed him suspiciously, then finally told him where the Flatray house was. It was the fact that he knew all about the cross-country trip in the pickup that convinced them.

"I might be stayin' here," she told him. "Cleve's run off and left me. I've got Mama's house if I want it. If I stay, why don't you stay, too?"

Loyal shook his head. "I ain't the stayin' kind, I guess, but if'n you need me, I c'n stick around a spell and do some handyman chores in exchange for bed and vittles. You got someplace me'n Petunia c'n sleep? I don't mean in the house. A night 'r two in a motel (he pronounced it *mo-tel*) reminds me why I don't care to live in no house. Makes me feel all pinched in, all squoze up."

Dorie laughed. "There's a shed out back of Mama's, and a chicken coop. Even an old outhouse. You can take your pick of the accommodations. I'm sure there's a hose in the garage that we can attach to an outdoor faucet, too. But if I'm here, you're welcome to use the indoor facilities. You can even take the windows down on the back porch and sleep there, if you want. Sort of a compromise."

"No thankee. Too civ'lized for my tastes. Too much of the soft life'll weaken a man like me. B'sides, Petunia'd lose all respect f'r me if'n I done that." Loyal looked doubtfully at Dorie. "You really gonna stay here, maybe? When'll you know? One more night in a motel's about m' limit."

"Tomorrow," she said, not knowing before she said it. "Tomorrow I'll decide."

Loyal got a kick out of Dorie's tales of her adventures in the bus with Brighty Lu and Bertram Pocock, though he was concerned about what the pair would do now that the world didn't end on schedule. He said he didn't notice a hybrid vehicle along the road anywhere. As for Madame Taji Mahi, he thought maybe he had worked the outskirts of a carnival with her "oncet somewheres." Only then she was Princess somebody or other. He guessed that maybe she looked more like a madame than a princess nowadays. And no, he hadn't seen her Volkswagen bus either.

"Holy Toledo," he said, "we've left car bodies strewed from heck to breakfast. We coulda opened a salvage yard."

"Yes," Dorie said dryly, "most people would just scatter bread crumbs. That's too easy for us. We gotta do things the hard way."

When Dorie told Loyal about Lily Dawn's plight, he was troubled. "Wisht I'd 'a knowed," he said, "I'd 'a snatched her on m' way through. Where's li'l Moses at?"

Dorie explained that the three bus people were going to handle that business. Rachel wanted to adopt him, but feared her lifestyle wouldn't sit well with the court. How that whole thing would turn out was anybody's guess. Dorie worried that she might be called in for questioning and could even be prosecuted herself, for bringing the baby out of Texas and failing to notify the authorities. "Maybe Rachel's lawyer brother can keep me out of it. At least I'm off the hook with Mama," she said, "and I've got a little cash in my pocket."

After they left the restaurant, Dorie took Loyal Bunce back to her mother's place on its quiet street of older homes and large trees. He checked out the somewhat dilapidated structures in back and said he could live there quite comfortably while he did the repairs she needed, though he wasn't used to having a permanent address. Dorie gathered that for him "permanent" was anything longer than three days. Then she took him over to meet Mrs. Eckersell. She wanted the meeting to take place before Loyal's appearance deteriorated, or worse still, returned to normal.

"Pleased, I'm sure," Mrs. Eckersell said, executing a girlish little curtsy.

Loyal bowed, quite elegantly, Dorie thought, and said, "Likewise, ma'am."

Mrs. Eckersell offered them licorice herbal tea, apologizing profusely for not having coffee in the house. "We don't imbibe, as you might know," she said, daintily opening

Minding Mama

her napkin, "but herbal tea is not forbidden."

Oh, yes, Dorie knew, because she had scarcely quaffed (her father's word) a cup of coffee, or even a coke, for that matter, since she arrived in Jericho. Which probably accounted for her headache, though she had plenty of other things to blame it on. Loyal, on the other hand, to Dorie's surprise, said he preferred herbal tea to caffeinated drinks, thank you, and that spiced licorice was his all time favorite. Why, he's a woman pleaser, Dorie said to herself. Put him in company with a female of his generation, and he's a regular Beau Brummell. Seth Johnson had nothing on him. It was a side of Loyal she hadn't seen before and frankly didn't expect to see again. She noticed, however, that if Mrs. Eckersell's presence improved his manners, and even his pronunciation, it had little effect on his grammar. Bad grammar runs deep. But then, Mrs. E's grammar wasn't all that great either. Truth be known, neither's mine, Dorie admitted.

Thirteen

Over the next few days Loyal Bunce and Petunia, accompanied by the trombone Matilda, settled into the shed behind Ruetta Flatray's house. He swept it out and tidied it, spraying around the edges to discourage spiders and rodents. Then he found an old cot in the cellar, which he hauled up and installed as a bed, across from the only window, complaining all the while that this high living would spoil him, make him soft. Dorie dismissed his good natured grumbling with a laugh, privately convinced that he was in no great hurry to move on.

She had hot water now, so she washed bedding and insisted that he take blankets, towels, and a bucket to the shed, along with soap, razor, and a piece of mirror she found in a drawer. Luckily, the old building was wired for electricity, and a single bulb dangled from a twisted cord in the middle of the room. Dorie gave Loyal money to buy whatever materials he needed for house repairs and supplies, including

Minding Mama

paint. As promised, a group of men and boys showed up on Saturday, ready to work. Truckloads of junk left garage, cellar, shed, and yard, headed for the dump. One of the men had a sanding machine, and he spent the day preparing the house's exterior for paint. Loyal said he could handle the inside. A couple of us will be back next Saturday to paint the outside, the man with the sander said.

By now Dorie had made a decision. She was staying. She couldn't believe it herself. Two weeks ago if anyone had told her she'd be setting up housekeeping in Jericho, Utah, she'd have told him he was crazy. It appeared to Dorie, however, that she was the one who'd lost her mind. When she called her boss in Atlanta to announce that she wouldn't be curling hair there any more, the woman confirmed the insanity diagnosis. So did Marybell, Dorie's Atlanta neighbor. "Honey, people with brains in their heads just don't do that," she told Dorie. Not even people whose husbands have run out on them, of whom there are more than a few. As if Dorie didn't know it already. As if she hadn't told herself the same thing several dozen times.

What's more, she was toying with the idea of doing cuts, perms, dye jobs, and shampoo-sets right out of her home. (Was it really *her* home?) Loyal said he could rig up a sink and cabinet in the laundry room (i.e., the back porch), which was plenty big enough because it ran the width of the house, and the house was wider than it was long. It was either that or go to work for some beauty shop in town. Or do something else entirely, though Dorie hadn't the slightest idea

243

what that might be. One thing was certain, she had to have gainful employment.

By the time she had sent Marva Grace her split from the coin sale, there wasn't a whole lot left to live on and fix the house up with. Much less buy a few more clothes and stock up on the basic foodstuffs. Dorie was grateful now that her mother had insisted on leaving the household furnishings in Jericho. She was also grateful that she herself had insisted on throwing out perishables like flour and cereals before the pair of them headed east. Since the mice and ants would come anyway, she saw no sense in issuing engraved invitations.

Oh, yes, Marva Grace had decided against contesting the will. Although Marva didn't out-and-out say so, Dorie gathered from her conciliatory attitude that Marva's attorney had advised her not to press her luck. In so many words he said that an ice cube had a better chance of surviving in hell than she had of getting money through the courts, or of forcing Dorie to sell the house. In any event, Marva Grace decided that a small rundown house wasn't worth the trouble anyway. Dorie knew then that she needn't have sent Marva Grace half the money from the coins, that her sister didn't have much of a legal claim to it either. But Dorie was glad she had sent it. At least she had shown good faith, even if Marva hadn't. In Dorie's view, the world was in a sorry state when sisters found themselves disputing with each other in court. She herself would take abject poverty any day. And so would her mother. No question about it.

Minding Mama

* * * * * * *

Early one evening, Dorie was putting the last plate from supper in the cupboard when she heard a sharp knock on the front door. Thinking it might be a solicitor, or the gallant Seth Johnson and his latest coin catalogue, she quickly wiped her hands and went to the door. Loyal had been painting the last few days, and she had the windows open to counteract the fumes. The day had been sunny, though still a bit cool. Squinting against the late sun's brightness, Dorie made out two figures on her front porch. They seemed familiar, but only when her eyes became accustomed to the outdoor light did she recognize the woman in the full ruffled skirt and the man in the dark suit and hat, though they looked far less perky and far more travel-worn than when she had seen them last. Brighty Lu and Bertram Pocock! They who were scheduled for angelic transport to heaven a good ten days ago.

The pair looked so pathetic that Dorie didn't know whether to laugh or cry. What do you do when your whole purpose in life depends on the world's ending at a particular time, and the world doesn't cooperate? When you are the one who got it wrong and the scoffers are the ones who got it right? Well, Dorie would soon learn that you do what the Pococks did. You choose a new date and you preach that because you don't know what else to do. It's all you're trained for. You figure you misunderstood the Lord once, but he won't let it happen again. He will shield his chosen servants from the world's slings and arrows. The Pococks were putting up a good front, but Dorie couldn't help noticing a slight drop in the confidence level of her visitors.

"We hoped you'd still be here, Dorie Grimes," said Brighty Lu in a businesslike tone. "We've come hither on the Lord's errand, to correct the information we gave you before. We think it our bounden duty to gather in the seeds of falsehood we innocently sowed through no fault of our own." She paused and glanced at her husband. "Bertie here heard the Lord wrong; he mixed up the dates, so we gotta retrace our steps and correct th' error. The world didn't end when we said it would."

"Yes, I noticed that," Dorie said. "Is there a new due date?"

"At present, we're importuning the heavens with might and main. We expect the Lord's official word to be revealed to us, his faithful servants, any day now; ain't that right, Bertie?"

"Right as rain," he chimed, making his customary rainfall gesture.

"Well, c'mon in," Dorie said, opening the door and directing the pair toward her mother's chintz-covered sofa. "How'd you get here? I didn't see your vehicle."

"It's a long story, ain't it, Bertie?" Brighty Lu sighed and sat heavily on the sofa. Bertram only nodded. "We hitched a ride this far with another couple of the gathered chosen who was headin' back to New Mexico to regroup, or maybe recheck the date with some aliens who're comin'

Minding Mama

in on a spaceship next week. But they wanted to go by way of Jacob's Lake, they said. So they left us off here at the junction. It's good your mama lived close by. We couldna gone much fu'ther with our luggage an' tracts."

"Aliens know the Lord's schedule?"

"Why o' course! He sends 'em here on errands all the time. My land, girl, don't you know anything?" Brighty Lu turned to Bertram. "The degree of ignorance amongst the general populace never ceases to amaze me, Bertie." He shook his head in amazed disbelief. "We called the Arizona highway people a few days ago, after we'd waited extra time for the end, thinkin' mebbe we'd miscalculated a teensy bit. Seems they towed our automobile to Turner and impounded it there, since it was pointed north and not south. We got to go get it over at the police place."

"How have you survived? Where and how did you eat and sleep?" Dorie's eyes and nose told her that they hadn't showered or changed clothes in some time.

"The Lord provides for his anointed," the evangelist said, raising her hand toward heaven. "We slept in the tents of the faithful and ate the food of the just."

"We begged, is what we did," Bertram mumbled.

"Hush up your mouth, Bertie Pocock!" Brighty Lu cried. "We blessed the tents and tables of the believers."

"Who came prepared in the event that the Lord changed his mind," Dorie said under her breath.

"And we held a revival meetin' or two at the Zion Park campground," Brighty Lu continued, "which netted us a little in operatin' expenses."

"Until the Park folks kicked us out," Bertram added. "Praises be, we made a good haul b'fore they got onto us!" Clearly, Bertram was the pragmatist of the pair.

Brighty kicked Bertram's shin. "Hush you now. B'sides, that money's mostly gone, and we still gotta get our vehicle fixed and outta hock. An' we gotta get t' Turner to do it."

"Well, you can't go 'til tomorrow, so you might's well bring your things in off the porch. I can give you food and a bed tonight. I've got a spare bedroom at the moment." Dorie decided not to mention Loyal, who always went to bed at sundown, wherever and whatever his bed happened to be. If the Pococks saw him in the morning, it would be plenty soon enough. With this pair, any time was too soon. She doubted he'd feel deprived.

* * * * * *

Four days later, the Pococks finally decided to leave, perhaps having realized at last that here in the dwelling of the unconverted, although they got three square meals a day, they were unable to get clear signals from above. The heathen roof was apparently blocking out any divine transmissions being sent their way. Dorie, fearing that the pair might take up permanent residence in her house, under squatter's rights law, offered to drive them to Turner in her Toyota pickup. They were both larger than either Lily

Minding Mama

Dawn or Ruetta, so it would be close quarters. Nonetheless, Dorie wasn't surprised when Bertram didn't offer to ride in the back with the luggage and boxes. How could he? His hat would blow off, unless it was glued on. Which it might be for all she knew. It was like a second head of hair.

Loyal avoided the Pococks after his first encounter with them at breakfast. Dorie could hear him pounding and sawing in the garage every day, but she let him be and took meals out to him rather than subject him to the evangelists. They predicted that an infidel like him would murder Dorie in her sleep and run off in her pickup. Brighty Lu avowed that she herself wouldn't sleep a wink knowing that Dorie was in dire peril. Dorie assured them that Loyal was harmless and that they needn't worry a moment over her safety.

With every passing hour Dorie knew more surely that she would not miss the Pococks in the least, even though they provided something in the way of grotesque entertainment. The trick was to take nothing they said seriously, absolutely nothing. But when the neighbors started complaining about Doom's Day revival meetings in the cemetery, she knew what the pair had been up to when they weren't exorcising the evil spirits in her house or catechizing Mrs. Eckersell.

Dorie had business of her own in Turner—finding Lily Dawn before the government offices closed over there. But by the time the Pococks got themselves organized and ready to leave, the hour was late. They had insisted, too, on a last minute snack, to build up their reserves for what might be a long period of sanctifying deprivation, Brighty Lu said. Dorie's errand was of little consequence to the evangelists, and there was no hurrying them. Once on the road, Dorie maintained a degree of composure by focusing on her personal errand rather than on Brighty Lu's discourse about ready-made, sure-fire salvation and joy for the converted and impending destruction and sorrow for the unconverted. Bertram, as usual, contributed little to the discussion. Dorie suspected he was asleep.

The evangelist said she was currently designing Doom's Day survival kits, with all the necessary user's guides and materials packaged in a container the size of a regular Cheerio box. Come to think of it, maybe she'd use Cheerio boxes and keep the Cheerio logo because what she was spreading was cheer. While Dorie wouldn't have called what was being spread "cheer," unless cheer came from the barnyard, she wasn't inclined to argue with the general premise about salvation for the faithful and destruction for the unrepentant sinner. Certainly, her mother had believed in something like that. But there the similarity ended. Dorie couldn't see much positive substance to offset the gloom and doom, not to mention the high jinks, that was the Pococks' stock in trade.

What in fact Dorie was thinking about all the way to Turner was not the Apocalypse but something a lot closer to home. Lily Dawn. And that would have been Mama's first concern, too, she told herself. Doing unto the least of

Minding Mama

these. In fact, Dorie took the Pococks in because that's what her mother would have done, regardless of the inconvenience, regardless of their cockeyed view of things, regardless of how unbearable they were. God is no respecter of persons, Ruetta used to say whenever she thought Dorie needed a refresher course in the matter. Dorie couldn't get Lily Dawn out of her mind. The girl left a lot to be desired when it came to breeding and polish, but there was a sweetness about her that tugged at Dorie's heart. An innocence that somehow rose above her circumstances. Dorie needed to find the girl, needed to know that she was all right. People like the Pococks would always survive. They knew how to use people to their advantage. Lily Dawn was quite something else.

* * * * * *

"Here's three hundred dollars," Dorie said as she bid farewell, after numerous delays, to Brightness Louise and Bertram Levi Pocock at the impound yard in Turner, Arizona. "Friends gave me the same amount when I was down and out," she explained, "and I'm passing it on to you. You go on an' do the same for somebody else when your fortunes look up."

Brighty Lu snatched the bills and stuffed them in her handbag. "We take this not for me and Bertie, here, but for the divine church and its holy purposes," she said with a haughty little toss of the head.

Marilyn Arnold

"I assume you'll use it first to rescue your vehicle, and that the church will have to get in line," Dorie said, instantly ashamed of her sarcasm, even though the comment flew right over the Pococks' heads. Religion wasn't something to be taken lightly. That much she had learned in the last few weeks. Only she decided that she much preferred the brand of it practiced by her mother and her mother's neighbors over that practiced by the capitalists of fear and doom.

Even so, Dorie doubted that she had seen the last of the Pococks. Her opinion of them had gone downhill with every passing hour since they arrived. They were not just ignorant. People like that turn up wherever human vulnerability or misery can be transformed into cash. When the twin towers in New York City explode, the Pococks of the world file false claims for compensation; when someone is dying of cancer, they come forward selling a magic elixir guaranteed to cure the disease; when a family is attending the funeral of a loved one, they burgle the family home. These are the people who scam the elderly out of their life savings with a promise of riches for a small investment. These are the people without conscience who preach salvation, of the soul, body, and bank account, for a hefty fee. The Pococks, Dorie could see now, were not merely misguided fanatics. She had no quarrel with the sincere misguided, even found them entertaining. The Pococks and others like them, regardless of what they peddled or claimed or perpetrated, were beasts of prey.

By the time Dorie got rid of the Pococks, the white collar

Minding Mama

portion of Turner had closed for the day. She had no way to track Lily Dawn. More than a little frustrated, Dorie started for Jericho, consoling herself by celebrating the Pococks' departure. That alone was worth the trip. But where was Lily Dawn, and how could Dorie find her? Furthermore, how could she make inquiries without raising red flags and making serious trouble for herself? Dorie knew she had to do something, she just didn't know what it was. She'd talk it over with Loyal. He had more common sense than most people, even if he was what police called a vagrant and what Cleve called a tramp. At least he lived up to his name, which Cleve didn't. A man with Cleve's name should make extra effort to cleave to his wife. The Bible said so, and Ruetta could have cited chapter and verse to prove it.

* * * * * * *

Weary and disappointed, Dorie approached her mother's home—her home now, Dorie reminded herself—at dusk. As the pickup lights swept the front porch ahead of the turning vehicle, Dorie thought she saw someone sitting on the top step. Loyal, she surmised, come out to enjoy the view from the front. The cold didn't seem to bother him much more than it did a polar bear. She pulled into the driveway and stopped, thinking to join him after she got a jacket. But as Dorie approached the figure huddled there she realized that it wasn't Loyal.

"Lily Dawn!" she cried, and rushed to the girl.

"What're you doin' here, girl?" Dorie sat beside Lily Dawn and embraced her, trying to soothe the trembling youngster. "You're cold. C'mon inside. I live here now. We got the place fixed up an' I live here now. Loyal's here, too. Out back." Dorie coaxed Lily Dawn to her feet and led her gently inside. The girl was wearing jeans and sneakers, so somebody had been looking after her. But she had no coat. Dorie hurried to the kitchen to heat milk for hot milk toast, her mother's remedy for nearly everything, including a broken heart. Then she brought a blanket and wrapped it around the girl.

Over hot milk toast at the kitchen table, an old red formica rectangle with sliding leaves and tubular chrome legs, Lily Dawn uttered her first words. "I run off," she said, staring at the bowl in front of her. "I got scared, so I run off. They said my grandmama she ain't never gon' get better." The girl stirred the torn toast pieces, but didn't eat.

"I thought you were goin' to a foster home soon."

"I was, while they looked for my daddy and stepmama. So I run off 'cause I can't go back there." She looked at her jeans and shoes. "A lady she gimme these clothes. She gimme a sweatershirt, too, but I los' it somewheres."

"But how did you get here? . . . Go on, now, child, eat."

"I walked over. I learnt the way when the bus people took me. Jus' in case."

"You walked!" Dorie heard herself screech the words. "When did you start?"

"A while back. I 'uz real careful to stay back frum the

Minding Mama

road mos' of the time so's nobody'd ketch me 'n take me back."

"What did you eat?"

"Oh, jes' stuff. People th'ows stuff outta their cars."

"Where did you sleep?"

"Oh, jes' places. I mos'ly sat somewheres. People even th'ows blankets outta their cars, or else they blow off. I done okay." Lily Dawn took a few bites, eating with her right hand and propping her head up with her left. Her drooping head was nearly in her bowl.

"Well, we'll talk tomorrow. You're gonna take a nice hot bath and go to bed. I'll find some of Mama's old pajamas for you." Dorie helped Lily Dawn to her feet, led her to the bathroom, and began running a tub of hot water. "You leave your clothes outside the door, an' I'll wash 'em tonight."

* * * * * * *

Once Lily Dawn was bedded down, Dorie put on a sweater and went outside. She needed some clear-headed thinking time. Loyal would be asleep, so she couldn't talk with him tonight. There was Mrs. Eckersell, but then Dorie really didn't want word about Lily Dawn to get around just yet. In any case, it would be awfully worrisome to Mrs. Eckersell. What would Mama do? Dorie asked herself as she paced up and down the front porch. Then it came to her, what Ruetta would do first off. She'd take her quandary to the Lord, and then with him on her side she'd act.

Dorie couldn't remember the last time she'd tried to pray. It was probably when she was small enough that her mother was still in charge of her spiritual life. Ruetta wasn't a Mormon in those days, but she was a religious woman just the same. As she used to say, she had religion all her life, she just didn't have the whole package until later on. Things were missing that had to be restored, she said. Dorie, however, wasn't interested. She preferred that her mother didn't discuss religion, but Ruetta managed to slip a lot of doctrine in edgewise during her eight years in the Grimes household.

Prompted by her mother's memory, Dorie embraced the large round support pillar next to the porch stairs and bowed her forehead against its smooth new paint. In stumbling phrases she addressed the personage her mother told her was listening, whenever any of us decided there was somebody up there smarter than we were. She spoke the words softly aloud, learning what to say and ask as she went.

She explained what a hard thing it was for Lily Dawn, and how sweet and strong she was in all the ways that counted. But she was only a girl, and she needed love and direction. She had come to Dorie because it seemed to her she had nowhere else to go, and now Dorie didn't know what to do to help her. So Dorie was coming to Him, after all these years, knowing she didn't deserve the slightest consideration, but asking it for Lily Dawn's sake. And then she thought to offer thanks that she had been favored with such a mother as Ruetta, and that Ruetta was safe now, and

Minding Mama

at peace, in her own promised land.

Pushing away from the pillar, Dorie felt lifted somehow, and assured. She descended the steps and walked to the street. The earth, lighted by the moon, was brighter than the sky, and she made her way through lacy tree shadows, up one street and down another. She had no particular geographical destination, but by the time she returned, she knew what to do.

* * * * * * *

The next morning, Dorie called Loyal in to breakfast, telling him she had a surprise for him. Lily Dawn was so happy to see him that, as he said, she nearly squoze the liver out of him. The two of them, detached from family and all things permanent and stable, had perhaps found something in each other that they had been missing. Dorie was amazed to see their genuine affection. Then she realized that her own attachment to them was probably just as amazing. They were all loose planets, she supposed, creating a solar system of their own to keep them spinning together instead of careening off alone into outer space. Moses, the bus trio, and even Madame Taji Mahi had been part of that system for a time. Yes, and maybe the Pococks, too, who were probably more desperate and alone than all the rest of them, more in need of connection and validation. Maybe I was too hard on the Pococks, Dorie told herself. I didn't walk in their shoes.

Marilyn Arnold

After breakfast, Dorie directed Lily Dawn and Loyal to the living room for what her mother called a "family conference." Ruetta spoke of such conferences, but Dorie couldn't recall that she and Cleve and Clarence Ross had ever had one. Their method of household governance was simple. In the beginning, Cleve made all the decisions; in the end, she did. Until the last one, that is, the one to abandon ship. Cleve made that, and it was a doozy. It made up for all the ones he missed in the middle and then some.

"We've got a problem here," Dorie said. "Lily Dawn's a minor, and she's run off. Legally, I got to return her to the authorities."

Lily Dawn let out a wail. "Not after I walked clean over here!" she cried. "I ain't goin' back to that place where the *Po*lice is an' where I don' know nobody!"

"Why cain't she jus' live here with you?" Loyal proposed. "That's th' on'y thing makes sense t' me."

Lily Dawn jumped to her feet. "Yes, Dorie! Lemme stay, pretty please?"

"Hold on, now, hold on. We've got to be legal. Just you bein' here could get me thrown in the hoosegow." Dorie gently pushed Lily Dawn back into her seat. "I've been doing some hard thinkin'—and prayin' too."

Lily Dawn interrupted. "I learnt me how t' pray in Bible school, an' I been prayin', too."

"Me 'n Petunia, we alluz prays," Loyal added.

"Here's what I think," Dorie said. "I think we've got to call your daddy and tell him where you are and what's

Minding Mama

happened. He'll know what to do. He's probably worried sick and already filed a missing person's report on you. Your daddy loves you. It's not fair to him, now is it? What if he'd run off and left you? That'd hurt your feelings, wouldn't it?"

Lily Dawn hung her head.

"Dorie's right. I vote we call your daddy, pronto," Loyal said.

"What do you say, girl?"

Lily Dawn sat silent for a long minute. "Oh, aw right," she mumbled, "but I ain't goin' back there to my stepmama and them evil-eyed boys a' hers."

* * * * * * *

Lily Dawn wouldn't let Dorie dial the home number, but consented to her making a call to the cell phone her father carried in his semi-trailer truck. She insisted, however, that Dorie do the talking. When Dorie finally reached Lily Dawn's father, after several tries, she learned that he didn't even know his daughter was missing. Near the end of his last run, his rig had broken down in Wyoming, leaving him stranded in Rawlins for nearly two weeks while he waited for parts and for a mechanic to come up from Denver who could fix it. When he called his wife, Lily Dawn's "stepmama," she hadn't told him the girl had left. He was only now headed back home and was a few miles outside of Nashville. He had to get the rig back, he said, but then he was flying out, and asked Dorie if she could keep Lily Dawn until he got to Jericho.

"I'll try," she said, "but I can't chain the girl to the bed post." Then she handed the phone to Lily Dawn. "Here, girl, talk to your daddy."

Hesitantly, shyly, Lily Dawn took the phone. "Is that you, Daddy?" she said. "This's me."

Fourteen

While Lily Dawn talked with her father, Dorie was silently flogging herself for not having insisted on calling him earlier. Then again, on that mad cross-country dash on wheels, she didn't exactly have limitless opportunity or time to devote to Lily's situation. All she could think of was getting her mother to Jericho as fast as possible. She should have known, though, that the girl's father would carry a cell phone in his big truck. After all, who didn't carry one of those annoying gadgets these days, except for a few throwbacks to the stone age like herself? And besides, every gas station had a pay phone in the vicinity for the technologically challenged, didn't it?

But then again, Lily Dawn had been adamant, and Dorie couldn't force her to make a call, or torture the information out of her, could she? She didn't even know the girl's last name, for Pete's sake, or the name of her hometown. So maybe it was best to wait until Lily Dawn got

lonesome enough or desperate enough to take the suggestion. For pure twenty-four karat stubbornness, you can't
beat the young when they get some notion stuck between
their ears. Reason and logic go out the window.

The question remained, however: What would become
of Lily Dawn? Dorie herself would hate to see the girl
returned to that soulless stepmother, if she was as bad as
Lily Dawn said she was. Then, too, there were the unsu-
pervised older teenage sons. Dorie had to think that Lily
Dawn's instincts were right about those boys, though she
had to wonder if running away was the best way to handle
the situation. Still, with her father on the road for long
stretches of time, the girl was pretty much at their mercy. It
was a dilemma then and it was a dilemma now. Maybe the
best solution, at least in the short run, was to keep Lily
Dawn here and get her back in school immediately. Dorie
worried that the girl was getting behind in her education.
She should have waited for summer vacation to do her running away. It was fortunate, but certainly unplanned, that
some of Lily Dawn's personal furlough coincided with her
school's regular spring break.

Lily Dawn handed the phone back to Dorie. "My
Daddy he wants t' talk t' you again," she said. "He's comin'
out soon's he c'n git here." She paused. "He's mad at me,
for runnin' off an' not tellin' him nuthin'. He says if'n I
feels inclined to run off ag'in I gotta tell him so's he c'n
talk me out of it."

Dorie nodded. "Sounds like a good plan t' me," she said

Minding Mama

and then addressed the voice on the phone. "Hello sir? Are you there? I don't even know your name. Lily Dawn has kept it a secret. You know how she is. She'd have made a good mule and a lousy politician."

* * * * * * *

And so it was arranged, at least as far ahead as the reunion of father and daughter in Jericho. What might transpire beyond that was anybody's guess, but Dorie was breathing easier. Somebody else could do the lion's share of the worrying now, people who were supposed to worry over each other. Family. Supposedly, that's what families were all about. She herself wasn't family to Lily Dawn by any stretch, so why did she feel responsible? Well, maybe because in a way she was responsible. Dorie couldn't deny that she had fed the girl licorice back in that church parking lot and allowed her to climb in the pickup cab and ride across the country next to Ruetta.

As Dorie applied her mother's heavy old iron to some curtains she had washed up for Mrs. Eckersell, she silently recited the litany of her crimes that pertained to Lily Dawn, the least of which were reckless endangerment and contributing to the delinquency of a minor. The official terminology came readily to mind because of Cleve. On a slow sports day, he watched all the detective shows he could find on the television, originals and cable reruns alike, and then threw fancy legal words like that around as though he had personally invented them as his contribution to the judicial system.

Speaking of Cleve, where was he? Dorie asked that question silently for about the thousandth time as she swept up kitchen crumbs late that afternoon. Especially at night, when she couldn't sleep, Dorie thought about Cleve. He came to mind a good deal more than Clarence Ross, though she had given birth to Clarence Ross and he was her own flesh and blood. For years now he had seemed like Cleve's child but not necessarily hers. She didn't know how that happened. And why was she more worried about Lily Dawn right now than about her own child? It didn't make sense. What kind of mother was she, anyway?

Clarence Ross was of age, yes, and way beyond. He was also what Marybell called, with apologies to Dorie, a chronic juvenile whose emotional growth was stunted at age fifteen. Even Ruetta, universal mother and grandmother, couldn't get through to him, though she tried for many months. In the end she opted to absolve herself, assign the blame to him for the impasse, pray for his soul, and stay out of his way. And rightfully so, Dorie supposed; but she herself—his natural mother—wasn't at liberty to do that. Well, at least she didn't ache over him so much any more— she got over that, finally. But that didn't mean she stopped loving him. Oh, no. Shoot, she told herself, I still love Marva Grace, and look what she is, a person who regards her only sister as an embarrassment.

Feeling suddenly a little lonely, Dorie left her ironing

Minding Mama

and went in search of Lily Dawn. She found the girl perched on an overturned waste paper can on one end of the back porch, watching Loyal Bunce plumb the cabinet he had built for Dorie's anticipated home beauty shop business. He had already put up a partial wall to divide the shop from the laundry area. Dorie sensed that Loyal was getting a bit restless, now that warmer weather was coming on. He said only this morning that Petunia had taken to pacing at night, but Dorie figured it was Loyal that did the pacing and the dog that joined in.

When Dorie looked in on the elderly man and the girl, worker and watcher, Lily Dawn was explaining that her daddy was going to fly out here as soon as he got home from his truck trip. Maybe in two days, or three. Soon as he could. He wanted to see his mama over there in Turner by the dam, too, to see if she was okay. Lily Dawn said her stepmama hadn't told him about her being gone or about her grandmama being sick, either. He said not to worry, he'd work things out. He even cried a little in his voice, she said.

"You love your daddy?" Loyal asked without looking up from his work.

"Yeah, I loves him, but not that lady he marri'd. She a mean one. She beat on me sometimes, an' sometimes for no good reason. Jus' outta chop-lickin' meanness."

* * * * * * *

Marilyn Arnold

The next day Dorie returned from the market to see a very familiar white bus on the street in front of her house. There on the porch were her three friends of the road, and baby Moses on Rachel's lap, sucking a bottle. Jonah spoke first.

"We wondered if you would still be here, or if you'd have returned to Atlanta by now." His eyes scanned the house. "The place looks nice. You've been working."

Dorie set her grocery bags down and hugged each of her visitors, especially Moses, whom Rachel delivered to her outstretched arms. "The house will look even better when I get these dead shrubs out and plant some grass and flowers," she said. "It's still a bit early for planting. We could have a bad cold snap."

Ishmael smiled. "Looks as though you're staying. I had a hunch you might."

Dorie shook her head. "Well, I sure didn't." She paused, not wanting to say what Cleve had done to her. "Then, I decided, why not?"

"Good for you, Dorie!" Rachel cried. "You're making your life instead of merely letting it happen to you."

Dorie sat on the top step, rocking and cooing at Moses.

Jonah spoke. "Uh . . . we've made a decision, too, and we wanted you to know. We're on our way to Texas. Rachel hopes to keep Moses, but she wants it to be legal. Did you say you found him in an abandoned warehouse outside of Amarillo?"

"Yes. Technically, it was Petunia and Loyal who found

him. That old mutt chased a squirrel in there an' Loyal went in to get her. It was almost dark and I was in such a rush that I didn't even know he had the baby until later." Dorie's voice was pleading. "By then, we were long gone, so I said we'd call the authorities when we landed in Jericho an' got Mama safely in the ground. Then you turned up an' in the hubbub I never got anybody called."

Ishmael nodded. "That's how we understood it, but we wanted to be sure. Is it all right with you if we leave your name out of it when we take him back? Things will be simpler if we say only that a transient found the baby and when our path crossed his we were asked to take him."

"I'll do whatever it takes to adopt Moses," Rachel said, "even if it means establishing residence in Amarillo until I qualify. With my training and experience, I can easily set up a profitable consulting business in my home." She smiled. "Once I have a home."

"You mean you'd give up the road for Moses? Your freedom?" Dorie was astonished.

"I'd give it up in a minute," Rachel said. "The three— I mean four—of us have been to the West Coast, we've seen several national and many state parks, we've put our lives back together, and we're all ready to move on."

"But the bus? . . ."

"We'll give it to some municipal organization, or some charity. They can repaint it and get good use of it," Jonah said. "It's time for Ishmael and me to take up our lives as fathers and citizens again."

Marilyn Arnold

"C'mon in for a bit, I've got a surprise for you, too," Dorie said, standing. Ishmael picked up her grocery bags, and the three friends followed Dorie into the house.

* * * * * * *

Surprise was too mild a term. Flabbergasted was more like it. First, there was Lily Dawn, sitting at the kitchen table reading to Mrs. Eckersell out of one of Ruetta Flatray's history books. Mrs. Eckersell was helping her with the unfamiliar words. In terms of grammar and pronunciation, it was a linguistic nightmare, this meeting of rural adolescent South and rural elderly West. But in terms of human interchange it was quite lovely. And then there was Loyal, who came in from the back porch to greet the friends he had met only briefly in a snowstorm in northern Arizona.

Ishmael threw his hands in the air and laughingly asked if Dorie were hiding the Pococks and Madame Taji Mahi in the bedrooms. Dorie asked if the trio had run onto the evangelists when they went looking. Ishmael confirmed that when the earth kept spinning after the advertised shut-down date, he and his companions had indeed stopped in Zion National Park out of concern for the evangelists. They had, in fact, caught part of a revival meeting in the campground and concluded that since the Pococks were already well into a revitalized campaign of piety and doom, they had rebounded from their disappointment. The trio had then

Minding Mama

gone on their way, satisfied that any help they might offer would be superfluous.

As for the Madame, no one knew her present whereabouts; but she, too, struck them as one who would weather any storm. Loyal hadn't met her, of course, but said that if she was anything like "them nutty preacher folks" who turned up here, he counted himself lucky to have missed her. Since Loyal introduced the subject, naturally Dorie had to relate her recent experience with the Pococks, confessing that she had passed her visitors' three hundred dollars on to them, so the pair could recover their vehicle from the Arizona highway department. She had come into a little unexpected money, she said, and would now like to repay the three travelers what they had given her. They refused it, insisting that in giving it to others in need, she had absolved the debt.

Having determined their course of action, and having learned that Lily Dawn would soon be reunited with her father, the travelers were eager to be on their way. Dorie, Loyal, and Lily Dawn walked to the bus with them, Lily Dawn giggling at little Moses as she went. She was certain he remembered her. As Jonah rounded the bus to the driver's seat, he noticed that someone had placed a crudely lettered yellow circular under the windshield wiper. It was advertising a revival meeting of the lost and found earnest seekers at Jacob Lake the following Saturday, all day. Featured testators would be Bertram and Brightness Louise Pocock of the Last Chance Holy Doom's Day Church.

With them, the circular announced, was a reincarnated fifteenth century nun, Mother Valencia Purina Florencia, who could see into the world beyond death and would tell new communicants (for a small fee) what awaited each of them in the next life. Jonah let out a howl and shared his delight with his friends. They all laughed long and hard. Madame Taji Mahi's fate, at least for the moment, was a mystery no longer. When Dorie protested that the Pococks and the fortune teller didn't like each other, Ishmael observed that even mortal enemies can become loving bedfellows if there is profit in it.

* * * * * * *

Lily Dawn's father came, as promised, two days later. He called from the Las Vegas airport to say that he was on his way, in a rental car, and should arrive by early evening. Dorie gave him directions and set about preparing supper. Lily Dawn sat on the front porch for at least two hours, jumping up every time a car turned down the sparsely traveled street.

"How much longer is it?" she asked when Dorie joined her after laying out the supper things.

"Not long, now."

"Is he gon' make me go back there? I'm dyin' t' see my daddy, but I ain't goin' back there."

"Your daddy's gonna do what's right for you, don't you worry." Dorie sat beside Lily Dawn on the top step and put

Minding Mama

her arm around the girl. "I can tell he's a good man. You're lucky. Not every child has a daddy who's a good man." She paused. "Or a good mama."

Lily Dawn bent low and picked at a dirty callous on her big toe. She was barefoot. "I don't got a good mama," she said, hesitating. "You got a good mama."

"Well, I did b'fore she up an' died on me."

"She still good, an' you still love her. She up there, lookin' out for you. My daddy says the good goes to heav'n an' looks out for them what's left."

Dorie nodded. "Yes, she is good . . . an' yes, I do still love her."

"You miss 'er, Dorie?"

"Yes, I do. Do you miss your real mama?"

"She run out on us, an' bust up my daddy somep'n awful. He try not to cry, but sometimes he couldn' help hisself." Lily Dawn left the callous and switched to a scab on the other ankle. "But sometimes she laugh, an' sometimes she sing, an' sometimes she kiss me. I miss her laughin' and her singin' an' her kissin'."

"I know. My mama was old, but I miss her laughin' and her singin' and her kissin', too." Dorie chuckled softly and brushed away a tear. "An' you know? Sometimes I even miss her preachin'."

Lily Dawn looked up. "Was your mama a preacher? I din't know that."

Dorie patted the girl's back gently. "She wasn't an official preacher, but she snuck preachin' in on me whenever

271

she got the chance. Kinda slipped it in, you know? The way she used to slip a chunk of parsnip or asparagus in my mouth when I was little and she had my attention on some bird outside, or some poem she knew by heart."

Then Dorie stood and looked toward the lengthening sun. "Here comes a shiny new car that's slowin' down. Get up, girl, I think your daddy's here!"

* * * * * * *

That was yesterday. Today, Dorie found herself at the curb again, bidding friends goodbye. First, father and daughter were going to Turner, to see his mother, the girl's grandmother. Then they were driving to Las Vegas where they would catch a plane back to Jacksonville, Florida. He had come to a decision, he told Dorie. He was going to wrap things up in Jacksonville as soon as possible and move west, to Turner, to be near his mother. If her mind wasn't too far gone, she'd remember him. And who knows, maybe she'd be well enough to come home for occasional visits. He and Lily Dawn would move into her home for the time being, and he'd get regular day work so he'd be home every evening. His wife, Lily's stepmother, might come later, after her sons turned eighteen and went out on their own—which they said often enough they intended to do. Husband and wife had talked it over before he flew west. She was feeling some remorse over how she had treated Lily Dawn and hadn't told him the girl had run off,

Minding Mama

or reported it to the police. She was hoping Lily Dawn would come back before her father got his truck fixed and came home.

Dorie couldn't help being a little skeptical, given the woman's past record in mothering, but she kept her doubts to herself. One thing she knew for certain, Lily Dawn's father would put his daughter first in his life. He would look after her and protect her and love her. And, when they moved to Turner, they'd be within spittin' distance (almost) of Jericho. Dorie could be like a second grandmother to the girl. She liked the sound of that.

* * * * * * *

When Loyal came to tell Lily Dawn goodbye, Dorie saw that he had his trombone and duffle with him, and that Petunia was by his side. A big hole opened behind her ribs.

"You're leaving," she said after the rental car pulled away.

"Yip, seems it's time, don't it? But we got the place fixed up, din't we?"

"*We* didn't, but *you* did. You know you're welcome to stay here permanently, don't you?"

"Shore do, and I thank ye, but me'n Petunia, we're gettin' restless. Mebbe the highway's too close. Nights we hear them big rigs a hummin', goin' somewheres."

"Everybody's leavin' at once. Can't you stay another week or two, maybe?"

"Warmer weather's comin'. We got to get futher north. Me'n Petunia, we kinda follers the birds." He hesitated. "Mebbe we'll be back through come October."

Dorie's eyes filled. "I'll watch for you," she said and stood a long time gazing at the shuffling figure as it grew ever smaller in the distance. And then it disappeared.

* * * * * * *

In the succeeding days, Dorie got her in-home beauty shop up and running. She applied for a business license and hung notices at Honey's Jubilee Foods, Denny's Wigwam, and a few other places. Word got around quickly, and soon she was back at her old trade. It seemed good to be in a routine, but evenings were lonesome. There were Mrs. Eckersell and Seth Johnson, of course. She even went to a church function or two with Mrs. Eckersell, and called Marva Grace a couple of times. Talking with her sister was never very satisfying, but it seemed to Dorie that Marva had softened just a little. One of her daughters was caught buying drugs in a sting operation, and the whole business had taken a toll on Marva Grace. Her perfect world of selfish superiority was discovered to have a bit of rot beneath the surface. Dorie found herself trying to give comfort and assurance, and was surprised to discover that whatever affected her sister also affected her.

It wasn't much, but in Dorie's view it was a start. At the end of Dorie's last conversation with her sister, Marva

Minding Mama

Grace had made a vague suggestion that maybe the two of them could get together sometime. Dorie had said she'd like that, wondering after she said it if she really would *like* it, that is, enjoy it. Dorie was happy to learn, too, that she wasn't glad that Marva Grace was experiencing a little comeuppance. Not too long ago she might have taken some perverse pleasure in her sister's misfortune, but not any more. Now she found herself willing to share the hurt. Ruetta Flatray had tried to teach her that charity was required of us, and that sometimes it was harder to extend charity to a family member than to anybody else. Marva Grace'll come around one of these days, Ruetta used to say. Just you wait and see.

* * * * * * *

It was late April, and spring had enveloped Jericho in a jubilee of new life. Desert marigold and cactus were in bloom, along with flowering plums and lilacs. The days were fresh and warm, the nights cool and full of stars. Dorie had taken to sitting on the front porch in the early evening, wrapped in a sweater or shawl. The desert had grown on her, with its dry air and pure skies. She thought she'd never prefer it over the miles and miles of green in Georgia, but it had wooed her like an insistent, irresistible lover. Was it the wind stroking her hair that won her, or the ever-changing face of the red bluff in front of her? Was it the smell of rain, its infrequency increasing the wonder and preciousness of it? Whatever it was, she was here, and she was staying. She was even beginning to find God in these rocks and canyons, and in the red brick church by the high school.

On one such evening, she saw a figure approaching from the direction of the highway, silhouetted against the rosy sky. Something about the figure struck her as familiar. The slouch of the shoulders, perhaps, or the slightly jerky gait. A backpack or duffle was slung over one shoulder. Dorie stood, her shawl falling to the porch behind her. She gasped and put her fist to her mouth in disbelief.

"Cleve!" she cried, running down the walk and into the road. "You've come! You've come!"

"I lost all the money," he said. "Me 'n Clarence Ross, in Atlantic City."

"Forget the money. You're here." Dorie said, laughing and crying at the same time. Embracing him, touching his face. "I've needed you."

"I've needed you, too. C'n you forgive me?"

"You're home. I'll kill a fatted calf."

* * * * * * *

The years of neglect and hurt seemed to disappear with the sunset the night Cleve came back to her. Dorie never thought he'd come, or that she'd take him back if he did. But he did, and she did. Things weren't perfect. They never are. But they were mostly good. She never threw it up to him, what he had done to her; and he never tried to explain why

Minding Mama

he and Clarence Ross did what they did. They closed that chapter and started a new one. The desert is a good place for fresh starts. The cleansing wind daily scours the sandstone and the people who live beneath its protecting walls. The first thing Dorie and Cleve did the morning after he came was visit the grave of Ruetta Flatray who, in spite of everything, had loved them both. Dorie knew by now that Clarence Ross had gone to beg Mona Fay to take him back.

Both Dorie and Cleve had the sense that Ruetta had perhaps been orchestrating, or at least influencing, a few things from her new station. If so, maybe she could lean on Mona Fay just a little, and straighten Clarence Ross up a little. Maybe she could even put in a word for Moses and Rachel and the others. And especially for Lily Dawn and Loyal, and yes, Petunia, too. Once her mind was made up about something, Ruetta could be mighty persuasive.

* * * * * * *

It was some weeks later, when Dorie was going through the old wooden desk that sat stolidly in one corner of the extra bedroom, that she had yet another revelation about her mother. And her father, he whom she had known so little. It explained why her mother had to make that last journey home and keep that promise tendered eight years ago. There, at the back of the lowest drawer were two packets of letters, one set addressed to him in her handwriting; the other addressed to her in his handwriting. The postmarked

277

dates on the envelopes spanned a good many years, and it would seem that the pair wrote each other whenever they were apart. There were also slips of paper that were not in envelopes. Each bore a date. They gave each other notes even when they were not separated.

Dorie sensed that she was treading sacred ground, but she read the top note, scribbled on the back of a shopping list. It was dated just three weeks before her father died. "Beloved Demont," it read, in Ruetta's distinctive hand, "I ran onto this bit of poetry when I was dusting books the other day. It's by Shelley. Do you remember it?" The two verses were then copied:

> Music, when soft voices die,
> Vibrates in the memory—
> Odours, when sweet violets sicken,
> Live within the sense they quicken.
>
> Rose leaves, when the rose is dead,
> Are heaped for the beloved's bed;
> And so thy thoughts, when thou art gone,
> Love itself shall slumber on.

Just that one little verse explained so much, and so much that Dorie hadn't known. Her father had seemed distant, always, and yet he and her mother had this. This enduring love. No matter that he had not accepted her religious conversion. No matter that Dorie never saw their private

Minding Mama

moments of affection—or, more likely, didn't notice the subtleties of their love. Their generation practiced reserve with the same intensity that moderns flout it. No wonder Ruetta had promised to come home to him for burial. No wonder he had exacted the promise. Dorie and Cleve had not had such a love, and would never have such a love, she realized. But they had love nonetheless, and perhaps it was enough. And they still had time to build on it. Forgiveness, she was learning, has reason to be sought and given from both partners.

Thus it was that a daughter kept her promise to a mother who had made a promise. She brought her mother home. But home was more than a house, more than a small plot of ground and a headstone. Home was memory, home was belonging, home was obligation, home was loyalty, home was selflessness, home was love, home was reunion. Dorie came to realize this bit of truth: When she undertook the journey from Atlanta to Jericho, she thought it was only to bring her mother home, to reunite her with her life's mate, but it wasn't. Wrapped in a lifetime of loving and caring, Ruetta Flatray was always home in the sense that really mattered. The journey turned out to be for Dorie's sake. It was, and had always been, Dorie's homecoming.

Other Novels by Marilyn Arnold

A Trilogy:
Desert Song
Song of Hope
Sky Full of Ribbons

Fields of Clover
The Classmates

Nonfiction Books by Marilyn Arnold

Sweet Is the Word: Reflections on the Book of Mormon
Pure Love: Readings on Sixteen Enduring Virtues
A Chorus for Peace: A Global Anthology of Poetry by
Women

Academic Books by Marilyn Arnold

Willa Cather's Short Fiction
Willa Cather, A Reference Guide
A Reader's Companion to the Fiction of Willa Cather, ed.
Willa Cather: A Reference Guide Update 1984-1992

Minding Mama was the 2004 recipient of
Mayhaven's Award for Fiction

Mayhaven's Awards for Fiction are unusual in the publishing world. Not only do we publish the book, we provide ongoing royalties in both primary and secondary markets. This important award has also opened doors for additional publications since 1997.

Our awards have been recognized in magazines, newspapers, on the internet, and in *The Writer's Market*. Applications for our Annual Awards for Fiction must be postmarked between May 1st and December 31st.

We feel these awards are important to both new and established authors and we will continue providing this unique opportunity.

Contact Mayhaven Publishing or our website for additional information on Mayhaven's Awards for Fiction.

www.mayhavenpublishing.com